Sisters

in

Spirit

(An Old-School Love Story)

Dorothy Griggs

Griggs Publishing

Chicago

Griggs Publishing

P.O. Box 3464

Oak Park, IL 60303-3464

This book is a work of fiction. Names, characters, places, and incidents are either the product of the author's imagination or are used fictitiously, and any resemblance to actual persons, living or dead, business establishments, events, or locales is entirely coincidental.

Cover Art by Brian Griggs.

ISBN: 0692206191
ISBN-13: 978-0692206195

DEDICATION

This book is lovingly dedicated to all of my beautiful sisters everywhere, in all their various shapes, sizes and colors.

Namaste

ACKNOWLEDGMENTS

While I dedicate this book to my sisters, I would be greatly remiss if I did not acknowledge my three wise men: Brian – who taught me how to soar high while remaining vigilant, so as not to scorch my wings; Nelson, whose quiet strength inspires and humbles me; and Freddy, who helps me to remember the value of a good belly laugh.

Thank you!

Winter, 2003

CHAPTER 1

The day is still in its infancy when she awakes, and she opens her eyes to darkness. Just as she has done for as far back as she can remember, before even so much as placing her feet on the floor, she whispers a brief prayer of gratitude, "Thank you, sweet Jesus, for another day."

Folding back a mound of blankets, she coaxes her body into a sitting position. Sliding sock clad feet into a pair of makeshift house shoes - lace less sneakers, the backs worn flat as pancakes – she pulls a tattered overcoat from the foot of her bed and drapes it over her thin blue cotton nightgown. Now she is ready to begin her day. "Sure is cold this morning, Charlie" she sputters, her ill fitting teeth clacking as the warmth of her breath gives shape to her words in the frigid morning air. As she moves through the darkened house, her cloaked, stooped silhouette is not the result of disease that plagues the elderly, turning ramrod backs into crescent moons; rather, in a rather ingenious survival technique, her body has curled inward into itself for added comfort and warmth.

She cautiously navigates the wooden stairs, bringing both feet back together on each step before descending to the next. As she slowly moves through the rooms of the darkened house, she greets each one with a silent hello. Clutching her overcoat close to her body, she inches her way through the narrow gap at the edge of the makeshift kitchen door—a green blanket tacked across the entrance, in a poor attempt to keep the cold drafty air from the larger outer rooms from penetrating the smaller room where she spends the majority of her waking hours.

Flipping on the kitchen light, she blinks rapidly as her eyes adjust to the sudden burst of light and color. The walls of the kitchen are painted sunburst yellow accented with giant red poppies painted on the walls and ceiling. Charlie had simply grinned and shook his head at her request for the addition of the large red flowers; but as was his way, he quickly acquiesced to any request that would make her happy. The end result bore a strange resemblance to a Warhol painting; but, of course, neither she nor Charlie knew who or what a Warhol was. The bold colors of the wall, coupled with the fuzzy forest green of the makeshift door, created a warm and cozy haven that she referred to as her 'private garden.'

Filling a copper teakettle with water, she places it on the back burner of the stove and ignites the fire beneath it. She turns on the remaining three burners, dials the oven to 350 degrees, and with cold, arthritic hands, pulls the oven door all the way open then beats a hasty retreat to the far end of the room, fearful that her loose fitting garments may ignite. She stands with her arms wrapped tightly around her torso, mesmerized by the leaping blue flames, and waits patiently for the chill in the early morning air to dissipate.

Once the room has warmed a bit, she removes the large overcoat and places it across the back of a nearby chair and inches nearer the stove with hands outstretched, letting the heat from the flames warm her stiff, swollen joints. Then slowly she raises her arms overhead and reaches with splayed fingers up toward the flowered ceiling. Her body pulls up out of her ribcage and lengthens to its full height of nearly 6 feet. In her private garden her previously bent body is miraculously transformed to one that is elongated and fluid. With arms still raised, and totally oblivious to the world outside her garden, she turns slowly round and round in a tight circle doing a strange little dance to an internal melody, while her shadow partner, leaping and twirling upon the walls and ceiling, keeps in step. As she dances alone in her private garden, her mind escapes the confines of her tiny kitchen, escapes the confines of her cold house and her tired, achy body and soars – free and untethered.

The whistling teakettle abruptly jolts her back to reality. The dance now complete, as she lowers her arms back down to her sides, her body automatically slumps back into its soft, stooped position. Turning off the oven and stove, she sets about preparing breakfast. Reaching into the kitchen cupboard for her ceramic cup with its chipped handle and faded roses, she lifts the edge of a towel covering a tray on the middle shelf and peers underneath. The delicate handle of a hand-painted porcelain teacup peeks out. She lingers for a moment or two, absent-mindedly caressing the cool porcelain, then drops the edge of the towel, "Don't want to risk ruining my good set," she says, "Gotta save it for special occasions."

After breakfast of tea and toast, she slips the overcoat back across her shoulders and prepares to make her way back upstairs where, in keeping with her latest daily ritual, she'll remove the coat from her shoulders and spread it back across the foot of her bed, then climb into bed and turn on the television and have it watch her as she drifts in and out of sleep. Today, for some unknown reason, she breaks from routine and stops off in the rarely used matchbox of a bathroom at the foot of the stairs. As she stands in front of the mirror looking dispassionately into her expressionless eyes, she feels herself once again becoming engulfed by an overpowering sense of despair. It is this dark, suffocating embrace that causes her to return to bed each morning, seeking escape in the only way she knows, through the suspension of consciousness.

She opens the door to the medicine cabinet and observes with childlike curiosity the row upon row of pills and capsules that neatly line the shelves. So many bottles, the overflow is stored in a shallow wicker basket that rests on the back of the toilet. "Look at all this here, Charlie," she says, sighing. "Not at all like when I was a chil' growing up in the South. Back then if you got sick, all you had to do was go out back and pull some herbs and roots from your garden and make your own medicine. Now they tell me I'm supposed to take a pill from each of these four bottles first thing in the morning, then I'm to take more pills from these two little bottles over here at noon after lunch – can't take 'em on an empty stomach. "Then..." she pauses and scratches her head, "Oh, yes! I'm to take another pill from each of the first four bottles again at night before I go to bed. Heck, truth be told, I haven't taken any of these pills for the last couple of months now and I feel just fine. But when I go and see my doctor, he'll be fussing and carrying on and knowing him, he'll probably give me a prescription for even more pills. I swear! I'm so sick of all these pills. One day I'm gonna be rid of 'em for good!" And just as that declaration clears her lips, an idea plants itself, like an errant seed, in the recesses of her mind and spreads so thoroughly and so rapidly that it chokes the life from all the beautiful thoughts and memories that reside there.

Moving now as if in a haze, she lowers the lid of the toilet seat and eases her tired body down upon it. Placing the wicker basket of pills onto her lap, she randomly selects bottles and twists off the plastic caps and dumps the contents of the brown plastic vials into the bottom of the basket, pausing periodically to sort the pills into little piles according to color, for no other reason except that she thought they looked prettier that way. With over ten bottles emptied, the bottom of the basket is now covered with mounds of little pills that look more like candy than the mood altering, symptom-masking drugs that they really are. As she struggles with the lid of the last bottle, it slips from her grasp and disappears behind the toilet. Placing the wicker basket across the top of the sink, she lifts herself up from the toilet, and with one arm braced against the edge of the vanity, stoops low while blindly reaching with her other hand for the bottle of pills. "Got it!" she yells triumphantly and as she straightens up a little too quickly, her hand lands squarely on the rim of the basket, tipping it onto its side and sending the little pills cascading like a shattered rainbow onto the floor. She drops to her hands and knees and frantically scoops the loose pills into a small mound. She suddenly sees herself in her mind's eye, and watches with a sense of detachment the sight of the poor pitiful woman hunched over on the tiled floor, eyes wild, limbs sprawled awkwardly about, bedclothes rumpled and disheveled. Then to her horror - or was it relief - she watches as the woman grab fistfuls of pills and crams them into her mouth. *Remember our wedding day? Remember what I promised your folks?*

She hears his voice clearly inside her head. Yes, she remembers that day half a century ago, just like it was yesterday. A day she recalls with a strange mix of emotions at the circumstances surrounding her marriage to a man twice her age; a man she neither loved nor desired. A man who, despite their dubious beginning, showered her with tenderness, love, and affection, all the while proclaiming, *"I know that you don't love me, but one day you will...you'll see."*

Tears of grief and shame blind her and as she cries out, and the little brightly colored pills spill from her gaping, twisted mouth back onto the tiled floor. The silent weeping turns into a mournful wail, that comes from someplace deep and raw as her body is racked with violent sobs. It is the first time she has allowed herself to cry, really cry, in over three years and she remains there on the cold tiled floor giving birth to all the longing, pain and sadness that has been housed in her body for so many years.

When she finally emerges from the bathroom she is exhausted and spent. Too tired to climb the stairs back up to her bedroom, she pulls the coat tighter around her shoulders and goes into the living room and stands in front of the large picture window. The world on the other side of the window appears vast and dark, and lately she finds herself frightened by the immensity of it all. It was Charlie's idea to keep the window bare and unadorned, loving how it created a sense of openness, helping him to not feel so hemmed in. Coming from the country, he was a big man used to being in big, open spaces. His idea about the window worked…almost too well.

The streets at this hour are quiet and barren. Over the years, the neighborhood has slowly given way to industry. Small manufacturing plants of one sort or another have moved in, spewing dark clouds of harmful pollutants carelessly into the air, driving out families and small family owned businesses. Their large house, sandwiched unceremoniously between two packaging plants, is one of the few that remains. Suddenly, a shadowy figure rounds the corner at the end of the block, walking fast and heading in her direction. Instinctively, she draws away from the window, afraid that she'll be seen. As the mystery man passes the house and continues on his lone trek, she crosses the room and gingerly lowers her body into one of two matching recliners. On a small pedestal table nestled between the two chairs is a framed picture of Charlie. In the photo he is leaning against his car and wearing a mischievous grin and a new herringbone overcoat - a birthday present from her. The photo was taken five years ago on Charlie's seventy-seventh birthday, two years before he fell asleep at the wheel of the very same car and while wearing the exact same coat as in the photograph.

Her shoulders and chest quivers as spasms continue to ripple through her body at lessening intervals, and she wipes her tear stained face on the sleeve of the overcoat. As she peers out the window through swollen eyelids, she sees that the blackened sky has given way to a pale shade of grey. Her eyes remain fixed on the sky, piercing it with her glare, silently willing it to reveal to her the meaning of it all. Then, almost as if in response to her plea, or perhaps simply as a reminder of the miracles that are manifested daily, a streak of amethyst appears on the horizon, followed by vibrant bands of pink and blue stretched like taffy candy across the early morning sky. *It might feel like yesterday, and it sure looks a lot like yesterday, but today is a brand new day.*

Though at that moment, she couldn't see how her continued existence in it would matter to anyone anywhere.

What she did know, however, was that God was not done with her yet, and that it was not quite time for her to put on her traveling shoes. Fresh tears streak her face as she picks up the photo of Charlie. As she delicately traces his smile with her fingertips, she softly whispers, "You were right, Charlie. I do love you."

Not wanting to return to bed, but not knowing what else to do, she heads back to the kitchen for another cup of tea. As she sits waiting for the whistle of the teakettle, she decides to take down her tea set and give it a thorough washing. Even though she kept it carefully stored away, it has been many years since she's bothered to wash it. It used to be that she would take the set down every couple of months or so, and tenderly hand washes each individual piece; infused during those brief moments with an inexplicable sense of peace and purposefulness. Today, longing desperately for a sense of either purpose or peace, she rises from her chair and pulls the step stool from the corner and places it in front of the cabinets above the sink. She takes a firm grip of both edges of the tray while keeping her mind completely focused on the task at hand, fearful of injuring either her self or the fragile contents of the tray. But for one fleeting moment her focus is temporarily distracted by what appears to be a piece of paper fluttering from the cabinet shelf onto the floor. *Must be an old piece of shelf lining,* she thinks, and quickly turns her attention back to the task at hand.

Planting both feet squarely on the floor, the tray securely on the counter top, she moves the step stool back into the corner and out of the way. Crossing the room, she reaches down to retrieve the worn piece of paper to dispose of it properly. As she slowly straightens her spine, she glances at the paper in her hand. "This here ain't no shelf lining," she says, fingering the sepia tinted paper that is folded into thirds. She unfolds the paper and squints at the images on its surface under the glare of the exposed ceiling bulb. Unable to read the fine print without the aid of her glasses, she carefully refolds the paper and places it in the pocket of her overcoat, patting the pocket of the coat to hear the reassuring crinkle of the paper inside. Her heart races as she slowly sinks into a nearby chair. She wills her heart to cease its pounding and her mind to slow down so that she can make some sense of her discovery. Because while she couldn't make out the fine print on the paper, there was one word she could easily decipher. Heading the top of the page in bold, elegant letters was the single word:

-Deed-

CHAPTER 2

Dressed in layers befitting the sub-degree temperature, she pulls on yellow rain boots, ties one scarf around her head and another around her neck. Into a plastic shopping bag she places her family bible with the address from the deed tucked safely between its well-worn pages, a handful of peppermints, and a change purse containing two dollars in coins and three neatly folded dollar bills.

Were it not for her stooped posture and her obvious disregard for fashion, she would be considered an attractive woman by most. And although she took little care with her appearance, she was not totally oblivious to it because for most of her life she had been referred to and identified by her two most obvious physical characteristics: her skin and her hair. She possessed flawless skin, as smooth and as dark as an eggplant. Black. Blue-Black. Just a couple of the words she's heard over the years to describe it. Skin so dark you would think that she had come straight from Africa, if not for her hair. Her hair spoke of a different past, a different journey. Straight, shiny hair that danced upon her shoulders, and that ironically, some Black folks referred to as 'good hair.' Hair passed down through generations where, if you traced back not too terribly far along the family tree, you would find limbs growing gnarled and twisted, representing offspring borne of legalized hated or illegal love.

As a young woman she had allowed these two characteristics to define her. The dark skin she bore with a deep sense of shame, while her hair she wore like a badge of merit. The value she internalized for each of the two physical traits was a direct result of the external responses they elicited. These days, she wears her sparkling gray hair in a thick braid, the tip secured with a rubber band then tucked into the hollow formed at the base of the braid.

Closing the front door behind her, she carefully makes her way down the street and over two blocks where she catches the bus. Taking a seat at the front near the bus driver, she stares blankly out the window as the bus lurches forward, then rolls steadily down the snow-covered street.

CHAPTER 3

The house sat in the middle of the street known as Ravenswood. The layout of the neighborhood was typical of most inner city neighborhoods - dwellings comprised of modest single family homes, two and four-family flats. There was the neighborhood drug store, pizzeria, public library, elementary and middle schools, and the omni-present liquor stores. The lack of any major grocery stores in the city gave rise to profit seeking immigrants whose knowledge about the people they served was gleaned through watching stereotyped caricatures on television. These convenience stores' aisles overflowed with tubs of lard and buckets of frozen chitlins. And, positioned prominently on nearly every check-out counter was an enormous jar of pigs' feet, where you could have your chosen foot wrapped up in wax paper glistening with coagulated fat, to take home for a mid-day snack. What was harder to locate within these stores was an adequate supply of basic, simple good foods, things like apples and oranges, and lettuce that was not wilted or moldy. But in spite of these and other disadvantages, or possibly because of them, there existed within the neighborhood a strong sense of community, where it was customary for neighbors to catch each other's slack, and watch each other's backs.

~~~

Jamela notices the old lady first. She is heading in her direction, stooped low to the ground and wearing a large coat with what looks like all the clothing she owns underneath it. An avid people watcher, Jamela is often seduced by imaginings of the lives of the well-to-do; rarely does she give much thought to what a day in the life of someone with less than her might look or feel like. Today is an exception, and the old woman in her line of vision gives her pause for contemplation. "Poor thing," Jamela sighs as the old lady comes nearer, "Wonder where she's headed on this cold day."

The old woman suddenly stops in the middle of the block, removes her bible from her shopping bag and double-checks the address. *7449. It's should be right along here somewhere*, she thinks, looking first to the left and then to the right, using the knuckle of her index finger to push her half-moon reading glasses back up on the bridge of her nose. "Oh, sweet baby Jesus, that's it over there!" she suddenly shouts.

When she started out on her adventure this morning, she only allowed herself to halfway believe that somewhere out there was a house that matched up with the address on the paper; she did not dare allow herself to entertain the possibility that she might actually find it. Stopping at the curb she looks both ways for oncoming traffic, then carefully makes her way across the icy street and stops and stands directly in front of the house numbered 7449. Catching her breath, she glances over and smiles at the young lady standing nearby tossing snowballs to a small child. *These young folk today*, she thinks, *don't she know she needs a hat on her head, cold as it is? Well at least she's got the little one bundled up good.* She studies the house a while longer, as she inches closer to the front walkway. Glancing back at the woman and child, now a mere few feet away, she notices for the first time the thick locs adorning the young woman's head. *What's that that chil's got growing outta her head. These young folks today. I do declare!*

Turning her attention back to the house, she stands with

her hands clasped behind her back silently surveying the two-story brick structure, from the soft grey smoke billowing out of the chimney, down to the front stoop and the cleared narrow path leading up to the concrete steps. Jamela watches the old woman curiously, while keeping one vigilant eye glued to her small son. *What is she staring at?* Jamela wonders as she searches the pockets of her jacket, hoping to uncover at least a few coins to give to the old woman when asked. Now that she has completed the initial inspection of the house, her house, she can no longer contain the joy that has been doing a slow build up from the moment she found the deed, "Praise Him! Hallelujah!!" she shouts. The sudden outburst alarms Jamela, and she automatically goes into a mode of heightened alertness. She has heard stories about the mounting pressures of living in the streets and how a perfectly harmless person can suddenly turn dangerous, if you happen to catch them on the wrong day. She grabs her child's hand, intent on walking quickly, not running – mind you, but walking briskly for the front door, when the old woman speaks.

"Hi there, young lady!"

"Damnit!" Jamela mutters, as she turns around and offers a too enthusiastic "Hello!"

"Do you know the people who live here?" the old woman asks, moving in a bit closer.

"I live here." Jamela responds, taking a step backward, wanting to keep a safe distance in case she had to grab her baby and run.

"You do?" the old woman responds, appearing weirdly delighted by this bit of information.

"And who is this handsome little fella?"

"My son." Jamela replies, giving his hand a little squeeze.

"Hi, baby. What's your name?" the old woman asks, leaning in and extending a gloved hand toward the little boy. The child responds by putting his free hand behind his back and burying his face into his mother's corduroyed thigh. Patting his shoulder reassuringly, Jamela clears her throat and replies, "His name is Shaka Mohammad."

"Shaka Mohammad!" the old woman exclaims, straightening her back a few inches and looking questioningly up into Jamela's eyes.

"That's quite a big name for such a little guy, ain't it?"

"I wanted to give him an important name. You never know. He might be the next president!" Jamela states proudly.

"Baby, when they finally elect a Black man for president, he's gonna have a common name. Something they feel safe with, like William or Theodore or maybe even Bob."

"Well if they want somebody common and safe, they can just keep electing old white men," Jamela snaps back defensively.

Realizing that she has hit a sore spot, the old woman reaches into her shopping bag and pulls out a peppermint candy.

"Here, little Shaka Mohammad," she says, extending the candy out toward the boy, "Would you like a piece of candy?" The tiny face suddenly reappears followed by an even tinier outstretched mitten. Jamela grabs the sleeve of the child's snowsuit and pulls the small hand back. "Sorry, Miss," Jamela states huffy, "but I don't allow him to accept candy from strangers."

"Why...no, of course not," the old woman replies, her high spirits suddenly deflated by the implication that she might do something to harm this sweet child. *Lord knows I'd never harm that baby*, she thinks, *but I don't suppose there's any way for her to know that. She's just protecting her baby, as any good mother would do.*

Uncertain of what to do next, the old woman removes the wrapper from the candy and places it into her own mouth. She stands silently eating the candy and enjoying being outdoors for a change, even in this inhospitable weather. She is even grateful for the unexpected company of the young woman with the strange hair, and the small child with the too large name. She looks down the street in one direction, then in the other direction, and finally back up at the house.

"Is there something I can help you with?" Jamela finally asks. She is now ready to go inside with Shaka, but she fears that the old woman is lost in more ways than one.

"Huh? No, baby. I was just about to leave, but that was mighty kind of you to ask," she says, as she places her bible back into her shopping bag and adjusts the handles of the bag up onto her shoulder. "But, on second thought," she says, adjusting the scarf on her head, "Would you be able to tell me who else lives here?" Feeling that she has already done her good deed for the day, yet feeling a strange compassion for the old woman, Jamela decides to oblige her for a few minutes longer.

"Well, one apartment is currently vacant. Then there's Miss Lewis, the school teacher," Jamela offers, "but she's moving out at the end of the month, so I guess I shouldn't even bother counting her. So all that leaves is old Mr. Henry and his wife. And me and Shaka, of course."

"So there are only two families that live in this big old house?"

"Yes, that's right."

"But there's room for two more?"

"Right again."

"And you say a Mr. Henry lives here?"

"Yes, ma'am."

"Mr. Henry." The old woman repeats, "I know a Mr. Henry..." she says, her words trailing off as she again stares off down the street trying to connect the name with a memory. "My Charlie had a good friend by the name of Jacob Henry. They worked together at the factory," she says, recalling now fragments of stories she's heard about Mr. Henry and his family. "I've heard Charlie talk about him so much over the years that I feel like he's an old friend of mine. But I don't imagine that this could be the same man."

"Well, here's your chance to find out," Jamela offers, "Why don't you go on up and ring the bell. That's the only way you're gonna know for certain."

"You say just go on up and ring the bell?"

"Just ring the bell."

"You really think that it would be okay for me to do that?"

"I don't see why not."

"Well then, I think I'll do just that!" The old woman says, suddenly feeling bold and courageous as she prepares to make her way up the four broad steps, generously sprinkled with salt. "Which one of these here doorbells belongs to him?" she asks.

"Lower left." Jamela answers.

"Thank you, sweetie. You've been such a big help to an old lady. I sure do 'preciate it."

"You're welcome, Miss..." The words trail off as Jamela realizes she's never bothered to ask the old woman her name.

Sensing her hesitation, the old woman replies, "Miz Mattie, sweet child. My name's Miz Mattie."

"Well pleased to meet you, Miz Mattie. My name's Jamela." she says, smiling at the old woman for the first time and feeling a tinge of regret at being so abrupt with her about the candy. It was obvious the old woman meant no harm.

"It was nice talking to you. Now you be careful going up those front steps."

"Uh huh! I sure will, chil'. I sure will." "Nice meeting you, little Shaka," she calls out as she prepares to carefully ascend the stairs. The child, who had broken away from his momma's grip, takes a break from patting a tired looking snowman to turn and offer a wave with a tiny, soggy mitten.

"Oh, one last thing." Miz Mattie says, stopping and turning back to face Jamela, having almost forgotten the very thing that brought her out in the cold and snow in the first place. "Do you know how I can find the person who takes care of this house?"

"You mean the landlord?"

"The landlord? Yes. Okay."

"Sure. You're on your way to see him now."

"Mr. Henry?"

Jamela nods her head yes.

"I do declare!" Miz Mattie exclaims, "Today is a good day!"

CHAPTER 4

Charlie had talked of Mr. Henry often. 'A good man,' was how he frequently referred to him. A man Charlie had befriended at the factory where he labored for 33 years after moving to the city and trading toiling the land and tending to cattle for a back breaking job hoisting steel auto parts in a concrete factory. Once inside the small square vestibule, Miz Mattie rings the doorbell to Mr. Henry's apartment and waits patiently. Through the windowpanes of the locked door she can see two interior doors with shiny brass doorknobs on the far side of either wall, separated by a wooden staircase. Wall mounted brass sconces illuminate the stairs and cast a soft glow on the polished wood. A tall, lean man appears in the doorway of the lower, left apartment. As he steps out of his open door, he runs one huge hand over the crown of his head, to smooth down the tuft of grey hair sticking up in the top, then pulls a Tiger's baseball cap snugly onto his head.

"Can I help you?" he inquires politely, though in a tone that suggests that he's been interrupted from an important matter.

"Hi! You Mr. Henry?"

"Yes. I'm Jacob Henry," the man replies, his brow furrowed in question.

"The same Jacob who work at the car factory?"

"Well...yes" he hesitates, "I worked at the car factory for many years, but I'm retired now. Are you here looking for a place to rent?" he asks, trying to steer the conversation to someplace logical.

"No. I have a place to live, thank you, although it's way too big and drafty."

"What I've come about is this piece of paper I've got with the address to this here house on it," she says, gesturing to her shopping bag, "I came by to take a look at the house, and I was also hoping to speak with the person who's in charge here. It was just my good luck that I met a nice young lady and her little boy out front. She told me that you're the landlord and that your name is Mr. Henry. When I heard the name Henry, I figured...well, rather I hoped that it was the same Mr. Henry who knew my Charlie."

"Charlie?" Mr. Henry asks, his face now a mask of confusion.

"Yes! Charlie worked at the automobile factory too, and he was always going on and on about Mr. Henry and his wife Lillian."

"*My* wife's name is Lillian."

"Then you're the Mr. Henry I've heard so much about!"

"I'm Mattie, Charlie's wife," she states proudly, removing her mitten and extending her hand in greeting.

"Charlie Kincaid?" he asks, recognition finally registering on his face in the form of a wide, gap-toothed grin.

"You're Mattie? Charlie Kincaid's wife?!"

"Yes sir! I sure am!" she answers, grinning back.

"Well, nice to finally meet you! Come in! Come on in out of the cold!" he says, grabbing her hand and pumping it firmly before removing his baseball cap and extending an arm to welcome her inside. She steps into the warm hallway and the smell of home cooking wafts out of his front door, teasing her nostrils and prompting her stomach to send her a noisy reminder that it's late afternoon and the only thing she's put in her stomach today was tea and toast. Stepping inside the warm apartment and her eyes are drawn, not to the large 42 inch television screen that occupies one full wall, but to the folding TV tray set up in front of the huge television. On the tray sits a steaming bowl of collard greens, a slice of golden cornbread with a healthy pat of butter melting on top, several pieces of golden fried chicken, a mug of iced tea, a large bottle of hot sauce, and a hefty stack of napkins. The television is blaring, and she instinctively covers her ears. The *Wheel of Fortune* is on, and Vanna is poised to flip over some vowels.

"Come. Please. Have a seat. You'll have to excuse the mess," he states apologetically, scurrying about the room removing cotton tee shirts and plaid flannel shirts from the backs of the sofa and chairs, turning down the television volume, and with his foot, pushing his toolbox out of the center of the floor into a nearby corner. "My wife's been out of town all week." he offers, by way of explanation. Then suddenly realizing how chauvinistic that might sound, hastily add, "Not that I'm waiting for her to return to clean the place up," he says laughing, holding up both hands in defense.

"It's just that we're in the process of moving. We're heading south to Georgia. My baby girl just had twin boys! She's the youngest of our three daughters, but the first to make me a proud grandpa!

"Here," he offers, remembering his manners, "let me take your coat." As he helps lift the overcoat from her shoulders, he recognizes it as the coat that Charlie had gotten for his birthday; a modest and frugal man, Charlie had been bashfully proud of the finely tailored coat. It was indeed once a very handsome coat. Mr. Henry starts to make a comment about the coat to Mattie, but suddenly loses his train of thought as he takes in her eclectic outfit: an array of colors peek out from beneath her plaid blazer, which is paired with stripped pants worn beneath a calf length wool skirt. He quickly changes his mind about commenting on the coat.

"Can I get you something to drink?" he says instead, "Something to eat?" he asks, gesturing toward his plate of food. "I was just about to sit down to lunch."

"No. Thank you. I'm not hungry." Miz Mattie replies,

smiling broadly.

Her stomach growls loudly as if to protest her blatant lie.

Mr. Henry pretends not to hear it. As a husband and a father of three girls, he knows firsthand how proud and stubborn women can sometimes be.

"It won't be no trouble. No trouble a'tall. I cooked it myself. And I can't eat if you're not going to join me – that would be rude.

"But I sure would like to eat," he adds coaxingly, " 'cause I am pretty hungry."

"Well, seeing as how it would be impolite of me to keep you from your meal, I suppose I wouldn't mind having myself some of them greens you got there. And maybe a piece of cornbread."

"Alrighty! Now we're talkin'! How about some chicken? Which piece would you like?"

"No. I don't want to impose any further, the greens and cornbread are plenty."

"What!? You mean you're not gonna try my chicken? I've got a recipe that's better than the Colonel's."

"Well, since you put it like that, I'll have a leg, please," she says "That's only if you're sure you can spare it."

"Oh, I've got plenty to spare, alright. Whenever I fry up some chicken, I always cook at least two birds. Cold fried chicken, in my humblest of opinion, is almost as good as hot fried chicken!"

"Ain't that the truth!"

"Charlie's wife! Good Lord, what do you know! After all these years we finally meet. Please, sit. Make yourself comfortable; I'll only be a minute," he says as he heads off toward the kitchen.

She eases her weary body into a comfortably worn chair and looks around. The house is in a state of organized chaos. In all directions, as far as she could see, boxes are stacked shoulder high along the walls. And although their home was in the process of being dismantled, it still possessed the loving energy of its current occupants; a place where, once inside, you were tempted to kick your shoes off and stay awhile. She sits listening to the noise of the television in the foreground, the clatter of plates, pots and pans in the background and is, at that moment, happy and content. She is thrilled to be out of her frigid home visiting with someone who knew her Charlie. How she had longed for someone she could sit with and talk to about the good ol' days; someone that she could sit with and talk to about yesterday, or even today, for that matter.

Mr. Henry returns carrying a steaming bowl of collard greens with a piece of smoked turkey leg perched on top, a generous square of the golden corn bread, and a golden fried chicken leg. *Yes sir!* she thinks, *today is definitely a good day!* Mr. Henry places the dishes down on top of one of the many available boxes while he sets up another folding tray. He places the tray before her and carefully arranges the dishes on top. Hurrying back to the kitchen, he quickly returns with a glass of iced tea, a knife and fork, and a mound of napkins all her own. He places these last items on what little remaining space there is left on the tray. He finishes with a flourish of his hand and a deep exaggerated bow before returning to his own tray of food. Miz Mattie brings the bowl of collard greens up to her face, closes her eyes and inhales. The steam from the bowl rises up to gently caress her face, fog her glasses, and remind her of the simple pleasures life still has to offer.

"Thank you," she says softly, overcome with gratitude by Mr. Henry's hospitality and her stroke of good luck, "You're very kind."

"It's my pleasure! The only thing I enjoy more than cooking a good meal is eating one," he booms, his face beaming brightly.

"So enjoy! Don't be shy, now! Dig in!"

He eats in silence, polishing off one chicken leg and starting on another before he speaks again. "So, how the heck is ol' Charlie? It's been a long time since he's showed his face around here. Why didn't he stop by here with you today? I've got some urgent business I've been needing to talk to him about." The eagerly anticipated tender greens never make it to

Miz Mattie mouth, as her fork drops from her hand and clangs loudly as it bounces off the metal folding tray and onto the floor, effectively silencing Mr. Henry's monologue. Henry looks up from his plate for the first time since he took his first bite and is alarmed by the stricken look he sees on his guest's face. When he sees her hand close around her neck, for a terrifying instant Mr. Henry fears that she might be choking on her food. He breathes a sigh of relief when he sees that she is just removing her napkin from one of her many shirt collars. As he gets up to replace her fallen fork, he notices that she's taken a hold of each end of her blazer jacket and is squeezing and kneading the heck out of it. It reminded him of the old saying, 'trying to squeeze blood from a turnip', that folks back home would say after the bill collector had departed. He becomes unnerved by this weird behavior, coupled with the sudden disengaged look in her eyes. *She may not be choking, but something definitely ain't right.*

"Are you okay?" he asks over the blare of the television commercial, which is transmitted at a higher volume.

No answer, just a continuation of the weird kneading thing she's doing with her jacket, coupled now with a barely discernible rocking motion of her upper torso.

"Mattie!" he speaks louder, "Hold on… Hold it a second, let me turn this damn thing down."

He picks up the remote control and mutes the sound before turning back to face her.

"Are you okay?!" he asks, a bit more forcefully.

"Charlie's dead, Mr. Henry."

"No!" he cries, and as if some invisible fist had just forcibly punched him in the gut, he stumbles backwards and falls hard back into his chair.

"What are you saying? That can't be, I mailed him a letter just last week."

"Charlie's been dead for three years now, Mr. Henry. I'm sorry, I thought you knew."

Henry suddenly leaps back to his feet, nearly toppling his tray of food in the process. He stares down at Miz Mattie in anguished disbelief, then begins pacing back and forth in front of the television set in large angry strides. His angst-filled pacing reminds her of a caged cheetah she once saw at a zoo. Trapped by invisible bars, its eyes told of its tortured soul. Her heart aches for Mr. Henry, just as it had ached for that beautiful, captured cat.

Finally, Mr. Henry slumps back down into his chair and cradles his head in his large hands, his strong fingers buried in the soft tuft of gray hair. He grabs a handful of napkins and roughly wipes his eyes and nose. Even though Miz Mattie can only see his face in profile, the pain etched there is almost unbearable to witness. Miz Mattie sits fidgeting with the paper napkin still clenched in her fists, feeling her own spirit starting a slow spiral back into the dark, vacuous hole it has occupied for the past three years.

"I'm sorry," she says again, at a loss of anything else to say, "I thought you knew."

Uncertain of what more to say or do, leaving suddenly seems like the only proper solution. Standing quietly to go in search of her coat, she realizes that she does not know where to begin to look, so she sits back down.

"You're leaving?"

"I thought that might be best."

"No, don't! I mean I'd appreciate it if you would stay for a bit longer, please.

"Alright, I don't mind staying. Are you okay?"

"Well, frankly, no. It's just that Charlie…" his chest heaves as he struggles to continue,

"… Charlie was one hell of a good man!"

"Yes," she says, nodding her head in agreement, "My Charlie was a good man indeed."

~~~

After getting over the shock of learning about Charlie's death, Mattie and Mr. Henry had managed to finish their meal and share a good, long conversation like two dear friends, too long apart. Mr. Henry shared with Mattie the little he knew about the house, because even though he and Charlie had shared a long-term working relationship, Charlie was a very private man and had offered up personal information sparingly, and Henry had quickly learned to respect these boundaries by not inquiring further. But what he did know was that in addition to the four-family flat on Ravenswood, over the years Charlie had purchased two other homes that Mr. Henry had helped work on. Each home had been painstakingly restored and then sold, with the profit gained from the sale used to purchase the next, slightly nicer home. Charlie's final purchase, and by far his largest restoration project, had been the four-unit home on Ravenswood.

Because both men had families and their full time factory jobs, the restoration process on this final home had been slow and laborious. But time apparently was not a concern to Charlie, who shared with Mr. Henry that he had purchased the home as a future investment for his growing family. He shared how he had envisioned how once the kids got older and wanted to test their wings, they could each have their own living space with the security of knowing that family was close at hand. *My Charlie*, Mattie thinks, *always the dreamer.* Even she had to admit that, in theory, his plan was perfect.

After the first unit was completely restored, Charlie worked out an arrangement that would allow Mr. Henry and his family to live there rent-free in exchange for keeping up the daily maintenance on the property. As each subsequent unit was restored and rented out, Mr. Henry had dutifully managed the property, collected and deposited the rent money, and forwarded the deposit slips on to Charlie. After many years and untold hours of labor, all four units were finally completely restored and occupied. As the years rolled by, since most of their business dealings were conducted by mail, the two men spoke occasionally on the phone, but only saw each other on rare occasions. It was not uncommon for them to go for many months without any contact; Mr. Henry hadn't realized that it had been over three years since their last contact.

When Mattie finally departs for home later that day, she

leaves with a full stomach, keys to all four units of the house on Ravenswood, a checkbook with more zeros than she's ever seen in her lifetime, and a newfound hope for her future.

CHAPTER 5

One month later, as the sun again transforms the dark sky with soft jewel tones of reds, purples and blues, Miz Mattie moves quietly through her house making her daily rounds. Today, however, instead of greeting each room with her customary good morning, she bids each room a silent and final good-bye.

CHAPTER 6

Jamela had known that Mr. Henry and his wife were moving away, but she had been shocked to learn that the old woman who she had initially thought was homeless, not only owned the place, making her the new landlord, but had moved in and was now her downstairs neighbor as well. "Momma was at least right about one thing," she says to her young son, "You sure can't judge a book by it's cover, 'cause who would've ever thought! That being said," she continues, as she takes his small hand in hers and heads down the stairs, "a welcoming visit is definitely in order!"

"Well looka here! I got company!" Miz Mattie cries out in obvious delight as she opens the door and ushers her two young guests inside.

"Hope you don't mind us stopping by." Jamela states, shifting Shaka from one hip to the other while looking around the crowded rooms.

"Goodness sakes, chil'! Y'all welcome to come by anytime. An old lady like me can always use some company!"

"We just stopped by to see if there was anything we could help out with." Jamela says, and noticing that most of the old woman's belongings are still boxed up, offers, "Like maybe help you unpack some of these boxes."

"Well, that's awfully nice of you to offer. Okay, yes. I most certainly could use some help, thank you." she says, genuinely touched by the young girl's kindness.

"I was just finishing up in the kitchen, so if you don't mind, we'll head on back in there." Jamela nods in agreement and follows closely at Miz Mattie's heels. With Shaka still on her hip, she expertly dodges the stacked boxes and maneuvers easily through the serpentine maze created by all the furniture that has been crowded into the small rooms.

Stepping into the kitchen, Jamela is enveloped by the welcoming scent of some wonderful spice wafting from the oven. She watches as Miz Mattie goes over to the oven, peers in, and then adjusts the temperature with the tiniest turn of the knob.

"Oh! You're cooking. Did we come at a bad time?"

"Huh? Oh, no chil'. Have yourself a seat and take that baby off your hip and give him a seat too," she orders, pulling a chair out from the kitchen table and sinking down into it as an audible huff of air escapes from her lips.

"I just got done lining these here cabinet shelves," she says, gesturing with a wave of her hand to the cabinets that line the wall behind her. "I was just about to put these here plates and glasses away, when I suddenly got a strong hankering to bake," she says as she places a large oven mitt on her hand and heads back over to the oven. As she pulls out one cookie sheet containing large golden squares, she simultaneous slides another dough-filled cookie sheet inside the hot oven.

"I ain't baked in such a long time, but there's something about the smell of cookies baking that always makes a house feel more like a home. I used to bake every day for Charlie," she says while gingerly tapping the tops of the cookies with her fingertips to test for doneness.

"Charlie's your husband?"

"Yes, that's right."

"But he's gone now." she adds hastily, reminded of the need to refer to her husband in the past tense when speaking of him to others.

"Talk about a sweet tooth. Lawd! That man sure had one. I would bake something for him most every day. Some days I wouldn't cook meat for supper; you know, give the digestive system a chance to rest. Most men would fuss, want a huge hunk of meat with every meal. But not my Charlie. He didn't mind. No sir! He was content, just so long as he had himself something sweet to eat! But after he passed on, I just quit baking. Stopped cooking most days too." she says, her voice trailing off as she stares vacantly into space, lost in memories and times past.

"Take these here teacakes," she says, as she gently separates the soft, palm size cookies with a wooden spatula where they've bled together to form one large perforated cookie. "These were Charlie's favorite…I don't know if this here batch is any good," she says modestly, "Like I said, it's been a while since I baked"

She gently lifts a teacake with the wooden spatula and holds it above her brow and peers at its underside and smiles, obviously pleased. She places the teacake on a saucer and hands it to Jamela. She places another one on a separate saucer for Shaka, and is poised to push the saucer in front of the little boy, who is up on his knees in his chair waiting eagerly, when her fingers suddenly freeze. "Is it okay for the baby to have one too?" she asks tentatively.

"Yeah, sure." Jamela mumbles, having already taken a giant bite out of her own. "He's had his dinner already, if that's what you mean," she says, taking another huge bite. But when she looks up and her eyes meet Miz Mattie's, the reason for the old woman's hesitancy becomes quite clear. "Oh, about that time when you offered Shaka the candy," she begins, feeling awkward and embarrassed, "I didn't mean nothing by it. It's just that I thought you were a..." she doesn't finish the sentence, stopping short of actually saying the words, "bag lady."

"I was just being careful."

"No need to apologize, chil'. You did the right thing. And had I not been so caught up in my own business, I would have asked you first if it was okay for him to have the candy. That would have been the proper thing to do."

"Here you go, baby," she says, pushing the saucer in front of the little boy, who grabs the teacake with both hands, bringing it up to his face to savor first with his eyes and nose before munching away at the crisp, golden edge. A smile of satisfaction spreads across Miz Mattie's face as she heads to the refrigerator to pour a cup of milk for the little boy, while remembering how her Charlie had also favored the cookies from the outer edge of the pan. When she returns with the cup of milk, she sees Jamela eating the crumbs from her plate with moistened fingertips while hungrily eyeing the pan of still warm cookies.

"These are really good. Is it okay if I have another one?"

"Sure, help yourself! It don't take no more than a minute to cook up a batch. I learned how to cook at my mother's knee when I was just a little thing, not much bigger than this baby," she says, affectionately stroking Shaka's head. "I always enjoyed baking best. Still do, I suppose." she adds, turning to put water on for tea. When she turns back around, she's pleased to see Jamela helping herself to two more teacakes, as well as placing another one on Shaka's saucer.

While waiting for the water to boil, Miz Mattie softly hums as she begins placing items on the freshly lined shelves. She goes over to a large box in the corner and returns carrying the sterling silver-plated serving tray with her precious tea set on top. Placing it down on the kitchen table, she stands there for a moment, beaming down proudly at its contents.

"Are we gonna have tea in those!" Jamela asks eagerly, discarding her slouched position and assuming what she considers to be the proper posture of a lady worthy of handling such finery.

"Oh, good heavens, no!" Miz Mattie exclaims. "This here is a wedding gift from my parents," she says, quickly removing the tray from the table and placing it on the bottom shelf of the cabinet.

"Here," she says, retrieving two mismatched coffee mugs

from the kitchen counter, "we can use these." With the aid of another teacake, Jamela quickly pushes down the disappointment that wells up inside of her.

"These are really good," she says again, with only a tinge of longing remaining in her voice, and her body unconsciously slouches forward and she places both elbows back on the table. "You're a great cook. I never learned how to cook."

"Well, thank you. I suppose I do okay," Miz Mattie replies, and seeing the empty cookie sheet, is reminded of the pan still in the oven and quickly makes her way over to it.

"When I was a young girl, all the women folk swore that the quickest way to a man's heart was through his stomach," she says, as she stuffs her hand back into her oven mitt.

"Well, things are a bit different these days," Jamela states matter-of-factly.

"Nowadays, a man don't care so much if you can cook or not. My momma always says that what a woman needs to know is how to take care of business in *another* room of the house, if you know what I mean," she says with lowered voice and raised eyebrow.

"Oh, is that so!" Miz Mattie replies, having caught the innuendo, and trying unsuccessfully to keep the shock and disappointment she feels from showing on her face.

"Well, no disrespect to your momma, but I personally think that's the last thing a young woman should be worrying about. 'Cause while it may work to get you a man, it sure don't do nothing to keep 'em!"

The instant the words had crossed her lips, Miz Mattie knew that she had erred in speaking so frankly. She barely knew this young girl, and here she was badmouthing her momma. She felt embarrassed by her behavior.

"Yeah, well, you're probably right about that," Jamela says, suddenly looking very tired and very vulnerable. A moment or two of awkward silence follows before she pushes away from the table and gathers her son back up in her arms. After thanking Miz Mattie again for the teacakes, she mumbles something about needing to get Shaka to bed, while looking around in search of the quickest escape route.

Miz Mattie leads her through the maze of boxes back to the front door, bids them both good night, and silently watches as Jamela climbs the stairs to her apartment. With the sleepy child's legs wrapped around her torso, Jamela looked little more than a child herself, a weary child with a very big responsibility.

Mattie felt bad. Real bad. Here she had finally gotten somebody to talk to, and she had gone and put her foot in her mouth and caused her to run off. She realizes now that she had probably hit a sore spot with Jamela. She didn't know much about the chil', but she had eyes, and she could see. And what she saw was a young girl trying to raise a child alone. What she didn't know, but wondered about, was the journey that had led Jamela and little Shaka to this house on Ravenswood; how Jamela came to be in this situation in the first place.

"But that really ain't none of my business!" she asserts to herself. "My job here is to try and manage this place as best I can, now that Mr. Henry's gone. But more importantly, my job is to be a good neighbor; someone folks are happy to see when they happen to cross my path during their comings and goings." Returning to her kitchen, she carefully wraps the remaining teacakes in tin foil, then ties the bundle with twine and finishes it off with a large uneven bow. Tightly clutching the polished handrail, she slowly makes her way up the flight of stairs to the second floor. Once there, she places the silvery parcel on the 'Welcome' mat at Jamela's front door. She lingers there for a moment to catch her breath before carefully making her way back home.

~ ~ ~

As she stands drinking in the beauty that is her sleeping brown wonder, the words of the old woman echoes in her head. She couldn't even bring herself to be too mad at Miz Mattie. There was something about her that felt strangely familiar and uncharacteristically comforting. Every since was a little girl, Jamela had longed for her grandmother. She had always believed that had she known her grandmother, either of them, her life would have been a bit easier... a little kinder. "Maybe..." she begins, but immediately stifles the thought, refusing to even allow herself the luxury of fantasy. "I'm so stupid," she chastises herself. "That woman probably has a boat load of grown kids, which means she's got an even bigger boat load of grand kids. She certainly ain't got no time for the likes of me to be hanging around."

Still, she couldn't deny how nice it felt just sitting and talking and eating those warm teacakes at the kitchen table. "I sure wish I knew how to bake those teacakes for Shaka," she says to herself, "Momma can't teach me, 'cause momma don't bake. Never even baked so much as a birthday cake for any of us kids," she sighs, as she climbs into bed and turns out the light.

CHAPTER 7

Before Shaka was born, Jamela lived at home with her mother and her two younger brothers. Things were far from ideal, but tolerable. But once she made the life-changing announcement that she was pregnant, living with her mother became downright unbearable. While there probably were many subconscious and, therefore, unspoken factors contributing to the friction at home, raging hormones no doubt played a major part.

On the one hand, Jamela's body was working to put the finishing touches on the new life within its womb, coupled with the fear that at some unknown hour, said womb would commence with mind-numbing, teeth-gnashing contractions designed to enlarge a tightly closed hole to the size of a bagel, in preparation for pushing out a head the size of a cantaloupe. All of these factors combined, resulted in Jamela being uncomfortably big, unimaginably frightened, and downright bitchy!

On the other hand, Jamela's mother's womb had just finished erecting a *'Going Out of Business'* sign, and her body was working round-the-clock to shut down her baby producing facility, resulting in her being extremely hot, extremely sweaty and, yes, downright bitchy!

34

CHAPTER 8

Although Jamela's doctor was aware of her desire to deliver her baby naturally, when Jamela showed up in the Emergency Room in labor and alone, she was doubtful that her delivery would be able to proceed as planned.

"Giving birth can be an extremely long and painful process, Jamela. Isn't there someone you can call to come and be with you - the baby's father? Your mother?"

To both inquiries, with eyes downcast, Jamela shook her head, no. Ten long agonizing hours later, her doctor breathed a sign of relief when Jamela's mother finally walked through the doors. But after an hour or so of witnessing her screaming obscenities at the nurses for not following *her* orders, "Forget what she told you she wants! What does she know about having a baby, she's just a baby herself! Now give her the damn drugs!" and upon realizing that the tortured look in Jamela's eyes was caused not so much from the physical pain of labor, but from the emotional distress caused by her mother's presence, the doctor tactfully, but firmly suggested to her mother that she leave and return in the morning.

"We're looking at possibly 5 to 6 more hours of labor before any pushing can begin. Rest and quiet," she continued, "is what's best for Jamela, at this point."

Her mother gave the doctor a cockeyed look, intended to her challenge her authority, but when she saw that the doctor didn't blink or take a step backward, she finally conceded but not before exclaiming loudly, "Well, fine! I'm tired any damn way!"

Throughout the night, it was Jamela's doctor who continuously instructed her to breathe, pant, and relax, until finally, after much pleading and bargaining from Jamela for the Lord to please have mercy on her soul, her doctor finally spoke the only word that Jamela wanted to hear, "Push!" The pain of the preceding grueling hours immediately vanished once they placed her newborn son on her chest. "Oh, God! He's beautiful!" she cried. *Surely things will get better once momma sees her beautiful grandson.*

Sadly, that hope was quickly dashed when her mother returned to the hospital and immediately began ridiculing the African names Jamela had carefully and consciously chosen for her son. She taunted Jamela for her unflagging commitment to continue to try and breast feed, despite her raw, sore nipples. And each time Jamela reached into the bedside crib to pick up her crying son, her mother yelled, "What 'cha doing, trying to spoil the boy?! You'd better let that child cry hisself to sleep!"

Still exhausted from the 21 hours of labor, and feeling under equipped and overwhelmed, Jamela had cried as she fought to explain to her mother that she was simply trying to honor her own inner mothering rhythm. Her mother had simply snarled and mockingly taunted, "Own internal rhythm."Jamela wasn't sophisticated enough to know, let alone articulate, that there was actual documented research that supported her parenting style – following what her heart was instructing her to do, she only knew that it felt right.

Once back at home, Jamela fought to keep the peace by repeatedly reciting The Lord's Prayer and The Ten Commandments, specifically the one about honoring thy mother and father. And despite the continued opposition from her mother, for the first 6 months of little Shaka's life, he thrived in the comfort of his mother's embrace, as she instinctively kept his little body close to her own. Her strong brown arms were the cradle that gently rocked him to sleep each night as she softly hummed long-buried lullabies, songs that had been tucked away in the dormant recesses of her brain, waiting for this precise moment to resurface. But as soon as Jamela had weaned Shaka from her breasts, her mother began a relentless campaign to get her to start dating again.

"What is the point of that?" Jamela had asked.

"The point," her mother spat, "is that now that you done gone and got yourself a baby, you need to find a man to look after y'all. You can't expect to stay up under my roof forever!" Though the thought of leaving home and living on her own was terrifying, Jamela saw it as a necessary step toward getting her life on the right track. She had always said she didn't want to end up like her mother - alone with a bunch of kids, each one with a different daddy. Yet, here she was traveling along a similar path; a different reasons perhaps, but the same path, nonetheless.

Another factor that made the decision to move easier was the fact the she wasn't too keen on her mother's latest male friend. Her mom had always dated decent enough guys, but lately it appeared as if she had started feeling desperate or less attractive, because her selections seemed to be coming from a pool of throwbacks - men that other women didn't want and threw back into the pool of potential mates. Her latest 'catch' was some joker named Joe. And even though Joe lived with them, most of the time anyway, the word on the street was that he had a younger woman on the side. Jamela knew enough to stay out of her mother's business, but after coming home one day and finding Joe parked out in front of the house with his PYT in the passenger's seat, Jamela felt that Joe had overstepped his boundaries. Even if the rumors were true, she was not going to sit by and let him be disrespectful in front of her mother's own home. It didn't matter that she wasn't there at the time, if Jamela had seen him, she was sure several of the neighbors had seen her as well.

After much soul searching and struggling with that 'honor

thy mother' thing, Jamela finally got up the courage to tell her mother that she felt Joe was taking advantage of her and setting a bad example for the boys. And, since they were already on the subject of his indiscretions, Jamela took the opportunity to address Joe's annoying habit of walking around the in his boxer shorts, a habit which she viewed as distasteful and disrespectful. She'll never forget her mother's amused expression nor the response that followed, "Darlin'," she began, in that exaggerated Southern drawl she used whenever she was being mean or sarcastic, "Darlin'," she had repeated for effect, "What that man chooses to do in the streets is his business. And so long as he keeps paying the rent, he can walk around the house with a pair of dirty drawers on his head too!" That was the defining moment when Jamela knew it was time for her to get the hell out of Dodge. And so, one month after her 17th birthday, right before her child had mastered the art of walking steadily on his little bowed legs, Jamela moved out of her mother's home and into the house on Ravenswood.

CHAPTER 9

The miniature light bulb inside the refrigerator illuminates her diminutive, boy-like frame with its soft glow as Jamela tilts her head back and drains the last of the orange juice from the carton. Quietly tiptoeing back down the hall, the silence that greets her tells her that Shaka is still asleep. A quick peek into his bedroom finds him tossing and turning in his crib, a reliable indicator that he'll be up soon, leaving her with just enough time to grab the morning paper and get breakfast started. "What's it gonna be today?" she asks rhetorically, already knowing perfectly well what the answer will be. Breakfast time was easy. Shaka wanted hot cereal every morning, even on the hottest of days, and Farina was his favorite. "Thank goodness I at least know how to cook that," she sighs, thinking back to last night's admission of her lack of cooking skills, plus the fact that although she has cooked Farina practically every day since Shaka started eating table food, she still has to occasionally mash out lumps before her bowl of cereal bore any resemblance to the smooth and creamy bowl pictured on the box. Filling a small, battered pot with a half of cup of water and a tiny pinch of salt, she places the pot on the stove to boil. With a few calculated minutes to spare, she throws her coat on over her pajamas, pulls opens the front door and is prepared to sprint unnoticed down the stairs to retrieve the paper, when she trips and stumbles and falls smack into the door of the apartment across the hall. Looking down she spies a silvery bundle resting midway the stairs. She pounces down the steps and, without breaking her stride, scoops up the foiled bundle, tucks it beneath her arm and continues her descent down the stairs.

Opening the heavy outer door, she reaches down and brushes away a thin layer of freshly fallen snow and retrieves the newspaper addressed to Mr. Henry. As she closes the door, she brings the silvery bundle up to her nose and sniffs. A smile slowly creeps across her face, as she turns sharply on her heels, intent on quickly retracing her steps and getting back upstairs, when she sees that the door to Miz Mattie's apartment is slightly ajar. She hesitates for a moment, before gently knocking.

"Come on in!" a voice rings out from the other side of the door.

"Morning!" Jamela calls out cheerfully as she pushes the door open further and sees Miz Mattie approaching her while drying her hands on a dishtowel.

"Thanks for the teacakes," Jamela says, gesturing to the package under her arm, "But you really shouldn't have."

"Oh shush, chil'. Like I said, I enjoy baking. I'm just glad that now I got somebody around I can share 'em with."

"Well, I just stopped in to say thanks. I didn't mean to take you away from whatever you were doing. Besides, I've gotta run. I'm sure my pot of water is boiling by now."

"You left that baby upstairs with a pot of boiling water on the stove!?" Miz Mattie asks, one hand flying to her chest and the other to her mouth in unveiled alarm.

"Well...yeah." Jamela answers. "But he's asleep. And he's in his crib, so even if he does wake up, he can't get into nothin'," she explains, becoming irritated for feeling the need to again defend herself to this woman, and thinking, *Damnit! That's what I get for stopping. In the time it took me to explain myself, I coulda been back upstairs with my baby.*

Miz Mattie bites down hard on her bottom lip try to keep from chastising Jamela.

Lawd, have mercy! she thinks, but because she simply could not hold her tongue, continues,

"'Cause if you ever needed somebody to look after the little fella, I'd be more than happy to."

Jamela, who had hastily turned to leave, now stops in her tracks.

"Oh?" She hadn't expected this. Her own mother wouldn't even watch Shaka without Jamela paying her up front first.

"You mean that?" she asks, eyes looking simultaneously suspicious and hopeful.

"Yes, of course. I wouldn't have said it if'n I didn't mean it."

"Well, thanks. I just might take you up on your offer," Jamela says, turning and bounding up the stairs and yelling back over her shoulder, "Thanks again for the teacakes!"

"You're welcome, baby!" Miz Mattie says, as she waves to her departing back, "Tell Shaka I said, 'Morning!'"

Back inside her apartment, Jamela places the package on the kitchen counter, tosses her coat onto the couch, and kicks off her shoes. She lowers the fire beneath the pot to a simmer and stirs in two tablespoons of Farina before heading back to the bedroom to check on Shaka. She's got one foot inside the bedroom door when she is greeted by a whooping yell. Jamela hurries over and swoops the small boy up into her arms and gives him a big, noisy kiss. "Good morning, baby," she says, nuzzling her face into the sweet dampness of his neck. "Miz Mattie told me to tell you good morning too"

"Cookies?" Shaka asks.

"That's right, baby," she answers smiling, "Miz Mattie's the lady who baked the cookies last night." After washing his face and hands, Jamela slides Shaka into his high chair, places his tiny hands in the prayer position, as together they say grace.

"God is good."

"God."

"God is great."

"Great."

"And we thank him for our food."

"Food."

"Amen."

"'Men."

"Good boy!"

Jamela slowly swirls the spoon around the outer edge of the bowl and patiently feeds her son. When all that is left is a small mound in the center of the bowl, she turns the spoon over to Shaka while she goes and retrieves the silvery package from the counter. She unfolds the tin flaps and looks down appreciatively at the mouth-watering treats. There's a baker's dozen. Some are now broken in half, and others are crumbling around the edges from being kicked down the stairs, but that doesn't deter Jamela, and she hungrily devours two and one half teacakes while still standing at the counter, then places another one aside for Shaka to have once he is done with his cereal.

She pours herself a glass of milk and sits back down opposite Shaka and watches adoringly as he feeds himself the remaining cereal, aware that only half of what is left will actually make it into his mouth. The other half will mysteriously find its way into his pajamas and his soft, sand colored hair. *Miz Mattie's a nice old lady*, she thinks to herself, *Nosy as hell, but nice.*

~~~

Jamela finds herself thinking a lot about Clyde a lot lately. Not that she intended to, but whenever she was not obsessing over something on her 'To Do' list, whenever her mind had time to drift freely. . . it always found its way to him. Clyde stops by three to four times a month to pick up Shaka and bring him to his, rather, his parents' house for the weekend. He is a good dad to their small son, and Jamela's heart swells, then breaks just a little, whenever she sees Shaka's face light up at the sound of his daddy's sputtering, beat up Chevy pulling into the driveway. Jamela makes a special point of having Shaka's bag packed and waiting by the door when Clyde arrives, so their encounters are always very brief. Never a need for more than the hand-off: "Hi. Here ya go. He's all set!" Then to Shaka, "Bye baby. Love you! Mommy'll see you soon." Kiss. Kiss. Big Hug. And they're out the door. Total Time: Two minutes. Three tops.

But lately, whenever Clyde stops by to pick up Shaka, Jamela feels awkward and exposed. And the once religiously packed bag is now mysteriously missing an essential item like Shaka's pajamas or his favorite toy train. Small oversights, done with the intention of keeping Clyde lingering in her home a bit longer. And while she's in the back searching for the missing sweater, the hat, or whatever is the excuse of the day, hopefully he'll grow tired of standing and sit and rest, like he has done on a few occasions in the past, unknowingly leaving behind the warm scent of his body in the cushions of her third-hand sofa. Then, once she's all alone, and her little apartment suddenly seems to lack the air necessary to breathe, she'll stretch out in all her nakedness along the full length of the sofa. With eyes closed and her face turned inward toward the rear cushions, she'll deeply breathe in Clyde's natural body scent mingled with the Egyptian musk he favors. And wrapped in her own arms, she'll gently stroke the fire that starts in her toes until it completely consumes her. Then, as her body arcs and strains for that elusive sweet release in the cheery light of the morning

43

sun, she'll silently cry tears of shame and regret.

If anyone were to ask Jamela what had happened to cause the demise of her relationship with Clyde, she would be hard pressed to answer why, just three months shy of giving birth to their child, she had felt it necessary to usher him out of her life. But one of the benefits of being out of her momma's house and, by extension, removed from its daily drama, was the fact that for the first time in her life, she could quietly sit and think. *Really* think. About important issues. About life. And it was during one of these reflective moments, when she felt she could bear the pain of the truth, that she had finally admitted to herself that the reason she had stopped seeing Clyde was because of her mother's hostility toward him, and her estimation that he was, in her words, "a possessed punk," and all because of a little star. Looking out from the center of Clyde's left pupil, surrounded by a disc of ebony, was a small ivory star. The outline of the star was so exact, it looked to have been cut by a stencil.

Jamela still recalls the day she took Clyde home to meet her family. Her mother had taken one look at him, and the lit cigarette dangling from her red lips had fallen to the floor as she beat a hasty retreat from the room. Confused and embarrassed by her mother's abrupt exit, Jamela had excused herself to seek an explanation and an apology, only to find her mother kneeling beside her unmade bed, hands clasped and eyes clinched, reciting The Lord's Prayer. She had not had any success in soothing her mother's fears. What was there that she could say, really? According to Clyde, the star had been there for as long as he had been in this world, possibly longer. So accustomed had he become to its presence that when he looked at his reflection in the mirror, he rarely noticed it. Only when he looked into the eyes of strangers and noticed the way their eyes suddenly dipped, unable or unwilling to hold a direct gaze, was he reminded that the irregularity of his pupil unnerved some people. Jamela, however, loved the star. When she looked into Clyde's eyes, she felt as if the star was her secret portal to peer into the depths of his soul. She once told her mother that when she was with Clyde, the world somehow made more sense. In her classic Southern drawl, her mother had replied, "Sweetie, let me explain something to you. The world is fucked up. Now, that's all you need to know about that."

Clyde was always kind to her, and she knew he would be a good father to their child. Yet despite knowing this, Jamela eventually broke under the pressure of her mother's constant barrage of insults, put downs and just downright meanness. Her mother had even found reason to taunt Clyde for planning to attend college instead of working full time. He had explained to Jamela that for the time being at least, school *was* his job. And that he and his parents, the reluctant yet excited soon-to-be grandparents, had worked out an agreement where if he maintained a GPA of at least a 3.0, they would shoulder the financial responsibilities of their grandchild until he finished college and found employment. And further, he explained, getting his college degree would better position him to provide for all of their future needs. This explanation made sense to Jamela, but when she had tried explaining it to her momma, she had simply sucked her teeth and hissed, "Momma's boy!"

As Jamela's stomach grew, and her battles with her mother intensified, she vented her frustrations by lashing out at Clyde with angry, biting words. But when she denied him the right to be present for the birth of their child, because her mother had already vehemently stated that Jamela had to choose - him or her, Jamela knew that her mother had succeeded in scoring the victory shot. And with that final piercing blow, Jamela's world ceased to make any sense. On the morning following Shaka's birth, Clyde received a phone call from Jamela's mother who unceremoniously announced: "It's a boy. You's a daddy now."

CHAPTER 10

"Damnit!" Vamp groans, as she kicks with both feet to free herself from the mess of tangled blankets. As her amber legs shoot free, the arch of her right foot comes to rest on something smooth and hard. Peering down toward the foot of her bed, she sees a couple of unusual bedmates - a lipstick stained shot glass and a whiskey bottle. Lifting her foot, she sees that the bottle, a fifth, is empty. Her brow wrinkles as she tries to recall how her bed got littered with all this crap. "Ahh, yes," she says as pieces of the previous evening come floating back, "Cat's little TGIF celebration." Her mouth is so parched that her tongue feels like a slab of cotton. Looking around the room she spies a half empty bottle of beer on the nightstand. She grabs it and takes a long, hard swig. "Ugh! That's God awful!" she says, wiping her mouth with the back of her hand. "But you know what they say," she reasons, "some shit about the hair of the dog that bit you. Wonder how that little cliché ever came to be," she says as she finishes off the flat beer then tosses the bottle onto a mound of discarded clothing. *Man, that must have been some gig last night,* she thinks. As her mind strains to recall the actual events from the previous evening, an unexpected loud knock at her bedroom door jolts her back to the present.

"Who's there?" she calls out a bit too loudly, her voice sounding like a stranger's, even to her own ears.

"It's me. Cat." her roommate replies while turning the doorknob to enter. With the agility of a feline that surprises even her, Vamp leaps from her bed and slams the door shut with the full weight of her body.

"Damn, girl!" Cat yells. "What the hell!? You coulda broke my friggin' nose!"

"Sorry, girl!" Vamp apologizes through the door, "I'm not decent. Give me a couple of minutes to throw something on and I'll meet you downstairs for breakfast."

"Breakfast? It's almost 4 o'clock!"

"Yeah, of course it is! Then in that case, we'll do an early dinner. I'll meet you downstairs in a few, and we'll figure out what we are going to do for dinner. How about that?" Cat's response is to not respond, and all Vanessa hears is the angry clicking of her descending high heels. *Man, that was close*, she sighs as she listens to Cat's retreating footsteps while she takes in her surroundings. *I don't know what happened here last night, but what I do know is that I can't have Ms. Cat coming in here and seeing all of this crap strewn about. She seems to take some perverse pleasure in seeing me drunk and disorderly. If she really thought I had a drinking problem, she wouldn't be throwing parties nearly every weekend to add fuel to the fire...would she?*

A sudden rise of bile interrupts her thoughts and brings her to her knees, *Ugh, looks like I might have to pass on dinner too.*

~~~

Vamp and Cat had known each other since high school, and had always engaged in what they termed, 'friendly competition'. So far, they were pretty much neck-and-neck with their professional achievements, but Vamp perceived Cat as having a slight advantage because her family had money. It wasn't like she was born into money; her folks had just gotten lucky and had hit the Big Lottery when Cat was a senior in high school. And even though their sudden good fortune had enabled Cat to go on to an expensive and reputable college, she still had plenty of street left in her that, under certain situations, wasn't a bad thing. During the last six months, both women had aggressively begun the pursuit of what they considered to be the next logical rung on the ladder of success: to become a respectable married woman, purchase a big house in the suburbs and give birth to no less than two, but no more than four, kids. Given the fact that they were not even competing for the same type of man, should have made this experience fun - Vamp liked her men handsome and sophisticated, while Cat preferred athletic bad boys. Yet, the competition had placed an unexpected strain on their relationship. They both wanted to win. And, winning trumped friendship every time.

Crossing the room on her hands and knees, Vamp catches sight of herself in the full-length mirror at the foot of her bed and winces. Her sandy brown hair, always impeccably coiffed, is matted to both sides of her head. Her hazel, bloodshot eyes are rimmed in black from smudged eyeliner and mascara. "I look like a clown," she says to her reflection, "A fuckin' psychotic clown, at that." The designer outfit she had worn last night lies crumpled in a heap on the floor beside her bed, and at some point had been replaced with a purple tee-shirt with the word 'Barbados' emblazoned across the front, and a pair of knee socks, although one had gone missing. Peering underneath her bed in an attempt to find her sock's mate, she finds an ashtray overflowing with lipstick stained cigarette butts, and the butt of what apparently at one time was one big ass joint. Vamp rarely smoked marijuana because it only made her want to screw, eat and sleep, usually in that order. And since she had been chaste for a few months now (an orchestrated move on her part to squash her 'party girl' reputation), she had not bothered to replenish her personal stash. Although at parties, it wasn't unusual for her to take a hit or two. Social toking, she called it, which she viewed pretty much the same as social drinking, done primarily to gain a sense of inclusion.

Abandoning her search for the sock, she crawls to the

window and peers up at the sky. A closet cloud gazer, Vamp could always find a modicum of peace in the blue sky with its white billowy clouds, one of the last remaining places on Earth left relatively untouched and unmarred by man. Today, the sky's somber colors mirror her mood and offer no sense of light or hope. Feeling suddenly very weary, she stretches out on the floor beneath the window and rests her head upon a pile of blankets, while trying to ignore the unsettling feeling in the pit of her stomach, and the small voice of alarm going off inside her head.

~~~

Vamp thought she had it going on. She had an MFA, drove a BMW, vacationed in the UK and the CZ, and wore clothes designed by D&G, L.A.M.B. and Y-3. In many ways she lived a duel life. When not working at her stuffy, conservative job, she lived and partied like a rock star, luxuriating in the fawning adoration of her many admirers. Everyone she met was impressed by some aspect of her life - what she looked like, what she wore, what she drove, where she lived, where and what she ate – everyone, except her parents. What she perceived as their indifference to her success, hurt. But she had discovered that it hurt a little bit less when she drank. And so she drank. She drank to the good times, the bad times, she drank just about all the time.

Having started drinking at a very early age, nowadays it was second nature, something she did by rote. Coming of age during a time when cigarettes were considered uncool, and alcohol was the new king, drinking marked her rite of passage. With the help of her older brother and his friends, acquiring alcohol had been easy. No one thought twice about sending the message that sometimes the only place relief could be found was in a bottle. No one told her how the destruction of families and the loss of jobs were often a direct by-product of the seductively packaged elixirs. Sadly, it appeared that no one present fully understood the far-reaching damage being done as they wiled away lazy summer afternoons, sprawled out on the hot grass passing a bottle from adult to minor and back again.

But things had changed quite a bit since the days of Vamp's drinking initiation in the neighborhood parks. She no longer drank beer or cheap wines with high alcohol contents, or rotgut, as they were appropriately nicknamed. Nowadays, she considered herself somewhat of a connoisseur of wines, but also had a personal penchant for smooth whiskeys, which she liked to consume in trendy new restaurants and the bars of 5 star hotels. This was in stark contrast to some of her childhood drinking buddies who could still be found hanging out at the park or standing on street corners drinking cheap swill straight from the bottle. The street corner nearest the liquor store was where all those who had slid to the lowest strata of drinking - social drinker turned wino - could be found. Their reason for choosing this particular locale was obvious, it was the most likely place to run into a buddy who had just scored a bottle. And if he happened to be having a good day, i.e., no monkey on his back, he would usually allow his closest comrades a swig or two, with the explicit understanding that when the day came when his funds were short and his supply dried out, they would return the favor.

Vamp was not so naive as to think that everybody with a drinking problem hung out on street corners. And while she never feared that life would take her to such low depths, she did realize that she shared something in common with those poor slobs on the corners. That she, like them, had a life which revolved around drinking. She first realized that she might have a problem when she began having what she termed 'lost nights.' These were nights where she had huge blocks of time that she could not account for; where the only thing she knew for certain was that when the evening began, she had been in the company of one of her two good friends, Jack D. or Jim B.

CHAPTER 11

She's falling through the darkened sky, barreling head first toward the cracked pavement below, trying unsuccessfully to grab hold of anything that will stop her descent toward an ill-fated demise – a star, a lamp post, a clothesline. "What?! What time is it?"

Luckily, mercifully, just as always in the past, she wakes up before having to subconsciously experience the horrors of the concrete absorbing the impact of her fall. She rubs her eyes, smearing mascara across the bridge of her nose and down her left cheek. She pushes a button on the side of her wristwatch. Sunday, 6:00 a.m., flashes in neon green. *Jesus! That can't be right! What happened to Saturday?* She presses the button again. Sunday, 6:01 a.m. *Another day of my life wasted,* she sighs wearily, already resigned to the fact that no amount of moaning and groaning would get it back.

Even though she has just awakened from a lengthy sleep, she feels tired and agitated. An attempt at some deep breathing exercises succeeds in slowing down her breathing, but fails to calm her mind or ease the tension in her body. Afraid to look head on at her situation, from the periphery she allows herself to contemplate some of the issues that led not just to this particular moment, but to all the other numerous fucked up moments just like it. *I have got get off of this merry-go-round. It's not even fun anymore, and it just keeps bringing me back to this same dark place.* Looking out of the window at the dark sky, she finds a moment of solace in the sight of the large snowflakes floating silently to the ground. *The end of another year is almost here. I'm going to be 33 years old next year. I can't keep living my life like I'm some spring chicken. Thirty-three is not old, but today I feel old as hell. Cat suspects that I've got a drinking problem. Well, maybe I have got a problem. In any case, I've got to get this shit under control before it completely destroys my life. I can't keep waking up like this, not knowing where the hell I am. This shit ain't cute anymore.*

Her thoughts are interrupted by the sound of the shower going full blast. "What's Cat doing up this early on a Sunday morning?" she wonders aloud. Katrina, or to her good friends, Cat, was not known for being an early riser. Most weekdays Vamp had to check in on her to make sure she was awake and out of bed in order to make it to work on time. So for Cat to be up and in the shower before 7:00 on a Sunday morning was very unusual indeed. Sunday mornings were normally spent hanging around the apartment, drinking coffee, reading the newspaper and indulging in some serious girl talk. It suddenly dawns on Vamp that Cat is flying to Las Vegas for a team building exercise sponsored by the marketing firm where she works. Apparently several women in her department were jockeying for a newly created Assistant VP position and a serious estrogen war had ensured, hence the team building workshop. Even though the seminar was only slated to run through Wednesday, Cat had informed Vamp that she would probably stay on a few extra days to try her hand at the black jack table. All of this was find and dandy, but for Vamp the real significance of the trip was that no Cat meant no visitors. And no visitors meant no Danny. *Thank you, sweet baby Jesus!*

Danny was Cat's latest beau. An okay guy, but someone who Vamp felt had taken to hanging around their place too damn much. Both she and Cat had the occasional overnight guest who had the good sense to discretely disappear before dawn's light, but Danny not only hung around for breakfast, afterwards he would just walk around in bare feet with uncombed hair like he was at home and she was the visitor! In truth, Vamp did not like Danny. He made her uneasy in his presence. It might have something to do with the fact that he was still married. Maybe it was because at their first meeting he had attempted to engage her in a conversation about bestiality. All she knew was that her patience toward him had long worn thin, and her nerves were starting to fray. Vamp decides to linger in her room a while longer and give Cat enough time to finish primping and packing and being closer to actually walking out of front door before she heads downstairs. As she waits, she savors the freedom that is only moments away. Her excitement is hard to suppress, and she feels a big, silly grin forming across her face, as she breathes a sigh of relief. The smell of freshly brewed coffee beacons her downstairs. Cat could not start her day without a cup of strong Colombian coffee; she swore by it, and had eventually made Vamp a believer. Vamp pulls on her bathrobe, slips her feet into her house shoes after first pulling off the one sock, brushes her hair back into a ponytail before unlocking her bedroom door and heading downstairs.

"Hey, you!" Cat calls out as Vamp enters the kitchen. "Whatever happened to dinner last night?" she inquires as she hurriedly finishes her breakfast of toast and black coffee.

"Oh," Vamp begins, "Yeah, that. Sorry, but I wasn't feeling too good, so I decided to just stay in bed and rest."

"Humph! I thought you were mad at me about something and had a bug up your ass," Cat responds, "You know how you sometimes get."

"Well, dear friend, you were wrong." Vamp answers sweetly, not feeling up to a verbal sparring match this morning. Then more to the point, "What time's your flight?"

"My flight leaves at noon, but I'm going to swing by my folks place first and get some money from dear old dad."

Cat glances at her watch. "Hey, could you be a dear and help me carry these bags to the door? I'm running late, as usual."

"No problem. Happy to oblige," Vamp answers cheerfully.

She grabs one of Cat's two over stuffed suitcases and drags it to the front entrance. "Do try and have some fun. I know it might be hard, it being Vegas, and all." Vamp teases, trying not to sound too excited as she watches Cat run out into the hallway and jam the elevator door open with one suitcase before returning for the other.

"I'll do my best to find something to do in that dull little city" Cat responds with a giggle, as she flips her freshly sewn weave over her shoulder.

The elevator begins to buzz loudly as other tenants summon it for a ride. "I feel like I'm forgetting something," Cat says, her eyes nervously darting around the room as she nibbles on an acrylic thumbnail. The buzzing persists, followed by an angry shout from below.

"Damn it! Gotta run!" she says, grabbing her purse and giving Cat a quick peck and hug and goodbye.

"Have a safe trip!" Vamp yells after her as the elevator doors are closing. Cat nods her head, waves goodbye and is gone.

Vamp scoops up the Sunday paper and carries it into the kitchen and plops it down on the counter top before pouring herself a steaming cup of coffee. Her tension headache is starting to subside and her mood is growing markedly lighter. She is right in the middle of a private debate over which is the lesser evil, refined sugar or artificial sweetener, when the telephone rings.

"Hmm…wonder who this could be." she says, heading to the living room, coffee cup in hand. She picks up the receiver and is surprised to hear Cat's breathless, "Hello." The muted sound of traffic in the background informs her that Cat is calling from her car.

"Hey, girl, what's up? Miss me already?"

"Yeah. You wish." Cat states, "But seriously, when I ran out this morning, I knew I was forgetting something. All that damn buzzing and yelling made me forget to tell you that Danny might be stopping by."

"Yeah, alright. Did you leave something here for him to pick up?"

"Umm…not exactly. I left my keys with him just in case he needs a place to crash while I'm away."

"You did what!" Vamp yells. Obviously she had not heard correctly… the noise from the traffic, and all.

"I said, I left my keys with Danny because he might need …"

"I heard what you said!" Vamp interrupts. The impact of Cat's words leaves Vamp's face flushed and stinging, as if she had just been slapped across her face by a wet, open palm. "Why the hell would you do that?!" Vamp screams into the receiver "Did it ever cross your mind to maybe check with me first? You've done some dumb shit in the past, Cat, but this time you've outdone yourself!"

"What the hell are you getting all bent out of shape about? It's my home too, ain't it?" Cat demands.

"Yes, of course it's your home too" Vamp replies in a quieter tone, "But you're wrong, girl. And you know it."

"What the hell's so wrong with me offering my man a place to stay for a few nights?" Cat asks, her voice now loud and defiant. "I had planned on discussing it with you yesterday, but your high yellow ass stayed in bed all day; I won't even begin to speculate why. Besides, I pay half the rent, so I think I've got some say as to what goes on there."

"Of course you do. You know you do, "Vamp replies, massaging her pounding temples, "But damn, girl!"

"Girlfriend, you need to loosen up and stop trippin'. I know you, girl, and I know how bitchy you get when you ain't been laid in a while. So while I'm in Vegas, why don't you do us both a favor and go and get yourself a good long fuck. You know the kind I'm talking about, that toe-curling, back-scratching kind."

Vamp's mouth falls open, but the words that swirl around in her aching head never actually find their way out. *Here it is you have fucked up royally, but instead of offering me anything vaguely resembling an apology, you're telling me to go and get myself fucked! On a*

56

different day, I might take you up on your advice, but today ain't that day!

Cat mistakes Vamp's silence as proof that she is on the right track, and that Vamp is mulling over who she can call that could deliver the goods. Feeling that things were somewhat back under control, Cat figures that now would probably be a good time to end the conversation. "Look, girl. I really should be concentrating on the road, so I'll talk with you soon. Ciao!"

"Cat," Vamp begins calmly, thinking that with a little more reasoning, she could get Cat to understand that this week of all weeks was not the time to dump Danny on her, "Listen, girl..."

Click.

"What the . . . ?! Oh, no she didn't!" Vamp states, knowing full well that she had. Suddenly the words, "Danny might be stopping by," begin to reverberate in her head and she feels herself slowly coming undone. She slams the receiver down with one hand, and looks at the steaming black liquid in her other hand. *I'm so damn angry! I want to just hurl this cup right through the fucking window!* While the idea seemed attractive enough, given her incensed state, she had not actually bargained for her rage overriding her good sense, so she can barely believe it when she sees the cup spinning through the air, spilling its contents mid-flight. Luckily, it misses the window and hits the wall with a dull thud. Part of her mind urges her to run and get towels, but the portion of her brain that has short-circuited insists that she stay and watch as the sand colored Berber carpet soaks up the dark Colombian coffee.

Though her body is numb, her mind is spinning, and she watches as it fast forwards for her viewing pleasure possible scenarios for the upcoming week.

Scenario 1: She is home relaxing in a tub filled with bubbles and sipping a glass of pinot noir. Her fragrant panties are still on the floor at the door where she'd left them, and she doesn't have a care in the world until she hears the jangle of keys and the sound of the front door opening...

Scenario 2: She's in bed tossing and turning from a bad

dream. She opens her eyes to escape the images that appear all too real, when she sees two shadowy figures towering over her bed - Danny in his birthday suit with a lusty grin on his face and a Great Dane at his side.

Having now completely freaked herself out, her mind races wildly as she tries to think of ways to circumvent this intrusion on her private life. Her first thought is to have a lock installed on her bedroom door. Better still, why not have the locks on the front door changed? *But if I do that, it might provoke some type of confrontation with Danny. I can see him now, out there banging on the door demanding that I let his sorry ass in. And if he doesn't go away, what do I do then?* The thought crosses her mind that maybe she should go away for the week. "Damn it!" she cries, as tears of anger and frustration spill from her eyes, "This is my home! Cat had no right to place me in this predicament!" she cries; sinking to her knees, content to wallow in her misery. But just as quickly, she's back up on her feet. "Fuck it!" she says, wiping the tears from her face. Filled with a new resolve and aided by adrenalin, her body, while not ready to fight, prepares to flee. "Just this morning I said that I needed to make some changes. I just didn't expect it to happen so quickly or for it to be this drastic. But a woman's gotta do, what a woman's gotta do!" Her decision made, she readies herself for action. "I'd better get moving, there's no time to waste! But first ... I need a real drink."

~~~

With Sunday's classified section tucked securely under her arm, she slips on a pair of Armani sunglasses to hide her red, swollen eyes and leaves the apartment in long, determined strides. Even as lousy as her body feels, she finds comfort in knowing that she looks good. With her firmly sculpted body and her expensive designer clothes, she is one of the few people she knows who can say that they look just as good butt naked as they do dressed to the nines. Even the hair, while it wasn't bouncing, was at least behaving. As a young girl, back in the day B.P. (before perm), her parents couldn't afford to indulge her in weekly trips to the beauty salon, so she had to endure weekly hair pressings at the hands of her unskilled mother. She can still vividly recall the crackle of the flames licking the greasy hot comb, and the stench of burning hair. By mid-week when most pressed hair starts reverting to its natural state, she felt blessed that her hair was not nappy, and that she could make it through to the next pressing by applying lotion to her hair and brushing vigorously. This trick helped secure her desirability, and gave her a definite edge over her darker classmates, whose natural nappy hair would not succumb to mere lotion. These days she wears her hair chemically straightened, and when she cannot make it in to her regularly scheduled weekly salon appointment, her new quick fix is to sweep her hair up into a classic French twist.

She jumps into her red BMW, cranks the music up full blast, throws the gear into first, and burns rubber away from the curb. Her agenda for the day is simple: Find a new place to live. The goal is to find an apartment that she can afford on her own, but one that offers the amenities which she has become accustomed to: concierge, exercise room and a uniformed doorman who stays in his place. All of these things, she knew, came at a price, so she had even managed to convince herself that she could make do with a studio apartment. But while the ads read studio, in her mind she saw lofts - big, airy and spacious. Six hours and five apartments later, she realizes that with her current salary and hefty credit card debt, she could not afford to live downtown, uptown, damn near in anybody's town! All of the apartments she had looked at so far were too small and claustrophobic, but the trade-off of getting more space by taking on another roommate, would be akin to jumping out of the frying pan and into the fire. She checks her newspaper once more and slowly reads over the last remaining ad highlighted there. She had circled this particular ad earlier in the day not because she had any intention of viewing it, but because of the peculiar way in which it was written:

If you are looking for a place to live, and you're a clean, honest, God-

loving person, come to 7449 Ravenswood and ask for me.

My name's Miz Mattie.

"What type of person writes an ad like this?" she wonders aloud. But with the sun going down and her options running out, she turns the car around and heads South. South, to the side of town where only Black folks lived and where her parents, brother, and most of her childhood friends still live. South, to where she'd grown up as a girl, playing Double Dutch on the cracked pavement in front of the house that she'd left 13 years ago, swearing to return only for visits.

Her current dilemma gives her a new appreciation of the expression, "Never say never," because as she was just starting to realize, you just never know. The truth of her situation had suddenly become alarmingly clear. If she was to stick to her original plan of moving out, then she would have to eat her words, right after swallowing her pride, and return South to her old neighborhood or the 'hood, as it was now commonly known.

CHAPTER 12

She locates the street and circles the block once, then twice, to survey the neighborhood. She parks her car across the street from the house listed in the ad and looks out at it from behind the safety of her sunglasses. *Not too shabby*, she thinks, cracking the window and breathing in the fresh, crisp winter air. Finally gathering up her courage, she exits her car and is halfway across the street when she sees the old woman sitting on the porch partially hidden from view by the brick pillar supporting the upstairs porch. She climbs the stairs to the front porch and feigns an obligatory smile in the direction of the old woman - lips pulled tight across her face in what is meant to represent a smile, but comes off looking more like a grimace, revealing the falseness of the gesture, as she quickly scans the names next to the row of doorbells.

"May I help you, sweetie?" the old woman asks.

"Yes, maybe you can," Vamp responds, "I'm here to look at an apartment for rent."

"Oh Lawdie! I'd done almost forgot all about that. You's the first person to come by to see about the place."

"*You* placed the ad in the paper?"

"I sho did," she states proudly. "Why don't you have yourself a seat for a moment? I was just about to go in myself, but my foot went to sleep on me. Tee. Hee!"

Oh man, this is going to be rich, Vamp thinks, looking around for a place to sit. There was not another chair available, so she gingerly settles herself upon the stoop, after first checking to make certain that she was not lowering her leather clad butt onto dirt or bird poop.

"I was just telling Miss Carlton, that's the woman who lives across the street...I'm sorry, sugar, what's your name?"

"Vanessa. My name's Vanessa."

"My, that's a pretty name. You young girls these days have some of the prettiest names. Well, Vanessa, like I was saying, Miss Carlton's the woman who lives across the street whose grandchild sometimes comes over and plays with little Shaka," the old woman begins again, barely pausing long enough to catch her breath, "I was telling Miss Carlton about Reverend Isaac's sermon on the radio this morning. Reverend Isaac's a big time preacher. He got hisself a big congregation, close to a thousand members, or so they tell me. And he drives a big green Cadillac, the color of money, or at least that's what he says on the radio, 'cause I ain't never seen it myself. Anyway, this morning he's preaching about how we all had better fall to our knees 'cause Jesus is coming back and he's mad! But I told Miss Carlton that there ain't no reason to fear God cause I don't believe that God is hateful or vengeful. And if'n' he is, then we're all in a world of trouble, Reverend Isaac included.

" 'Cause when he sends his son back to walk 'mongst us, you know that's what the bible says he's gonna do, and it could be any day now; but when he comes back, I don't suppose that it'll be for the purpose of seeking revenge. Now, that ain't to say that he won't have plenty of work to do. No sir! 'Cause Lord knows we sho done made a mess of this here place."

What the hell is she yammering about?! Vamp silently screams as she sits stiffly on the hard concrete stoop listening to the old woman prattle on. She had only come by to check out an apartment. She didn't want to hear about God, his son, or his slick, Cadillac driving, self-appointed talking head. Feeling anxious, fatigued, and thirsty, Vamp wants nothing more than a cool drink of water and a safe, secure place to lay her head. Her inability to fulfill one of these basic needs is the only thing that keeps her rooted in her uncomfortable spot on the stoop enduring the mindless ramblings of an eccentric old woman.

Luckily, she quickly realizes that her undivided attention is not required for what is essentially a monologue, and as she tugs at the neck of her sweater and shifts from butt cheek to butt cheek, she starts to focus on the activity going on around her. Ordinarily, shopping for a place to live during the winter months did not allow for a true assessment of the flavor of a neighborhood, since most everyone is indoors cocooning. But today's weather feels more like an invigorating spring day, and the neighbors are out en masse. Even though she has been at the house for only a brief amount of time, she immediately notices one startling difference, aside from the obvious economic ones. Here it seems like everyone knows each other, talking and sharing a laugh in a causal, easy fashion, while back at her uptown apartment, folks kept pretty much to themselves. In fact, it was pretty typical to not know the name of your next-door neighbor, even though the only thing that separated you from some of the most intimate and personal aspects of their lives was a single sheet of gypsum board. She tunes back into the old woman's ranting long enough to inject an, "uh huh" in the silent gap left open for her response, coupled with an affirmative nod, even though she has no idea of what she just agreed to. *This old woman has obviously spent a lot of time at church too*, she thinks, observing the ease with which they both fall into the call and response cadence exclusive to Black churches. Even though she felt her rear end starting to go numb, sitting there in the sun being a participant in the rhythm of the block felt almost right. Maybe it was because of the many sunny afternoons she had spent sitting on a similar stoop at her parents' modest brick home. Or maybe the familiarity was due to the many sermons she and her brother, Marc, had endured together during their youth.

Growing up, every Sunday morning their parents had insisted that they attend church. Bible study coupled with morning service wouldn't suffice. Oh, no! We're talking all day church, here! Hour long bible study would segue into the morning service, which typically lasted for an hour and a half. Then there would be a good two hour break before mid-day service began, followed by another substantial break before the final evening service, which was also broadcast live over the radio. Following the morning service, most members of the congregation would head home, having had their fill of religion for the week. Still others would go home, relax and enjoy a meal before returning for either the mid-day service or the evening service. Then there were the hearty, die-hard sect; those members felt it their obligation to spend the *entire* day at church. Vamp's family was a part of this latter group. During the breaks, she and her brother occupied themselves by playing with the other children who were also being held hostage at the church by their parents, while the parents mingled with one another talking about church business, church politics, or good old church gossip.

And while all of this was taking place out amongst the pews, in the back kitchen a dedicated group of women would converge and trade in their mink stoles and high heels for aprons, hair nets and house slippers. Then they set about frying up chicken, mixing up bowls of potato salad, putting cans of soda into ice-filled wash tubs, and proudly slicing and arranging the homemade pies and cakes baked by the Mothers Board. Dinner was served up by these smiling, shiny, plump women who took your money in exchange for a plate of food and a, "God bless you, child." Not a bad deal for $3.00. Afterwards, everyone would trek back out front and take a seat in the wooden, folding chairs, which came equipped with tattered paper fans featuring an advertisement of the local funeral parlor on the front. The evening service was the only one that Vamp had actually enjoyed because that was when the choirs sang. Now mind you, they had sung during the morning and mid-day services too, but when the service was being broadcast over the airwaves in the evening, the young adult and adult choirs came together and they *Sang*!

Accompanied by the organist and the choir director, they always gave an electrifying performance. They would sing sweet songs of surrender that caressed you like the brush of an angel's wing, and alternatively rock the little church with shouts of *Joy!* and *Praise Him!* And as the organ music swelled to a soul piercing shrill, men, women and children would get hit by the Holy Spirit and leap from their seats as if hit by lightening, cutting a mean step across the floor, they would take out everything and everyone in their paths. Vamp enjoyed watching the Spirit at work, but had always been terrified that it might one day hit her too, sending her running down the church aisle in wild abandonment.

She had not realized it at the time, of course, but Vamp's childhood had been pretty sheltered and carefree. Her earliest recollection of being genuinely worried about anything happened at around the age of six when she had fretted over how Santa Claus would get in to deliver her presents, since their house did not have a fireplace. Then at age nine, it was whether or not Chris, the boy down the street, really liked her as much as her best friend, Mary, swore he did. And later in junior high school, she had stressed over whether her parents would buy her the red Chuck Taylor high-tops sneakers that all the cool girls at school wore stuffed with layers of knee socks that made their calves appear disproportionately larger than their thighs. She smiles now at the memories, and wonders if her current problems will ever, in hindsight, appear as trivial and insignificant.

"Baby, do you know that Jesus died for your sins?"

"Huh?" She sits up straight, as if she had been poked in the ribs. "Yes ma'am" she stammers, nodding her head in agreement. She had almost missed her cue that time. Her mind had been a million miles away or, more accurately, four miles and a couple of decades away. Almost against her will, Vamp finds herself relaxing and becoming slightly amused and entertained by the old woman; a mood definitely not in keeping with her usual one of annoyance and impatience when dealing with what she perceives as uneducated individuals. But sitting on the stoop in the sun, hearing the familiar hum of church-speak, she surrenders to her mental and physical fatigue and breathes a sigh of relief at knowing that, unless the place was a total and complete pig sty, her search might soon be over. She watches as the women on adjourning porches laugh and talk while keeping a casual, watchful eye on the small children playing nearby. Further up the block, she spies a group of guys engaged in a serious game of hoops in a vacant parking lot, while another group of young men hover over the engine of a car parked in a driveway, its greasy innards piled on a drop cloth on the ground. The young girls strolling down the street smile and show their appreciation for the young brothers by laughing a bit too loudly, while the bolder ones that take a pause in their journey to stop at the house with the disemboweled car, or stand at the outskirts of the parking lot cheering on their favorite players. The men are by no means oblivious to the attention from the girls, and every now and then one of the guys from the makeshift basketball court will glance in the direction of the cheering females to see if anyone noticed that he just got some serious air, never mind the fact that he didn't score any points. And the guys hanging out around the car slap each other's palms and bump chests, their way of broadcasting to any onlookers that they've just discovered where one of the many mystery pieces of the engine fit. It appears as if the spring like weather has sparked the premature arrival of the mating dance.

The familiar cadence of the voices and the rhythm of the bodies in motion fill her with an unexpected sense of peace. She shakes her head in amazement at how little things have changed since when she was a teen, as she sits on the stoop taking in the flow and vibe of the neighborhood, unaware that the watcher is also being watched.

She focuses back in on the voice coming from the porch just in time to hear, "My husband left me this here house before he passed on. God rest his soul. Now, the type of person I'm looking to rent to ain't gotta be the richest or the smartest person in the world; they just gotta be good people.

And by that I mean good where it counts - right here," she says, stabbing at her chest with a bony finger. There follows a short silence as she turns away and looks off into the distance, then adds softly, speaking as if to herself, "And I thank God everyday for Charlie and for this here house. 'Cause ain't no telling what talking to yourself and pictures on the wall all day can do to a person over time.

"I'm sorry," she says, returning her gaze to Vamp, "forgive my manners, I never introduced myself. My name's Miz Mattie, and like I said earlier, I own this here place. Now, what you say you name was again, sugar?"

~ ~ ~

"Well now, I don't suppose you came all the way here just to sit and listen to me talk, now did you? You'll have to forgive me, but I've gone so long without having anybody to talk to, now it seems I can't keep my mouth shut. Alright now, let's go on up so that you can have a look at the place." As she follows closely behind the old woman, who is climbing the stairs at a turtle's pace, Vamp finds herself again becoming anxious, and impatient that she had not had the foresight to take the lead. *I can't possibly get around her now, not on this narrow staircase. Even if I could, I would still have to wait for her to make it to the top. But I would at least have a better view.*

Once they both have reached the top landing, Vamp inquires about the price of rent and is shocked when Miz Mattie quotes a price that was a mere fraction of what the studios downtown had been asking for. She further learns that the place has not just one bedroom, but two! Vamp's elation quickly gives way to suspicion, as she logically evaluates the situation. *Okay,* she tells herself, *let's just think about this for a moment. Now, granted, the building is not in my preferred part of town...but still, for a two-bedroom apartment, she could easily get double the amount she's asking. And since she's asking for so very little, I can probably expect to find holes in the walls along with a host of uninvited guests.*

Hearing music coming from across the hall, Vamp wonders

about the person who resides behind the closed door. Almost as if the old woman had read her thoughts, Miz Mattie announces, "That apartment across the way is rented out to a very nice young lady and her small son. I'm sure you two will get along nicely. I stay downstairs. I can't manage these stairs like you young folks. The apartment across from me is empty too. I've been toying with the idea of fixing it up into a sitting room, unless you'd rather take that one," she says, looking over her shoulder at Vamp.

"No!" Vamp yells, rather too empathically. "I mean…no, thank you. The second floor is perfect for me. Good for your heart. You know…all those stairs…good aerobic workout," Vamp says, smiling awkwardly while thinking that she wanted to be as far away from those rambling sermons as she could possibly get. As she stands waiting patiently while Miz Mattie tries out what has got to be at least 1 dozen keys, self-doubt begins to gnaw at her confidence. *If I were to leave now, there would still be time to enact my original plan and have a lock installed on my bedroom door before nightfall.* But just as she is about to thank the old woman and quickly bolt down the stairs, she hears the lock click, and as Miz Mattie pushes the front door open, a beam of sunlight comes pouring out.

As she steps inside the apartment, her mouth drops open when she sees that the apartment is large, airy and clean! Once she is able to close her mouth, she becomes aware of the vague scent of fresh paint lingering in the air. Her silent critic kicks in to provide her with sufficient evidence to reject the apartment, and draws her attention to stray droplets of paint on the windowpanes in the living room. Common sense takes one giant step forward to remind her that the dried paint can easily be removed with a putty knife; a butter knife will even do in a pinch. Critic: The hard wood floors are dirty and lackluster. Common Sense: A good scrubbing and a coat of wax will bring them to a nice gloss. They move on into the kitchen, which is white and boring, but a large distressed wooden cabinet built into the far corner of the kitchen adds character and an unexpected old world charm. The refrigerator looks like a collector's item, but when she sticks her hand into the large empty box, a blast of cold air affirms that it is in good working order. *At this stage of the game, that's all that matters.* She heads toward the bedrooms and is disappointed to realize that neither of the two rooms are large enough to hold her king sized bed and armoire. Luckily, common sense is still in the house, "My bed can go in the larger and sunnier of the two rooms, and the smaller bedroom down the hall will hold the armoire nicely," she says aloud to herself, as Miz Mattie stands gazing out the window at the street below. The bathroom is pretty nondescript, but it contains a large claw foot tub and is clean and bug free. To Vamp's surprise the building, although old, has apparently been well cared for, evidenced by the polished hand railings, to the unmarred condition of the hard wood floors. While the old woman continues to chatter, Vamp walks from room to room, trying to envision herself actually living in this space. Could she give up all the perks and amenities she has grown so fond of and move back to the South Side and live in this old building with this talkative, old woman and some other lady and her kid? *Heck, I bet they won't even deliver pizza here mid-day,* she thinks, whereas at her current residence, she could order anything from sushi to crème brulee delivered right to her front door, day or night.

She knew she needed to move forward or, as they used to say when she was growing up, shit or get off the pot. But the thought of starting over on her own caused an actual physical ache in the pit of her stomach. Over the years Cat had become the sister she never had, a narcissistic irresponsible and unreliable sister, but a sister nonetheless. And then there was the gossip that was guaranteed to ensure. She was certain that some of her friends would get a good chuckle over what they would view as her descent on the social ladder. Laughing and joking about how the mighty Vamp has fallen. She had seen it done before, was even guilty herself of having participated in the gleeful celebration of someone else's misery. The mere thought of actually putting this life altering move into motion, coupled with the possible aftermath, drains her of all her remaining optimism, and just when she thinks that it is time to tuck tail and crawl back home, the image of Danny showing up unannounced in the middle of the night pops into her head.

"Okay. I'll take it!" she says, instantly feeling a sensation of relief. The hardest part was over. The decision had been made. Determined now to plough full speed ahead, she asks, "Do you have an application that I can fill out, and will you accept a personal check for the credit check?"

"Chil' there ain't no application for you to fill out, and what you mean by a credit check? If you say you want the apartment, then it's yours. You look to me like a good Christian woman, so I trust that you'll respect your neighbors and pay your rent on time. That's all I need to know. Now is there anything more you need to know?"

"Yes!" Vamp responds eagerly, suddenly feeling elated and free. "How soon can I move in?"

CHAPTER 13

The next morning is a mad whirl of chaos and commotion as Vamp frantically searches for a moving company. The first dozen or so places she contacts tell her they cannot accommodate her request on such short notice. Just when she is about to go into panic mode, she hits pay dirt when Billy, presumably the B in M, B & J's Moving Co., agrees to immediately send over one large moving van with driver, plus one additional man. Billy charges her the company's normal going hourly rate, plus an addition $300 for having to call his men in on such short notice, or, what he secretly refers to as a 'stupid tax.' For anyone else, two burly men to move one single woman would have been plenty sufficient, but because Vamp wants to get her stuff out of the apartment she shared with Cat as quickly as possible, she searches her BlackBerry and is able to quickly summon the help of three male companions. Though not committed to any of the men, she keeps close contact with all of them just in case she needed a little *some'um, some'um*.

With everyone on board and instructed of the game plan, Vamp orchestrates their movements like a mad conductor, never once breaking a fingernail or a sweat. Six hours later will all of her earthly possessions packed, loaded, and en route to

Ravenswood, she manages to secure a moment alone with each of her muscled friends to thank them with a passionate kiss and softly murmured promises. Each, not surprisingly, offers to help her with the unloading and unpacking, but each time she declines, preferring to enter her new home alone, free, and void of any unnecessary baggage. Vamp stands alone amidst the unsettling emptiness in the place that for the past five years she has called home. Because most of the furnishings belonged to her, the apartment now seems unusually large and barren. All that remains in the living room are two CD towers and a large neglected umbrella plant, its dried leaves littering the carpet like confetti. With all of the furniture gone, the new focal point of the room is the large unsightly coffee stain. Vamp stares down at the spot and wonders how Cat will feel when she comes home and discovers it. She knew that the sight of the empty apartment would wound her, but the sight of that ugly ass stain would be equivalent to pouring salt into a fresh wound. She regrets not taking the time to properly blot the stain yesterday while it was still fresh. Her attempts at cleaning it earlier today had only made it appear worse.

A wave of sadness hits her and her fingers linger on the doorknob, as she wonders one last time whether she's doing the right thing. It all suddenly felt so final... so extreme. She feels a lump growing in her throat, and the urge to collapse right on top of the huge repulsive stain and cry a torrent of tears for the weekend that had gone so wrong. The only thing that keeps her moving and up on her feet, is the fear of running into Danny. She had managed to find a place to live, pack up all her stuff and move it across town, all without crossing his path once. The last thing she wanted was to run into him now. She returns to the kitchen and drops her set of keys on the countertop, and daring to tempt fate a few moments longer, she jots down on a notepad a few lines of explanation/apology for her now ex-roommate.

Cat -

Sorry that I had to split so abruptly, but with Danny staying here while you're away tells me that the winds of change are a blowin'. It's been one wild ride! Thanks for the fun memories.

She starts to sign the note, Love, Vamp, but instead draws a heart, pierces it with an arrow and prints her full name beneath it.

~ ~ ~

As she passes by the living room window, Jamela notices a large moving van attempting to squeeze in between two parked cars. She backtracks and stops in front of the window and sees two men seated inside the front cab of the truck eating donuts and drinking coffee. It does not take long for her to see what they are waiting for, as moments later the red BMW returns. Jamela is surprised to see her back so soon, and with a moving van in tow, no less. "She sure didn't waste any time," she says, "I wonder what she's running from."

With one hand securing her red beret from the blustery winds threatening to blow it from its cocky perch on her head, Vamp jogs over to the parked van. Even from the vantage point of her second floor window, Jamela could tell that this woman was not like anyone she personally knew. She looked and dressed like a black version of the models in the fashion magazines that Jamela once hoarded. Magazines where all the models had alabaster skin and bodies built like pre-teen boys. Models who Jamela yearned to be like until she got rid of her old magazines and got ahold of ones with Blacks folks on the covers, and subsequently changed her name, her hair, and her attitude.

Vamp sticks her head inside the open window of the van and the man in the driver's seat jumps to attention, nearly scalding his balls in the process, as the hot liquid sloshes from his cup and onto his lap. He hurriedly climbs out of the cab of the truck, as his partner follows suit, and heads to the rear of the van where he lifts up the sliding rear door in one big *whoosh* and starts hauling boxes. Vamp runs ahead of the men to unlock and open doors so that the men can move her things right inside her apartment as instructed, and not set them down in the dirty, wet street. As she bounds up the stairs, she looks back over her shoulder and sees that the driver of the van is right on her heels. *Slow down, Sampson*, she thinks, *there's just the two of you now. Stop trying to impress me and pace yourself.* She watches in amazement as the huffing figure struggles with the two boxes labeled Kitchen. *If you think those are heavy,* she thinks, rolling her eyes in disgust, w*ait till you get to the boxes containing my free weights.* Looking back up toward the door ahead of her, she is startled to see a young woman suddenly appear at the top of the stairs. *This must be the girl Miz Mattie told me about. She could at least have warned me about those,* she thinks, spying Jamela's locs poking out from the top of a colorfully patterned scarf. *I wonder if she put those God-awful things in her kid's head too,* she thinks, trying hard not to let her face reveal her aversion to Jamela's natural hair, *Ugh, let's pray not.*

"Hi!" Jamela offers brightly as Vamp reaches the second floor landing, which spans the length of approximately 6 feet.

"Hi," Vamp responds, her back turned to Jamela as she fumbles with her set of new keys.

"Umm ... I'm Jamela. I'm your neighbor."

"Vamp. The name's Vamp." she says in reply, briefly glancing over her shoulder and looking over the top of another pair of designer glasses while jiggling a key in the keyhole. The door opens and Vamp rushes inside.

That was awkward, Jamela thinks, as she steps back into her own apartment for fear of being crushed by the box-laden men trampling up the front stairs. As she closes her front door, a hard shiver runs up the length of her spine. She wasn't sure if it was from the cold blast of artic air from below, or the icy reception of her new neighbor.

CHAPTER 14

Later in the week as she is returning home from a quick trip to the corner drugstore, Jamela sees Miz Mattie coming out of the vacant apartment across the hall and making her way back to her own apartment.

"Whatcha doing?" she asks, as she kneels down and unbuttons Shaka's coat, "Is someone *else* moving in?"

"Huh? Oh, no chil'. I ain't hard pressed for more tenants. I don't really need the money. What I need is more space. There is so much furniture in here, it makes it kinda hard for me to move about. So I thought I would spread out a little by moving some of the bigger pieces across the hall."

As they stand surveying the nearly vacant apartment, Shaka squeezes past both women and runs from the living room toward the rear of the apartment, pulling on an imaginary conductor's bell, delighting in the sound of his "choo-choo's!" echoing off the walls.

"Shaka! Come here, baby! You know you don't belong back there!"

"Let the chil' be. He ain't hurtin' nothing. Besides, he got the right idea. The last time y'all stopped by got me to thinking that the little fella needed a place to run and play, especially with it being so cold out. It ain't fair to ask that he sit still for too long, them young bodies are made for moving. And I want y'all to keep coming by to visit Miz Mattie, without you having to worry every minute about what the baby is up to.

"So, next time y'all come to visit, you won't have to keep Shaka glued to your hip. Cause if I told you once, I done told you twice, you keep carrying that chil' around on your hip like that and you gone end up lopsided.

"Yes..." she continues, while looking around, "This front area can be our sitting room, or what rich folks used to refer to as the parlor. You and Shaka are welcome in here anytime. Just think of it as an extension of your home.

"Thank you. It's real sweet of you to go to all this trouble."

"It ain't no trouble at all. Like I said, I enjoy your company and I want y'all to keep coming by to visit. I'd visit you sometime too, but those stairs are murder on an old woman's knees. So in truth, you could say my motives are a bit selfish. Go on in and take a look around. I had two of those fellas who are always across the way playing ball help me out by moving that big sofa in here yesterday. Today I was just in here pittlin' around, trying to see what else I can do to make the place more homey. But right now, I think I'll take a break and have myself a cup of tea. Would you like to join me?"

"I was just about to put Shaka down for his nap, but if you don't mind waiting about 15 minutes, I'd love to join you."

"He only naps for 15 minutes?"

"No," Jamela replies giggling, "It'll take him about 15 minutes to fall asleep."

"Oh. You're not planning on leaving him upstairs alone are you?"

"Well...yeah, I was. But I was going to leave the front door open. That way I'll be able to hear him if he wakes up."

"Why don't I just fix him up a spot on the couch? Then we can go on into the kitchen and have our tea, and he'll be within earshot and eye shot too. I don't know why I didn't think to fix up one of those bedrooms for the little guy. I'll have those young men come back tomorrow and take care of that. And while I'm at it, I'll see about having them move that big table over in here too. I'll figure all that out later on, but for now, y'all make yourselves comfortable while I some clean sheets and a blanket for the baby," she says, flashing a satisfied, denture free grin.

Miz Mattie returns with the sheets and blanket in a matter of minutes, and it quickly becomes apparent that the conversation did not cease just because she left the room, "...brought home jars and baking soda. The next time I bake some teacakes, we'll have a little party. Me, you, Shaka and Vanessa."

"Huh?" Jamela responds, as she drapes the sheet over the sofa and removes Shaka's shoes, uncertain of how much of that last sentence was intended for her.

"A tea party! It'll be fun!" Miz Mattie says, clapping her hands together like a small child. "Back home when I was a coming up, that was how people courted. Afterwards if you really liked the boy and your parents approved, he could come back for dinner. Then soon after that, you got married."

"Is that how you met your husband, Charlie?"

"No. My folks were strict, God-fearing people who didn't allow parties of any type, she says, suddenly recalling long forgotten memories

"But I heard they was nice...the parties, that is."

"Okay, count me in, but who the heck is this Vanessa you're gonna invite?"

"Vanessa. The new tenant." Miz Mattie replies, waiting for some sign of recognition. "The young lady who lives across the hall from you. I figured you two would have met by now. You must have seen her moving in."

"The person I saw moving in told me her name was Vamp."

"Vamp! What kind of a fool name is that?"

"Beats me. I'm just telling you what she said."

"I was planning on telling you that we might be getting a new neighbor, but one day she's here looking at the place, and the next day she's back with all her stuff. Now as much as I enjoy your company, you don't have to worry about me getting in the way of you young folks. I'm figuring that in no time flat, you two will be as thick as thieves."

"I don't know about that," Jamela replies with a smirk on her face. "I know Ms. Thang's type."

"And what type is that?"

"Let's just say that we come from different sides of town. I just don't think we're gonna find we've got too much in common."

"Well, regardless of where we all come from, we here now. You two just need a little bit of time to get to know one another, that's all."

"If you say so," Jamela replies glumly, "Just know that I ain't gonna hold my breath."

CHAPTER 15

The massive dining room table sits in its new home adorned with a mouthwatering heap of teacakes, a pitcher of old fashioned lemonade complete with floating lemon slices, and a hodgepodge of glasses, mugs, and saucers. The invitations were informal, yet the tone of the delivery revealed that for the hostess, this event was of special importance and highly anticipated. Both of the young women had accepted Miz Mattie's invitation to come to the tea party - it would have been heartless to refuse. But in truth, Vamp's acceptance was based solely on the fact that she had nothing to do and nowhere to go because she had not yet summoned the courage to inform her friends of her new zip code. For Jamela, this is the first party that she has been to in the 18 months since Shaka's birth, and although it's just a small group having tea and cookies, she cannot deny the hint of anxiety she feels as she showers and dresses in a pair of clean jeans and a black turtleneck that is missing a noticeable saturation of color.

Smoothing down her moist hair, Jamela absentmindedly starts twisting the new growth at the base of her locs while contemplating the upcoming party. Shaka, who has been sitting on the floor unsuccessfully trying to cram his left foot into his right shoe, abandons his efforts and comes over and pull her hands away from her hair, "Play with me, momma," he implores.

"Sorry, baby, momma was lost in thought. Come on, let's get you ready for Miz Mattie's party," she says, as she lifts him up onto the bed beside her. Taking the small shoe in her hands, she expertly applies it to his foot while slowly explaining in a calm, soothing voice the process involved of first loosening the strings, then pulling back the tongue of the shoe to make room for the foot, inserting the foot, and finally, placing the tongue flat and pulling the strings tight. She repeats the process with the left shoe. Now, proceeding even more slowly, she explains the procedure for tying the shoestrings into a bow. Once done, without explanation, she takes the two loops of the bow, crosses one over and under the other and pulls tight. The end result is a snug knot, because for the last two months, Shaka's latest obsession has been taking off all his clothes and running around the apartment yelling, 'nekkid boy!' The streak usually started with the removal of the shoes. Jamela was hoping that if she could keep the child in his shoes, she might be successful in keeping his clothes on as well.

Gently wiping his runny nose, Jamela pulls a clean shirt with a slightly frayed collar over his head, and lovingly brushes the little tight curls of his cottony soft hair. She stands him before her for a final inspection. "My, don't you look handsome!" she beams, as she takes his little face gently in both her hands and kisses his shiny forehead. He responds with a gap-toothed grin and grabs her cheeks with his tiny dimpled hands and kisses her back. She believes the target of the kiss was meant to be her forehead, but the wet smack lands right in the middle of her right eye, leaving her amused and momentarily blinded. Her heart swells with love for him, and she says a silent prayer that one day she will be able to find the words to adequately express to him just how much she truly loves him. But as she gazes into his wide, innocent eyes and sees the bottomless well of love that she feels for him mirrored back to her, she suspects that he already knows. Despite all of the things that she could not currently afford to buy for her child, the one thing there has always been a surplus of was love.

"Okay, I think we're all set. Are you ready to go to Miz Mattie's party?"

"Ready."

"Okay, let's go," she says, taking his small hand in hers and heading for the door.

"Oh, just a second, sweetie," she says, as she quickly runs back to the bedroom. Rummaging through the top dresser drawer, she pulls out a rarely used tube of coral lipstick. It is the one piece of makeup that she owns, which she bought on a whim at the Dollar Store. She applies the lipstick slowly, being careful to stay within the border of what she views as her thin and unimpressive lips. She purses her lips as she examines her reflection in the mirror. "There, I suppose that's a little better. This is, after all, a party."

Across the hall her neighbor, clad only in panties and bra, stand against the frame of her open closet door admiring her handiwork. After finally getting all of her possessions off the moving van, getting her wardrobe organized had been her first line of business. She knew how to motivate men, and for as long as the van held any of her belongings, she had addressed the moving men with her silky smooth voice. And just as the last load was being deposited inside her front door, to her horror and amazement, the sweaty brother with the pregnant gut and yellow smile had found the balls to ask her out to dinner. Too tired now to continue playing the damsel in distress, her smile quickly vanished and was replaced with a sneer, as she responded curtly, "Sorry, but I only date professionals."

"I can 'preciate that," the mover replied, "Any self-respecting sista needs to know that a brother's working hard and getting his pay honest. I've been on this job for over 5 years now. It's steady work and the pay is decent," he stated proudly.

"Oh! No, dear," she says, fighting to suppress her laughter, "When I said professionals, I meant college educated men with multiple degrees like myself. Then in an attempt to softly her response added, "But thanks for asking."

She couldn't quite make out what he said after that, because his back was to her as he descended the stairs for the last time. But if looks could kill, that look he shot back over his shoulder at her would have caused her to drop dead on the spot.

Now well past the fashionably late stage, she stands gazing lovingly into the closet at her clothes. She owns so many clothes she has had to divide them between the two bedrooms - fall and winter clothing in her bedroom closet, spring and summer clothes in the armoire in the spare bedroom. The clothes are grouped according to color, and within each color grouping, the clothes are further separated by hue. At the first sign of spring, the closets will have to be reversed - spring and summer clothes to her bedroom, fall and winter clothing to the armoire. While some would view it as a lot of unnecessary work, to her it was well worth it because her clothes were a part of her well-honed identity. And as the old saying goes, clothes maketh the man…or in this case, the woman.

Her clothes obsession started innocently enough with the purchase of her first designer outfit. A Donna Karen classic black pantsuit with understated elegance. When she wore it to work the first time, she had been acutely aware of how people treated her differently. Co-workers who had never parted their lips to mutter so much as a "hello" in the past, now struck up animated conversations about anything they thought would hold her interest. And the day she strode down the halls in her red-soled pumps was the very same day that she was invited out for drinks after work to the latest "It" spot, the place where the beautiful people went to see and be seen. The women showered her with compliments on her impeccable sense of style. The men appreciated her clothes too, though not so much for the cut and style, but for the way the little knit dresses clung to her shapely buttocks, or the way the winter white cashmere sweaters molded themselves to her bountiful breasts. She could tell from the moistened-mouthed stares of both the men and women that she was the object of their secret fantasy to partake of just a wee bit of chocolate. They did not want to take the whole box home; just a small discreet sampler would suffice. But the moment that stood at above the rest happened one particular Friday evening while she was out drinking with her new friends. The leader of the tight little clique, a petite blonde with high, pert breasts and a paralyzed forehead, had made her way over to where Vamp was sitting at the bar. She ordered a martini and they sat together, drinking and laughing, bare thigh brushing bare thigh. Suddenly, little petite Blondie leans forward, secures her hair behind her ears and whispers in a slightly slurred, conspiratorial tone, "I really like you, you're different from the others." Vamp had taken a small sip from her glass and smiled back appreciatively at her new BFF, as a warm glow spread throughout her belly, in part from the whiskey, but mainly from her sense of satisfaction at being validated by one who she felt was worthy of emulating – a virtual square peg that Vamp could never squeeze her African hips into, but that did not stop her from trying.

"Oh, what the hell!" Vamp exclaims, finally deciding on casual wear, "Even in this, I'll probably still be overdressed. I don't know why I'm going to such lengths, it's not like there are going to be any men there," she says as she slips a gold cuff on her right wrist and a few thin gold bangles onto the left. "And even if there were, it would just be some of the fellas from the neighborhood." She slides her bare feet into a pair of soft, suede loafers. "And while those brothers who hang out across the street shooting B-ball all day are definitely *fine*, with their tight little asses and chiseled arms, I don't see any of them being serious relationship material, not for me anyway," she says as she expertly swipes a $26 tube of coppery bronze lipstick across her full, pouty lips. "Too bad for them my days of 'hit it and quit it' are over," she says as she grabs her keys, blows herself a kiss in the mirror and finally heads downstairs. As she nears the downstairs landing, the sound of laughter drifts up to greet her, and she enters the open door to the apartment across from Miz Mattie's apartment without a knock or a moment's hesitation. The sight that greets her so deeply assaults her sense of aesthetics, that it actually knocks her back a step. Directly inside the front entrance to the apartment, sitting smack dab in the center of the living room is a mammoth dining room table. She takes a few halting steps forward and pokes her head around the bend and sees Miz Mattie in the dining room sitting in an overstuffed lounger-rocker. The old woman is wearing a contented smile, and her hands are folder atop a round mound of excess flesh. Still unnoticed, Vamp examines the remaining decor of the room, feeling a bit like *Alice in Wonderland*. Atop a large floral rug, whose faded colors speak of better decades gone by, sits a brown corduroy sofa, complete with lace dollies on the armrests and flanked by matching tables, each holding a too large lamp topped off by an even larger lampshade, covered in antiquated plastic. Vamp squares her shoulders and is just about to make her grand entrance, when a little brown-faced boy suddenly appears at the far end of the dining table wearing nothing more than his shoes and socks and a fat, drooping diaper.

"Hi!" he yells loudly, revealing a mouthful of crumbs as he starts toddling over in her direction.

"Vanessa? Come on in, chil', I didn't see you standing there!" Miz Mattie beams, attempting to rise to greet her newly arrived guest. When her knees fail to cooperate, she surrenders to the struggle and settles back into her chair, extending both arms in welcome. Vamp smiles nervously and quickly moves forward, grateful for the opportunity to escape the clutches of the fast approaching diaper boy, but now uncertain of how to handle this too intimate of a greeting. The short distance she has to navigate does not allow much room for ingenuity, so she simply grasps one of the old woman's hand between both of her own and shakes firmly.

"I believe you two have met," Miz Mattie states, gesturing with her free hand toward Jamela who is sitting on the rug, Native American style, encircled by wooden train tracks on which sits a blue tank engine, a green gondola and a red caboose.

"Yes, we've met," Vamp replies, still pumping the old woman's hand, glances over and feigns a smile in Jamela's direction. Jamela subtlety nods her head in a gesture of hello. *What a fuckin' snob, marching in here like she owns the place! But, wow, nice shoes,* Jamela thinks, taking in Vamp's soft suede loafers and the form fitting black pants, which stop just above the ankle, revealing a delicate gold chain. Her eyes move up to the silk blouse and the perfectly styled hair, before stealing a shy glance back down at her own outfit. Even her Doc Martens, which everyone knows gains character with age, have long passed the well-worn look, and are well on their way to the broken-down look. She feels her face starting to flush, and she knows that even with her copper skin, the rims of her ears are turning noticeably red. Just as she feels herself starting to emotionally withdraw from her present company, she is suddenly bowled over by twenty pounds of unbounded, kinetic energy – no doubt the result of a recent sugar spike.

"Hey, baby! Where're your clothes?!" she asks laughing and grabbing the little boy in a bear hug and deftly lifting him above her head before attacking his exposed stomach with belly blasts.

Over the squeals of Shaka's laughter, Jamela can hear Miz Mattie talking to the new girl, "...and he's just the sweetest little thing. He knows his ABC's and he can even count to 20. Well he sometimes skips a number here and there, but it's still pretty good for a little fella his age." Jamela glances up and sees Vamp nodding her head with a blank, disinterested look on her face. Jamela stands Shaka back on his feet, wraps her arms around his torso and directs his attention to the woman before them.

"Shaka, this is our new neighbor, Vamp. Can you say 'hello?'"

He looks at Vamp curiously, but offers no greeting. Normally, Jamela is quick to admonish Shaka when she feels his actions are disrespectful, but she suspects that her child has just picked up on the new neighbor's negative vibe, so she dismisses his slight as good intuition.

"Come on, sweetheart, let's go change your diaper and find your clothes," she says, rising to her feet and gingerly stepping over the now jumbled train set.

"Excuse us," she says in the direction of her host, and takes Shaka's hand and leads him to the small bedroom that Miz Mattie, as promised, has furnished with a twin bed and small chest of drawers. " 'Bye," Shaka calls, with a small wave as he is being led away by his mom. Then, quicker than a June bug, he pulls away from Jamela and lunges for Vamp, tightly wrapping his arms around both her knees. Vamp stumbles backwards then forwards, arms flailing wildly as she struggles to retain her balance. Miz Mattie covers her mouth with both hands to stifle a giggle as Vamp, looking both mortified and stupefied, finally managing to steady herself, bends over and pries the little boy's arms away from her knees. Shaka promptly responds by wrapping his arms around her midriff and burying his face in the front of her blouse. Jamela is totally confused by this unexpected display of affection, and feels slightly betrayed by her baby boy. But when Shaka shows no signs of letting go, she steps forward and intervenes.

"Okay, okay, let the lady go. Now please go and find your clothes for momma. Thank you, baby."

Shaka obediently releases his hold on Vamp and heads off toward the living room, where he retrieves his half eaten teacake from the dining room table and disappears beneath the draping tablecloth.

As Vamp straightens her blouse back up on her shoulders and tries to gain her composure, she notices the smudged fingerprints on the front of her blouse. She glares over at Jamela, and Jamela answers the look with a defiant glare of her own, as their eyes lock and they each silently size up the other:

Vamp:

It doesn't surprise me that she can't control her boy, got him running around the place naked like he's straight out of Africa! Thank God I don't have kids, I couldn't be bothered with such madness. I ought to make her pay to have my blouse dry-cleaned, but from the looks of those run down shoes, I don't think girlfriend can afford it. Look at her with her nappy hair and wild child; it's women like her that gives Black women a bad rap.

Jamela:

Why'd she get all dressed up? Who is she trying to impress? I hope it ain't me, 'cause I don't swing that way. And from the way she looks at me, like I'm a pot of warmed over chitlins, it's obvious Ms. Thang thinks she's better than me. Yeah, I know her type, met her too many times before. She's lucky she didn't say nothin' out of line to my boy or else I would'a had to check her fake ass! Women like her make it hard for real sistas to get the respect they deserve.

Miz Mattie remains seated in her chair, seemingly oblivious to the thickening tension in the air. But this subtle, non-verbal exchange is not lost on her, these days very little is.

"Ladies, and Shaka," Miz Mattie begins in her slow genuine southern drawl, "I'd like to thank y'all for coming to my little tea party. Why don't we just head on into the living room and have ourselves a seat." Vamp takes the lead and pulls out the nearest chair and sits down. Jamela goes to the head of the table where she first pulls out a chair for Miz Mattie, then another for Shaka, and finally, one for herself, leaving Vamp sitting alone at the far end of the expansive table.

"Well, y'all just help yourselves. I baked us a batch of teacakes and made us some fresh lemonade. There's hot water on the stove for tea, if you prefer something hot to drink. "Forgive me if I appear a little nervous, but this is my very first party."

"You're kidding, right?" says Vamp.

"No, baby. I wouldn't kid you."

"You must have at least been to a birthday party or two," Jamela adds.

"No. Like I was telling you the other day, my folks believed that a worthy life was one spend serving God and family. That was it, and in that order."

"Yeah, but it just seems like they should have understood

that a young person need to have friends and to be allowed to have *some* fun, says Jamela, struggling to understand, "You know… like what you said about Shaka, him needing a place to run and play."

"Well, if my parents were alive today, I'd like to think that they would have come around to understanding that it is not God's plan for us to deprive ourselves of a little joy."

"Oh, God intends for us to have fun. You can trust you me on that one," says Vamp, authoritatively.

"I think I would have gone a little crazy, being restricted like that," replies Jamela.

"Well, there were times when I felt mighty lonely, especially when I'd overhear the other girls talking about the fun they had. They'd be all aflutter," Miz Mattie continues, "talking about the good time they had eating and laughing and listening to music. So, in recognition of my first party, I thought it might be nice if we had us some music to listen to also," she says, turning slightly in her chair and reaching out her arm, lifts the lid of a small wooden cabinet that stands unobtrusively along the wall, and carefully sets the needle down on a small vinyl disk. For several long moments, the only sound that fills the room is a gritty, scratchy noise. The scratching finally recedes to the background, and the room becomes filled with some down home soulful longing, better known as the Blues. As the music builds, Miz Mattie closes her eyes and gently rocks her head from side to side, letting the music transports her back to a time long past, but obviously not forgotten.

"I would have never had you pegged as a Blues woman, Miz Mattie," Jamela states.

"Well chil', when you've lived as long as I have, there's bound to have been some blues in your life.

"I can still remember the day I heard my first Blues record, I just sat down in the middle of the floor and cried."

"What were you crying about?" Jamela asks quietly, her forehead furrowed with concern.

"Oh chil', I don't even remember! But what I do know is that every woman's had times in her life when she's just had to sit down and have herself a good cry! Ain't you?"

"Well, now that you mention it, I suppose I have," she answers with a sheepish smile.

You poor, pitiful women, Vamp thinks, rolling her eyes in disgust. *Crying the blues. And over some man, I would bet!*

When the record ends, Miz Mattie carefully returns the record to its paper jacket before placing another record on the spindle and gently lowering the needle. Although this one is a Gospel record, it has the same haunting longing as the first.

"Eat! " Shaka yells, no longer content to just sit and look at the mountain of teacakes piled high on a platter beyond his reach. He has long finished off his first teacake, and all that remains of it is a small scattering of crumbs beneath the table.

"Give that chil' a teacake, sugar." Miz Mattie instructs Jamela, then adds, "That's right, Shaka, you just eat till your heart's content."

"Oh, please don't tell him that, " Jamela protests half-heartedly, obviously pleased at the loving attention being bestowed upon her child.

"Since I only have Blues and Gospel records, next time we have our little tea party, why don't y'all bring down some records to play," says Miz Mattie, "That way, I get to hear what it is you young folks are listening to these days."

"Next time?" Vamp asks, thinking that this was a welcoming party that surely did not bear repeating.

"Why, yes…" Miz Mattie replies, now uncertainly, "I was thinking that we could get together every week to sit and talk… or once a month, maybe…

"Well, whenever y'all feel like stopping by, you's welcome! These days I got more time than I know how to fill up, but I can't expect you young folks to want to sit around listening to scratchy old records and eating a bunch of sweets that, if you ain't careful, will have your belly looking like mine," she says, her belly gently rising and falling with each chuckle.

Sensing the sadness behind the empty laughter, Jamela quickly respond, "Well, I don't know about Vamp, or Vanessa, or whatever your name is," she throws in Vamp's direction before turning her attention back to Miz Mattie, "but you just name the date and the time and me and Shaka are here!" Jamela says with extra enthusiasm hoping that it will put a smile back on Miz Mattie's face - it does. "And," she continues, feeling jazzed now, "I'll bring along some of my music. Turn you on to some Al Jarreau and The Black Eyed Peas."

"Baby, I know about black-eyed peas, I cook a big pot of them every year. Folks back home used to say that if you eat them on the first of the New Year, it'll bring you good luck."

"Nooooo. Not the ones you eat!" Jamela says, laughing.

"I'm talking about a phat music group. That's their name, The Black Eyed Peas!"

"Oh…well, sugar, you have to educate an old lady about these things."

"And I'll bring along my CD player too, 'cause I don't own no vinyl, just cassettes and CD's. Suddenly feeling like she's coming off as the 'bad guy,' and certainly not about to be outdone by Jamela, Vamp chimes in, "You know, when I was packing up my things, I ran across an old stereo system that I had completely forgotten. I stopped using after I got a bonus at work and celebrated by buying myself a state of the art stereo system. It cost me a small fortune, but I digress.

"Anyhow, seeing as how I have absolutely no use for my old system now, the next time I'm on my way out, I'll drop it off down here. If that's okay with you, Miz Mattie," she adds, taking a sip of lemonade from a chipped coffee mug, her pinky finger extended.

"Yes, chil', that will be fine. Thank you."

"Oh, and Jamela," Vamp continues, "in addition to being able to play vintage records, it also plays CD's and cassettes, so you won't have to bother lugging your boombox down on your shoulder because even though my old stereo system is well over 10 years old, it is a quality piece of equipment."

"Oh, and mine ain't!?"

"Well, I don't know… does yours have a subwoofer and an equalizer?"

"Huh?"

"Alrighty, then. Moving on, " she says, turning her attention back to the head of the table. "Miz Mattie, I didn't mean to imply that I don't ever want to do this again. Actually, I think it's rather sweet. It's just that I assumed this was a one time 'Get to Know You' type of party."

"Well, yes chil' it is. But do you honestly think we can all get to know each other in just one night?" Miz Mattie asks with open sincerity.

"Hardly!" Jamela blurts out.

"Like, for instance, that first day I met you in the hallway, you said your name was Vamp." She stops and takes a big bite from her teacake before continuing, "And when I mentioned you to Miz Mattie she didn't know who the hell…oops, sorry! She didn't know who the *heck* I was talking about. So, is your name Vanessa or Vamp, and either way, what's up with the Vamp? You fancy yourself a movie star or something?"

"Movie star?" Vamp asks, confused. "Oh, I get it! Vamp - vixen - movie star. Cute." she says, not amused. "No, that's not it at all. My given name is Vanessa and that is the name I use when conducting business. Hence, that is the name I used when applying for this apartment. Vamp is a nickname given to me by friends of mine. It's short for vampire."

"Vampire!?" Miz Mattie asks, now completely confused.

"You ain't into none of that Satan worship stuff are you?" Jamela asks.

"What? No! Besides, what does one have to do with the other? Forget it! Don't even bother answering that. My friends call me Vamp because I don't like to be out in the sun too long. And as you know, or maybe you don't, vampires can't go out in the sunlight or they'll die."

"You won't die from being out in the sun, will you chil'!?" Miz Mattie asks, suddenly becoming alarmed.

"No! Of course not!" Vamp answers impatiently, while thinking, *Who are these backward folks I'm living with?!? They are truly working my nerves! I wish I had some vodka in this lemonade!*

"I don't get it," Jamela says. "Why won't you go out in the

sun?"

"Why?" asks Shaka, not so much interested in what's being said, but wanting to be included in the conversation.

"I do go out in the sun," Vamp explains, "I just don't stay out in it longer than is necessary."

"Oh, okay." says Miz Mattie, satisfied with this explanation.

"'Kay." Shaka mimics.

"Why?" Jamela demands, obviously not satisfied with Vamp's pat answer.

"I love the sun," says Miz Mattie, "I don't think I could live without it."

"I like the sun too, and I do sit outside, as long as I'm in the shade," Vamp says, feeling Jamela's piercing eyes demanding that she expound further. "I don't sit in the sun because I don't want to tan. Alright!?"

"Tan?!" Jamela repeats, confused.

"Yes, tan." Vamp replies, stretching out an arm and appreciatively contemplating it's light complexion.

"Oh, snap! Now I get it!" Jamela practically shouts, "You don't want to be in the sun because you don't want to get black!"

Vamp responds by glaring back at Jamela.

"Ha! That's pretty funny!" Jamela continues, "You want a good piece of advise? Next time someone asks about your nickname, stick with my explanation!"

"Thanks, but I truly don't ever see myself needing any of *your* advise," Vamp replies with an audible smirk and a haughty look in her eyes.

Jamela cocks her head to the side and grins through a lopsided sneer while thinking, *Yeah, Ms. Thang, I've peeped your number!*

As Miz Mattie removes the album from the record player and carefully places it in a plastic sleeve and then back into its faded cardboard cover, she notices Shaka rubbing his eyes with his fists. *The chil' needs a nap. Probably just as well, 'cause it looks like we're going to have to take this getting acquainted in little baby steps. It makes me sad to see these two young women going at each other like bulls locking horns. Just don't make no sense.*

"The little guy's getting sleepy," she announces to her guests.

"I think it's best we wrap this party up for now. Thank y'all again for coming."

CHAPTER 16

The weatherman announces the temperature at five degrees below zero. Add in the wind chill factor, and it feels more like 25 below. Jamela does not have a car and the thought of hopping buses with her baby in sub-degree temperatures is unbearable, but the business at hand is urgent, so Jamela finally decides to take Miz Mattie up on her offer and leaves Shaka in her care.

That morning Shaka is treated to something other than his usual bowl of farina for breakfast. Miz Mattie cooks him a small stack of pancakes and two strips of bacon. *The way the little fella attacked his plate*, Miz Mattie thinks, *you would swear the chil' hadn't eaten in weeks!* But Miz Mattie knew that Shaka got nourishing meals, he just got fed too much of the same old thing. She felt honored to have been entrusted with looking after Shaka because she knew that Jamela thought the world of her son; so, by extension, that must mean that Jamela thought that she was pretty okay too. *But Lawdy, she sho is sure protective of this boy*, Miz Mattie thinks. *She gotta be careful not to smother him with too much mothering. Gotta give the little fella a little breathin' room. Otherwise, first chance he gets, he gone spread his wings and fly away, long before she wants him to, and long before he's ready.*

~~~

When Jamela returns home and stops in to pick up Shaka, it's immediately apparent to Miz Mattie that she's been crying.

"What's the matter, baby?" Miz Mattie asks, coming over and putting her arm around Jamela's slouched shoulders. "I need a job." She says with a determined edge to her voice. "I went to the social welfare office today and the people there…it's like they assume just 'cause I'm broke I must also be stupid. And since I'm stupid, then that apparently makes it okay for them to treat me like a piece of shit! I'm sorry…crap! That it's okay to treat me like crap! I just want for my son the exact same things that they want for theirs. I don't see why that is so hard for them to understand," she says, wiping her nose on the back of her mitten.

"You having money problems, baby? I can cut back on your rent for a few months if that will help you out."

"Thank you, but no. You're too good to me already. Clyde and his parents have been helping to cover rent. They knew that in order for Clyde to be able to have a relationship with his son, he needed to be able to visit him without having to confront my momma each time. I get food stamps and health insurance for Shaka through the agency I visited today, and momma will occasionally take us shopping when Shaka's outgrown his shoes or he needs a new winter coat.

"It's just that I want to find a way to provide for our needs myself. I don't like being totally dependent on others. I know how to work, and I don't mind working. When I first moved here, I actually had a little money saved up, but that all ran out after the first year. Having a baby makes it really hard to go out and get a full time job. Who's gonna look after Shaka all day? Clyde's in school, and his parents are already helping out, plus his mom has health issues and can't chase after a toddler all day. Momma's working all week and on her off days, she just wants to be free. I can't be mad at her, she already raised three kids on her own.

But the thought of dropping Shaka off with a stranger just

tears at my heart. Not to mention the fact that whatever little money I might be able to make will go directly to whoever I hire to watch Shaka. There'll be nothing left over for anything else, so basically I would be working to pay someone to look after my child, while I'm away from said child working, and not working so that I can get paid and have money to take care of my child. This society is sick and twisted. You're damned if you do, and damned if you don't!"

"Don't stress yourself, baby, things will work themselves out. You'll figure it out, you just gotta believe and know that God specializes. Shaka's still napping, so you and me gonna sit right down and have ourselves a nice cup of hot tea."

Thankful for the opportunity to vent her frustrations before having to resume caring for her child, James sits quietly sipping her tea. As she feels the tension slowly seep from her body, she settles back in her chair, kicks her shoes off, and curls her feet underneath her. "Miz Mattie," she begins hesitantly, why is it that no one ever tells you how hard it is to raise a child? I mean, once people find out you're pregnant, everybody's got a horror story to tell you about labor, "'I was in labor for 96 hours, then they had me pushing for 2 more days till I burst a blood vessel in my head! And then, don't you know, after all of that, they wound up giving me a C-Section!'" Jamela mimics, laughing.

"But seriously, no one tells you how much time and energy it takes to raise a child, especially when they're small and can't tell you what they want or need. Their cries are the only way they communicate, and it seems like they're crying all the time. So you gotta try and figure out, is that a hunger cry? Is he wet, too hot, too cold? Is he bored? Does he want to go outside? Is he ready to come back inside? Is he teething? They're constantly teething, you know. Does he want his toy? Which toy does he want? No kiddin', this round the clock, 24/7! "And let's not talk about feeding the boy!" she continues, "The child was hungry all the time! Luckily, I had some really good nurses at the hospital that took the time to teach me how to get him to latch on properly. 'Cause if you do it wrong, it's over before it begins. All your hard work and good intentions go right out the window, and all you're left with is a hungry, crying baby and scabby nipples.

"My Momma tried to discourage me from breastfeeding, said it would make my titties sag. But I figured that God's design couldn't be wrong. Besides, a woman's body ain't never gonna look the same after she's had a kid anyway, whether she nurses or not. Some women get shrunken, sagging boobs, others get serious varicose veins, others have stretch marks that go from here to China, and still others get left with a poon-tang that's big enough to drive a Mack truck through it!" she says, laughing wickedly.

"I'm sorry, but you know it's true! So the way I see it, all things considered, I got off pretty easy. I never had much in the boob department to begin with and now, after twelve months of nursing, I ain't got none. But I ain't complaining 'cause at the end of the day when I'm putting my little brown baby down to bed, even after a rough day when he's run me ragged and I'm ready to pull all my hair out - one loc at a time, I just look into his little sleepy eyes and I feel that all is right with the world.

"But why am I telling you all this, you already know how it is. So, just how many children do you have, and what about grand kids?"

Miz Mattie looks first at her, then turns and stares out the window as she replies; "I ain't got no chil'ren, baby. I was never able to have any."

"I am so sorry, Miz Mattie. And here I am just rattlin' on like a fool!"

"Now, chil' it's okay. I probably should have said something sooner myself, but I never know how to bring it up in a conversation. It's all right...really." Miz Mattie replies quietly, lovingly, but the little smile on her face can't mask the pain in her eyes. Jamela gets up and goes and puts her arms around the older woman and gives her a big hug. Then she sits back on her heels in front of Miz Mattie's chair, looking up at her, "You're so good to me and Shaka, I just figured that you had lots of experience loving and caring for children."

"No, baby. I ain't had no experience at all taking care of babies."

"So how is it that you're naturally more loving than some women who have given birth?" Jamela asks, thinking of her own mother.

"I don't know the answer to that, baby. I suppose that it might be because I try and live Christ-like."

"What do you mean by that?"

"You don't go to church much, do you baby?"

"No, ma'am."

"You do know that Jesus Christ is the Son of God, right?"

"Yes ma'am."

"And you know that Jesus walked the Earth just like we're doing now, right?"

"Yeah? Okay."

"Well, whenever I have to do something and I'm not sure which way to turn, I just ask myself, 'Self, what would Christ do?'"

"Hmm," Jamela responds, sitting quietly absorbing the words of the older woman.

A low whimper comes from rear where Shaka is sleeping, and Jamela excuses herself and returns a few moments later.

"He went back to sleep. I guess he's still a little tired; he didn't sleep very well last night," she says, sitting down cross-legged on the floor.

"I don't know much about the bible and all, we weren't raised up in the church, but I remember times when my momma would be feeling blue, and she'd gather us kids all together and talk about God. She'd ramble on for a while and neither me or my brothers paid much attention to what she was saying. But we knew when she was done because she always ended by saying, 'God is Love.'"

"No truer words have ever been spoken."

"We'd just sit there and wait to hear those words, 'cause then we knew we could be dismissed. It's kinda weird that I would think of that now after all these years."

"Miz Mattie, since you ain't got no grandkids, and I ain't got no grandmother…well, none that I know of anyway, what say you to being my honorary grandmother?"

"Honorary grandmother? Baby, how do I do that?"

"Well, we're not related by blood, of course, so it would mean that in your heart, you would adopt me as your granddaughter, and in my heart, I would adopt you as my grandmother."

"Why, baby, I'd be proud to be your grandma!" Miz Mattie gushes, taking Jamela's hands in her own and giving them a tight squeeze.

"Great! Then I suppose that would also make Shaka your great-grandson."

"Well, then, I suppose it does at that!" Miz Mattie replies, beaming with the unexpected joy of becoming a grandma and a great grandma all in one day.

"Well, then," Miz Mattie begins, as she pats Jamela's hand while she gathers up her nerves, since now we're all related, it makes it easier for me to say what I've been wanting to say to you for some time," she says, her eyes steady and serious. "Shaka and I had a good time together today. In a short time, I've grown to love both you and that boy as if you were my blood relatives. I want to help you get on your feet and be able to provide for your son. So what I'm asking is that you let me help you out by doing some of the things that a real grandma would do. I spent many a nights crying over the fact that my womb would never carry a chil'. But I'm often reminded of something my momma used to always say, and that was that the Lord works in mysterious ways. "So, baby, I just want you to know that I would be happy and honored to look after Shaka for you, just like I did today. So whenever you find that job, I want you to know that grandma is here for you."

"Thank you, Miz Mattie. I sure do appreciate you," says Jamela, eyes bright with tears.

"That boy's getting so big," Jamela says with a loud sigh. "I love him so much. Pretty soon I'll have to start thinking about him going off to school, and trying to teach him about this crazy old world we live in.

"One of the things that's starting to weigh is how I'm going to explain to him about America's unwritten Amendment. You know the one: If you're White you're right, if you're Black, get back. Seriously, I struggle with the whole African American history bit; like how, for example, am I gonna explain to him about how our people even got over here in the first place. I tried talking to my momma about it once, but all she said was, 'Go on away from me with that nonsense.' Her response probably had something to do with that white guy she was dating at the time, but still…it's not nonsense."

"Baby, people don't want to talk about it because it brings up such painful memories."

"I get that. I get that there's a lot of pain and shame tied to our history, but *not* talking about it don't help none, cause even if people ain't talking about it, they're thinking about it. Maybe they're not thinking about the past history, maybe they're just thinking about the injustice they heard about on the television yesterday. But that's why you gotta still talk about it, because it's all related.

"You're right, baby. I can't deny what you're saying," agrees Miz Mattie, "And it's true that some day you'll have to explain that ugly truth to your son. I suppose it's good that you're thinking about it now. This way you've got time to pray for words to say that will speak the truth, buffer the pain, and teach him not to hate…others or himself.

"Lawdie, that's a mighty tall order for anybody to fill. I never gave much thought before to how Black mothers gotta educate they babies about so much more than just reading, writing and 'rithmetic.

"But since you do, you might want to begin before the school starts handing out those history books. Those books will tell 'em all about half naked Africans being rounded up, shackled and sold alongside animals, working from sun up to sun down, stripped of they land, they language, they religion and they families. Dear Lawd, they took everything but they souls! But if they coulda found a way, I'm sure they woulda took them too! And when they teach the chil'ren from those history books, it makes the little babies feel self-conscious as all eyes turn and stare with pity. Those babies can't hide, their dark skin makes it impossible for them to blend in and go unnoticed. But those same history books never really tell 'em much about the takers. What it was about they religion, they families and they souls that allowed them to convince themselves that what they was doing was good for the country and sanctioned by they God? That's the part of the story I want to read about, but that's the part that's always left out.

"Maybe one day somebody'll have courage enough to fix those history books and finally tell the whole story. Then those pitying eyes can stop staring outward and start lookin' inward."

Miz Mattie and Jamela sit in silence for a long moment before Miz Mattie continues.

"And what you said earlier about there being a lot of pain and shame tied to our history, you're right, there's no denying the pain. But don't go getting yourself confused, 'cause we ain't got *nothing* to be ashamed of, you hear me chil'! So when it comes time for you to have that talk, you make certain you tell your baby that.

"Amen to that, grandma. Amen to that."

"But you know something, grandma," Jamela continues, giving voice to years of unanswered questions and unspoken musings, "Sometimes I just look and wonder…I wonder what others think when they see pictures of men, and women with their children gathered casually around a tree bearing the "strange fruit," that Billie Holiday sang about, and I wonder what they feel when they see pictures of Emmett Till - I'm not talking about the smiling, pretty brown boy in the 'before' pictures, I'm talking about the boy in the 'after' pictures.

"I just… sometimes…wonder."

"I don't know, baby. All I know is that everybody's time on this here Earth is limited, and we each gotta find ways to make peace with whatever it is that's burdening our soul. So my advice to you is to keep the focus on yourself, and try to live your life in a way that will make your Father proud."

"That's easier said than done, since I don't know who my daddy is."

"Baby, it don't matter who your daddy is, all you gotta remember is that you's a chil' of God."

CHAPTER 17

Sunday morning, the day of the week that Vamp and Cat had dedicated to sitting around drinking coffee, polishing one another's toenails, and catching up on the drama of the week or, as Cat liked to refer to it, "talking shit!" Now on her second cup of coffee and just finishing polishing her own toenails Passion Flame Red, Vamp grabs the phone from her nightstand and tries calling Cat again. Again, no answer. In the three weeks since she moved out, Vamp has called Cat 21 times - one call per day. She had strategically varied the times she called in the hope of actually talking to Cat instead of getting her recorded message instructing callers to, 'Holla Back!' Vamp never left a message. She didn't want to appear desperate, despite the fact that she knew that Cat knew of every incoming call, "Thank you, Mr. Caller I.D." Vamp was fairly certain that Cat had to have been home at least a few of the times she had called. Where else would she be at 10:00 p.m. on a Thursday evening, 7:30 a.m. on a Saturday morning, and now at 2:00 p.m. on a Sunday afternoon? "It's not like she's hanging out at her man's place, because her man ain't got a place! Which is exactly why I'm here and she's…fuckin' wherever!"

Carefully walking on the heels of her feet, wads of cotton

stuck between each crimson toe, she heads to the kitchen for a bite to eat. The kitchen is orderly and pristine, with everything in its designated place, just as she likes it. Vamp was not much into cooking, she preferred to have others cook for her. But when that was not an option, pre-packaged foods, namely breakfast cereals and dried noodles, were her main means of sustenance. When she lived with Cat, now that sister (she had to give her her props), could cook her butt off! It was like it was encoded in her DNA, and whenever Cat had an exceptionally good weekend, translation: mind blowing sex, she would get up early Sunday morning, put on a pot of strong coffee, wrap herself in her candy-striped apron, turn on the CD player and girlfriend would go to town! Hash browns with omelets and freshly squeezed orange juice. Smothered chicken and biscuits with a bowl of hot buttered grits on the side! The only stipulation to these Sunday morning food fests was that Vamp would help out by cleaning up the mess. Compulsively neat and tidy, this task suited Vamp just fine, and armed with a steaming cup of coffee, Vamp happily washed dishes while Cat chopped and diced and threw into the sizzling pans a little bit-o'-this and a little dab-o'-that. It had not even seemed like work, with her keeping pace with Cat and never letting the dishes get out of control. The aroma of the food mingled with their laughter and the sound of Stevie in the background singing, "Rocket Love," or Luther crooning, "If Only for One Night," made the time fly by! And before they knew it, they were both climbing atop the kitchen stools and bowing their heads in grace, before pushing up their sleeves and chowing down!

As she pulls a couple of frozen waffles out of the freezer, Vamp yearns for one of those home cooked meals, dirty dishes and all. But more than the actual food, Vamp realizes that she truly misses Cat. "I wish she'd just talk to me!" she yells in frustration at the near-empty freezer. The thought of driving over to her old apartment and confronting Cat directly flits through Vamp's mind. The only thing that stops her is the thought of Danny being there, which would make a heart-to-heart talk with Cat impossible. *If I could just get her to talk to me, I know she'll understand. She would probably even agree that, had the situation been reversed, she would have done the exact same thing. Okay, maybe she would not have done the exact same thing, but I'm sure I can make her understand,* Vamp thinks, as she removes the waffles from the toaster and scrapes away the burnt edges. Topping the waffles with a pat of frozen butter, she opens the kitchen cabinet in search of the syrup. She stands there for too a long moment gazing up into the cabinet, past the bottle of white rice vinegar, past the bottle of hot sauce and unopened spices, past the brown bottle of maple syrup, and on further back to the rear of the cabinet where she stores her liquor. She is fastidious about always having at least one bottle on hand, telling herself that the hallmark of a truly good hostess is to always have something on hand to offer an impromptu guest. But Vamp has not had any guests. She recently turned down a request to visit from her own mother because she had not yet mustered up the courage to tell her parents that she had moved. She has not even had any of her eager male friends over, knowing as she did that they would arrive with the expectations of more than just a drink. And right now, a drink was all she was willing to offer.

As she stares into the cabinet, her voice of reason reminds her of a promise she made to herself to cut back on her drinking. That voice is quickly interrupted by a different, louder voice that argues that the promise was to cut back on drinking, not to cut it out completely. Satisfied with what she felt was a strong, logical argument, she shoves the spices and syrup aside and pulls the liquor bottle out from the dark recesses of the cabinet. Tossing the burnt waffles into the trash, she pours herself two fingers of whiskey and proceeds to drink her breakfast – straight, with no chaser.

~~~

"Hello?"

"Vamp. It's me, Cat."

"Cat?" Vamp asks, bolting upright and rubbing her eyes while quickly trying to assess where she is. It is now 5:00 p.m., and she is startled to see that she is still wearing her nightgown from the previous night. *I must have fallen back asleep after breakfast*, she thinks, conveniently dismissing the fact that she had gone back for seconds and thirds.

"Hey, girl! What's happening?" she asks, trying to sound alert and upbeat. As she props herself up against the headboard, the reality of where she is and why she is talking to Cat over the phone, suddenly comes barreling back.

"Oh, hey…thanks for returning my call," she continues, her initial cheeriness now replaced with seriousness, as she contemplates what is at stake – the complete and total loss of her best friend. Her sudden understanding of the gravity of the situation leaves her unsure of how to proceed. Luckily, Cat saves her the trouble of having to figure it out.

"Look. I'm only calling to give you a chance to say whatever it is you need to say, so that you can stop calling *my* house at all hours of the day and night." Her voice is cold and unforgiving; it's a tone that Vamp has heard before, but never had it ever been directed at her. I sinking feeling in the pit of her stomach let Vamp know that the prognosis does not look good.

"Listen, girl," she begins, "I'm sorry I moved out, but I had been looking forward to having the place to myself…I *needed* to have some time to myself," she continues, struggling to fight back tears and maintain her composure so that Cat would not know just how totally miserable she has been. The crack in her voice betrays her.

"Damn it!" she continues, "You gave Danny the keys to our home, and you didn't even bother to discuss it with me first! We've never done anything like that before, so when you called me from the road to tell me about it as an afterthought, I lost it. I fuckin' lost it!

"That much was apparent."

"Yeah, well, I was feeling..."

"Just what were you feeling, Vamp?!"

"I was feeling..." she's hesitant to reveal what she truly felt, realizing that the truth might mean the complete and total demise of her friendship, when all she wanted was to try and save it. *I've come this far,* she thinks, *I think she at least deserves the truth.*

"I was afraid, Cat." she confesses in a small whisper.

"Afraid? Afraid of what?!"

"I was afraid of what Danny might do in your absence. The two of us alone...together...at night."

"What?! Are you saying that you were afraid that Danny would want to fuck you simply because you were there and I was out of town for a few nights?! Wow! You really need get over yourself, girlfriend!"

"Cat!" Vamp pleads, while thinking, *the truth doesn't always set your Black ass free!*

"No! Cat, my ass! You've got a whole lot of fuckin' nerve!"

"Cat, I don't want to fight with you," Vamp says, openly crying now, "I only called to say that I'm sorry things turned out the way they did."

There is a long awkward silence as each searches for a way to undo all the damage that's been done, while at the same time realizing that Life doesn't always give you a do over.

"Yeah, well, I'm sorry too," Cat responds, her voice quiet and thick with pain, "But your ass didn't have to go and fuckin' move."

Vamp's mind is whirling, frantically searching for just the right words that will ease her friend's pain, and help steer them to the path of healing.

If I could just get her to laugh I know that will break the ice. I know, I'll sing her one of our favorite songs that we used to sing while we cooked together on Sundays, Vamp thinks, and she clears her throat, closes her eyes and melodically croons the opening lines to TLC's, "No Scubs."

"Listen," Cat interrupts, "Danny's home. I gotta go. 'Bye."

Click.

"Okay. 'Bye," Vamp replies, then thinks, *maybe I should have picked a different song.*

CHAPTER 18

The following morning, it is the ringing of her alarm clock that jolts Vamp awake. Getting up with a lurch, she stumbles down the hallway to the bathroom where she falls to her knees and heaves into the cool cavity of the toilet, relieving her churning stomach of its contents from the previous day: amber liquid mingled with green bile. After her brief conversation with Cat last night, self-pity had prompted her to revisit the kitchen cabinet, and she had spent the remainder of the evening huddled in her bed crying into her glass. Even through her stomach has rid itself of its offender, she still feels nauseous, in addition to feeling spent and disgusted with herself. Stepping carefully out of her soiled nightgown, she goes back into her bedroom and phones the office, leaving a message for her boss informing her that she has contracted a stomach virus, and won't be in today.

~~~

Downstairs Miz Mattie is busy whipping up another batch of teacakes. She has been baking like crazy lately. If there are no teacakes left over from the weekend, it has become her new custom to bake a fresh batch first thing Monday morning; she didn't want little Shaka asking for some, and for her to not have any to give him. With the platter of warm teacakes in hand, she shuffles across the hall to the parlor where she puts on water for tea, before settling into her rocker lounger to listen to her gospel albums. Even though she has played those old albums hundreds of times, when played on Vamp's record player, or turntable, as she's been told it's called, she hears subtle elements of the music that she has never heard before. And on those mornings when particular songs stir up old, melancholy feelings that have her missing Charlie real bad, those two babies, Shaka and Jamela, *God bless their little souls*, will always just happen to stop by. Most days Jamela was content to just sit and nibble teacakes, as she sipped tea and nodded her head to the music ever now and then. Other days they would launch into spirited conversations about anything under the sun. After discussing or debating at length whatever topic they had stumbled upon for the day, they would usually settle on an answer or solution that was satisfactory to them both. Some days they couldn't agree, but that was okay too. During these conversations, Shaka, usually with a teacake in hand, would run off to his auxiliary bedroom which, in addition to the preliminary furnishings, now held a bookcase overflowing with children's books, and one shelf dedicated to a row of brightly painted toy trains.

Miz Mattie hears the sound of footsteps descending and smiles to herself. She waits to see Jamela's dred locs appear in the doorway. *It's funny*, Miz Mattie thinks, *how something that at one time appeared so strange, doesn't anymore.* In fact, she actually rather liked the rope-like hair, and felt that they enhanced Jamela's unpretentious, natural beauty. She remembers asking Jamela for permission to touch her hair, and how surprised she had been at the strength of each individual loc; amazed that hair so strong could adorn the head of a young woman whose soul at times appeared so wounded and fragile. The face that peers around the corner and greets her this morning, however, is not the one she was expecting. It is the face of her new tenant, Vanessa, and she is not looking quite herself today. Breaking with her usual modus operandi of full dress and make up before even cracking the front door, today Vamp had simply washed up, slipped on a clean nightgown, donned her bathroom and a pair of thick wool socks, then crept quietly downstairs. After phoning her job earlier this morning, she had suddenly felt so desperate for company that even the thought of listening to Miz Mattie recount yesterday's sermon was preferable to remaining upstairs alone. *She said to stop by anytime. I sure hope she meant it,* she thinks, as she peeks her head inside the door.

"Hello?" she inquires in a small, hesitant voice and this time, actually waits for a response before entering.

"Morning, Vanessa!" Miz Mattie says, waving her in.

"Come on in, baby. Come on in. I'm so happy you stopped by. I was hoping that our first little get together hadn't scared you away for good."

Vamp responds by pulling the belt of her robe tighter, and unconsciously biting her lower lip.

"Pour yourself a cup of tea and help yourself to some teacakes," Miz Mattie instructs, "I was just about to put on some music. With this here new turntable, I can feel the music all the way down to my toes; before, it used to stop at my belly," she says, smiling broadly as she carefully places the needle into the groove of the album, filling the room with the unmistakable voice of the Queen of Soul singing, "Precious Lord, Take My Hand." For a long moment, no one speaks, as the words to the song wrap each woman in a cocoon of private thoughts. Miz Mattie finds herself thinking about the despair she felt during those last few days she spent alone in her old home. Vamp's thoughts are on her best friend, Cat, and how impulsive decisions made on a Sunday morning, damaged a valued friendship and drastically altered both their lives. As she sits across from the old woman in silence, Vamp is not certain whether it is the hush of the early morning hour, or the mesmerizing sound of Miz Mattie's humming that slows her breathing and eases her pain. She is only grateful that she has a safe place where she can come to rest, a place where she can feel free to be herself without being the fear of being criticized or judged.

The dining table in the living room is awash with a broad band of sunlight and a thin, almost invisible reed of steam rises from the platter of teacakes, gently beckoning her. Without speaking, Vamp goes over to the table and picks up a teacake. Slowly she turns the warm cookie over in her hands admiring the golden color, while quizzically observing its irregular, rectangular shape. Bringing the cookie to her face, she discreetly sniffs the square before taking a bite. The cookie melts in her mouth and brings a smile to her face. Sinking into the nearest chair, she slowly devours the golden square, while thinking back to how her mother loved to bake, and how she and her brother had always fought over the batter left in the mixing bowl. *That seems like another lifetime*, she thinks. When she finally looks up, she sees Miz Mattie staring at her with a curious expression on her face. Vanessa blushes as a nervous laugh escapes her lips. "Sorry." she offers, "I suppose I was daydreaming."

"No need for an apology," Miz Mattie assures her, "daydreaming is the mind's way of taking a little break. But if you don't mind my asking…where did you go?"

"Where did I go?" Vamp repeats, "Home," she answers, "I went back home.

"Not the place I just moved from," she clarifies, "but my childhood home. Believe it or not, I grew up not too far from here."

"Is that so?"

"Yes. Most people are surprised to hear that I grew up in the inner city. Most assume that I grew up in a middle-class family. I know it's not politically correct to admit this, but I love it when that happens."

"Oh?"

"Yes. Is it so wrong to want to get away from your past?"

"I suppose that would depend on why you're trying to leave it behind," Miz Mattie answers.

"By the way," Vamp continues, wanting to shift focus and not dwell too much on all the stuff that she had left behind,

"The cookies, what are they called again, teacakes?"

"Yes, baby, that's what they're called."

"Teacakes. Hmm…interesting name. Are they called that because they're served with tea?"

"Could be. I just happen to like mine with tea, but they're also good with milk or coffee. I like 'em served warm or cold, and sometimes with peanut butter spread on top."

"You don't say?" Vamp replies, and cannot help but smile at the engaging simplicity of the old woman.

"Well, some day I'll have to try that – the peanut butter, that is. They really are delicious. I didn't get any the last time I was here. Do you mind if I have a few more?"

"Help yourself, chil'. That's the reason I bake 'em, so that y'all can enjoy eating them. So anytime you smell a fresh batch baking, just stop on by. The door is always open."

"Thank you, that's real generous of you." Vamp replies sincerely, and then helps herself to a cup of tea and another teacake. She's humming along to the music with Miz Mattie now, munching on her teacake and slowing stirring cream into her cup when the peace and quiet is suddenly shattered by an anxious loud voice urging, "Hurry up, baby!"

Vamp looks up from her tea, eyes suddenly wide with alarm as her heart begins to race. She jumps up from the chair and the sudden movement sloshes tea over the rim of her cup. "Damn it!" she swears quietly as she searches for a napkin or paper towel. Seeing neither, she grabs the hem of her robe and quickly wipes up the spilled tea. Jamela is on her way downstairs. *I don't think I can take Ms. Rasta Revolutionary this early in the morning,* Vamp thinks, as she mutters an abrupt goodbye to Miz Mattie.

"What's the hurry, baby? It's just Jamela and little Shaka."

"I know," Vamp replies, "I'm just not in the mood for a lot of chatty conversation this morning."

"Okay, baby. I understand. You two just got off on the wrong foot, that's all."

"Yeah. Maybe so." Vamp responds, pacing back and forth like a trapped animal.

"I hope to see you again soon. But before you run off, why don't you take a few of those teacakes with you."

Vamp, who has one foot across the threshold, stops and runs back to the table, grabs three of the golden squares and gingerly places them in the pocket of her bathrobe. "Thanks!" she says with a grateful smile and disappears out the front door and quickly dashes up the stairs past her neighbors.

"Who was that wild woman?!" Jamela asks with feigned alarm as she enters the parlor carrying Shaka on her hip. "Wait! Before you say anything," she says as she lowers Shaka to the floor, "I'm only carrying him because we almost got knocked down by the caped, or should I say, robed crusader! Get it! No? Okay. So, what did you do to her anyway?" Jamela asks playfully. Miz Mattie simply smiles and shakes her head. "She was just in a bit of a hurry."

"I'll say!" Jamela says, as she leans over and places a kiss on the old woman's forehead. "But enough about the Pale One. How are you this beautiful morning?"

"I'm just fine, baby." Miz Mattie replies. "And it looks as if you're feeling pretty good yourself!"

"Why, as a matter of fact I am!" Jamela replies, grinning from ear to ear. "My little guy here..." she says, reaching down to stroke Shaka's head, only to find that he has already wandered off. She shrugs her shoulders and continues, "My baby boy is turning two next week, and I've decided to throw him a birthday party!"

"Oh, that's wonderful!"

"I'm just planning on having a few people over to sing Happy Birthday and eat cake, nothing big or fancy. Last year I bought him a little cream-filled cupcake, stuck a candle in it, and sang "Happy Birthday" to him. It was kinda nice actually, just the two of us. But this year I want to do things a bit differently.

I'm inviting my mom," Jamela continues, her face scrunched up now, as if the mere thought hurts, "I'd like you to meet her."

"I would love to finally meet your mother."

"And I've been thinking about inviting Shaka's daddy too. What do you think?"

"About what?"

"About me inviting Clyde."

"Why wouldn't you invite him?"

"Well...I don't know. There's a lot of unfinished business between us, and I just don't want things to get too...awkward. I'm still undecided, but maybe you'll get a chance to meet him too."

"I would like that. I've caught a glimpse of him a few times when he's come by to pick up Shaka. He seems like a very nice young man."

"Yes," Jamela replies softly, half to herself, "He is a very nice young man."

"So," Jamela continues, "you think you'll be able to make it?"

"Can I make it? I wouldn't miss that baby's birthday party for all the world!"

"Excellent! Would it be okay if I have the party down here in the parlor?"

"Absolutely! That's a wonderful idea! That way I won't have to battle the stairs, and I'll be able to help you prepare for the party. This is so exciting! Now let's see...what do we need to do?"

"Well, we'll need to hang up streamers and blow up balloons."

"I'm sure I can blow up a balloon or two."

"Then there's the ice cream and cake."

"That's what I can do! I'll bake the birthday cake!"

"Oh, the cake..." Jamela stutters, "Umm, no, you don't have to bake the cake."

"Oh, baby, it won't be no problem at all."

"I know. Thank you, but...well, I was actually planning on baking the cake myself," Jamela says.

Miz Mattie slaps her hands to her thighs, "There I go again assuming things. You just tell me what you need me to do, baby, and I'll do it. I just got a little carried away, that's all. "

In all her years, Miz Mattie had never baked a birthday cake for a child before. But despite her initial disappointment, she quickly understood that that task was rightfully reserved for the mother.

"But I was kinda hoping that you would agree to help me. I've never baked anything in my life before, and I would like for it to be suitable for eating," Jamela says, laughing. The spark in the old woman's eyes returns, and her face fills with joy as she gushes on and on about a little white cake that is not too difficult to make, that can be topped with a simple, yet delicious, cream cheese icing. She's off and running now, listing ingredients and talking about mixer speeds and oven temperatures, but all of that is lost on Jamela, who sits nodding and smiling happily, thinking about how blessed she is to have this dear old woman in her life.

CHAPTER 19

The day of the party has arrived, and instead of feeling elated, Jamela is in a funk. Her only desire today is to spend the day alone with her son. But since she, not to mention Miz Mattie, had spent weeks preparing for this day, to pull the plug now would be selfish and insensitive. Veering from her usual routine, she puts Shaka down for his mid-day nap in her bed and climbs in alongside him. He falls asleep within minutes, but she has no such luck. She is both anxious and excited about the party. It has been over a year since her mother and Clyde have shared the same space, so how today's party would unfold was one big question mark. Abandoning her plans for a power nap, Jamela climbs out of bed and goes to her closet and inspects the two dresses hanging there. One is a size 18 denim jumper that she wore when she was pregnant. The other is a terra cotta colored, free flowing dress that swirls around her ankles when she dances with Shaka. Although it is better suited for summer, it is the one she will wear to the party later today. But as she takes it out of the closet, she can't suppress her yearning for a newer, prettier dress to wear, something like the ones she sees her neighbor wearing – form fitting, contemporary and stylish. *I've still got a pretty decent figure for someone who's had a baby*, she thinks, though she is aware that she has been so consumed with caring for Shaka, that she had unwittingly let her appearance slip a bit. Just how far it had slipped, had not been apparent to her until Vamp moved in. But today she wanted to look special. Truth be told, she wanted to look nice for Clyde. *Does he still find me attractive?* she wonders, does *he ever wish for what we had before things got crazy and complicated?* Living on her own had given her a new perspective on her life. And one thing she now knew for certain was that she wanted Clyde back in it. She knew that if she took a little extra care and fixed herself up, she might be able to entice him back into her bed. But the real question was, would he ever let her back into his heart.

Jamela runs her fingers through her freshly washed locs. Her thick hair is still slightly damp. She spritzes it with a light oil-based moisturizer that smells of coconut, and prepares to begin the methodical and cathartic process of "tightening" her locs. It's a slow process, and one best performed during times when she's unhurried and uninterrupted, aka, Shaka's naptime. In the living room she closes the blinds and lights her special 'Ocean' scented candle. The candle had been a gift from one of the nurses at the hospital. The nurse had just appeared at her bedside one afternoon, sat the candle down on her nightstand, gave Jamela's arm a light squeeze and disappeared. Jamela suspected that the nurse had probably witnessed her mother's clownin', and had given her the candle because she felt sorry for her, but the scent was so heavenly that Jamela no longer cared if the gift had been borne out of pity. She uses the candle judiciously because once it burned out, she did not know where she could obtain another. The label on the bottom read, Carol's Daughter. *But that's no help to me*, she thinks, *since I don't know either Carol or her daughter.*

Sitting cross-legged on the floor, she buries her fingers into her hair and gently massages her scalp. Then using the tips of her fingers, she gathers the puffy new growth of hair at the base of each loc, and incorporates the new growth into the already loced hair by using a gentle counter-clockwise twisting motion. As Jamela twists, she visualizes how she would like the day to proceed: The birthday party is a great success. Clyde, as the proud father, compliments her on everything - the decorations, the cake, even her appearance. And, to top the evening off, he offers to stay behind and help her clean up. While cleaning, he asks if it would be okay for him to help her put Shaka to bed, it being his special day and all.

Her mother, the proud grandmother, is cordial and polite, even to Clyde, and showers Jamela with praises of what a great little mother she turned out to be. When introduced to Miz Mattie, she greets her with exuberance and a warm embrace, and thanks her for providing her daughter and grandson with such a loving, nurturing environment. Miz Mattie beams lovingly at everyone. There's plenty of good food, good music, laughter and photo opportunities, and everyone is having a fabulous time. The party wraps up after exactly two hours, as planned. Shaka's grandma departs graciously, kind words and hugs dispensed to everyone on her way out. Miz Mattie retires to her rocker lounger in the dining room feeling tired, proud and happy. Jamela, along with Clyde, who is carrying a happily exhausted birthday boy in his arms, bid Miz Mattie good night as, arm in arm, they slowly climb the stairs to her apartment. Once upstairs, they put their sweet love child to bed – a simple loving act performed nightly by millions of parents around the world, but one that they had never performed together, until tonight. After shutting off the lights and tiptoeing out of his bedroom, in the darkened hallway Clyde and Jamela silently stand face-to-face, toe-to-toe. They are so close that Jamela can feel Clyde's warm breath on her lashes. Her breath halts as Clyde gently strokes her cheek and then brushes her lips with his thumb. She closes her eyes and allows herself to slowly melt into his enticing caress. She moistens her lips and bites her lower lip in anticipation as he urgently pulls her supple, willing body into the hardness of his own. He wants her and he is not in the mood for playing games, so he does the one thing that he knows for certain will let her know exactly how he feels. Her breathing quickens, then suddenly catches as he...

Buzz...Buzz...Buzz...

The alarm on Jamela's wristwatch goes off, rudely jolting her back to reality. "Hour's up," she says as she blows out the candle, "Time to get this party started."

With only 40 minutes remaining before the party is scheduled to start, and with Shaka likely to awaken at any moment, Jamela quickly dresses and heads downstairs to borrow bowls from Miz Mattie, and finds her standing at the kitchen sink thoughtfully dunking a teabag into a cup of hot water. On the kitchen counter sits the cake that Jamela had baked last night with Miz Mattie's help. She looks at the cake, then over at Miz Mattie, then back at the cake again and grins her silly grin that always puts Miz Mattie in mind of a sweet, insecure schoolgirl.

"Damn it!"

Miz Mattie looks up, brows knitted together, not exactly the type of language she would expect to hear coming out of the mouth of a sweet schoolgirl. *But then,* she reminds herself, *Jamela ain't no schoolgirl, she's a grown woman.*

"Sorry! I forgot the candle!" Jamela says, turning to run back upstairs to get it, then apparently changes her mind before changing her mind again, and in the process has literally turned herself around in a complete circle.

"Slow down, chil'. Slow down! You running around here like a chicken with its head cut off!" Miz Mattie says, taking hold of Jamela by her shoulders.

"Take a deep breath."

Jamela complies.

"Another!"

Again, Jamela complies, but this time with a silly, exaggerated roll of her eyes.

"You don't want to pass out before the party starts, do you?"

"No. Okay, I'm better now. Thank you. I just want everything to be perfect."

"It will be, baby. It will. But you need to calm yourself down a bit. Your baby's turning two today, you're not having the Queen over for tea. Not to say that this is in any way less important, cause it ain't, but everybody who loves Shaka will be here giving him lots of love, and that's what matters most."

"You're right. Of course, you're right," Jamela says, inhaling deeply and exhaling loudly. "How do I look?!" she asks, hands urgently patting her hair, and smoothing down her dress.

"You look beautiful, baby," Miz Mattie replies, and then cautiously ventures, "Is it because of Clyde that you're all in a tizzy?"

Jamela blushes the answer.

"There's no shame in wanting to look good for your young man. If I had somebody who was sweet on me, I'd be trying to look good too," she says chuckling, then asks, "Where's the baby, still asleep?"

"Yes, ma'am."

"Well, let's get this stuff on across the hall before the guests start to arrive."

Jamela lifts the cake from the counter and proudly surveys her work. Miz Mattie said she had done a good job. The cake did look pretty. It was a little lopsided, but otherwise, it looked like a real birthday cake. She crosses the hall and enters the parlor, where she places the cake in the center of the dining room table. Miz Mattie follows behind her with a stack of saucers, napkins and forks.

"Wow. It looks pretty in here," Jamela says in a surprised tone, as if seeing it for the first time, when in fact, she was the one who had stayed up late last night hanging with great precision and care the blue and yellow crepe paper and the huge Happy Birthday! banner. "I sure hope Shaka likes it," she says wistfully.

"Shaka is going to love it!" Miz Mattie declares.

"You think so?"

"I know so. Now go on upstairs and get that baby ready. We can't have him being late for his own party!"

"Okay!" Jamela exclaims, and suddenly feeling re-energized, happily bounds up the stairs to retrieve the birthday boy.

Even though she is totally inexperienced with playing the role of hostess, Jamela believes that she can hold it together for two hours. *Anything beyond that, and I can't be held accountable,* she thinks. And just as she is starting to pace, fretting that everybody was gonna be on C.P. time, the doorbell rings. It was Clyde. *It's just like him to ring the bell at exactly 2:00 p.m. sharp, the official starting time of the party. Oh dear, precious Clyde. Why did I ever let you go?* she wonders as she watches him make his way across the room in long, sure strides, arms outstretched beckoning to his son, while mouthing a smiling hello in her direction. *Whoa, he looks good,* she thinks, as she waves back, while checking out the curve of his buttocks in his jeans, and the ripple of the muscles in his forearms as he effortlessly lifts Shaka and tosses him into the air a few times before wrapping his strong arms around the boy's tiny torso. Shaka wraps his tiny arms tightly around his daddy's neck and, as Jamela stands witnessing the depth of Clyde's love for his son, she is once again wracked with guilt.

After Shaka runs off toward the sound of the ringing doorbell, Clyde casually saunters over to where Jamela is playing deejay. She sees him heading in her direction out of the corner of her eye, and quickly places in the cassette player a tape that she has already fast-forwarded to her favorite track, the song that asks the million-dollar question.

"Hi, Clyde," she says smiling, "Glad you could make it."

"I wouldn't miss it. Thanks for inviting me."

"You're welcome," she says, hearing Sade's plaintive cry, "Is It A Crime," in the background, and hoping that Clyde will recognize that the plea is intended for him.

"Wow," she says finally, after the song has ended, "Shaka's two years old day. Can you believe it?"

"I know," Clyde says, shaking his head in disbelief, "It's pretty hard to believe. Just look at him. He's definitely a big boy now."

"Yeah, he's no longer my baby."

"You know he'll always be your baby." Clyde says smiling down at her.

"Yeah," she says, smiling up into his eyes, "You're right."

"Grandma!" Shaka suddenly yells, causing Jamela to look

up in time to see her mother walking in the room carrying Shaka in her arms with a cigarette dangling from her lips.

"Just look at this boy," she tells Jamela, "He sure is fine. Kinda looks a bit like your brother, Junior who, by the way, said to tell you hi." Shaka reaches out for her, and as Jamela lifts him from her mother's arms, ashes from her cigarette tumble down the rear of his shirt and onto the floor. Her mother scuffs the ashes with the toe of her boot, grounding ash and melting snow into the polished hard wood floors. Jamela grimaces at the sight of her mother's carelessness, after having recently witnessed Miz Mattie on her hands and knees painstakingly scrubbing and polishing the floors.

"Baby, get me an ashtray." her mother commands.

"Mom, could you please not smoke inside...There's no smoking here...No one here smokes." Jamela hears herself stumbling over her words and hates the way she sounds. *I've got no reason to be apologetic*, she thinks, *this is my home*.

"The smoke...second hand smoke isn't good for Shaka. So if you must smoke, can you please do it outside on the porch," she finally manages to say with confidence and self-assurance. "And, if you could please wipe you feet before coming back inside...I'd appreciate it...Thank you." This last part stated with just the slightest hint of timidity, which did not go undetected by her mother.

"Well, la-dee-da! Excuse me!" her mother replies loudly and sarcastically, and snuffs the cigarette out on a paper saucer and puts the butt inside her purse while looking around. "Cute," she says, gesturing toward the hanging streamers, in a tone that sounds more condescending than complimentary, "Who decorated the place?"

"I did," Jamela replies, shrinking slightly under her mother's critical eye.

"I thought you lived upstairs."

"I do. This is what we call our parlor; it's like a big rec room where everybody can just come and hang out together. Besides, having it down here just made more sense because then Miz Mattie wouldn't have to climb the stairs. Come on,

Ma! I've been dying for you to meet her," Jamela says grabbing her mother by the hand and leading her into the dining room where Miz Mattie is seated in her favorite chair.

"Ma, this is Miz Mattie," Jamela states proudly. "She's the lady I told you about who bakes those delicious teacakes. She even offered to teach me how to bake 'em," she adds as Shaka climbs out of Jamela's arms and onto Miz Mattie's lap.

"Well, well, well..." her mother replies, looking down at Miz Mattie, who sits smiling up at her from her chair. "So you're the woman who's taken my place with my daughter and, from the looks of things, I'd say you're trying to steal my grandson away from me too." she says accusingly. Miz Mattie continues rocking and smiling and thinks, *This must be the sort of thing that folks say when they don't know what else to say.* But when the sneer on Jamela's mother's face remains fixed, Miz Mattie stops smiling and rocking and an odd expression clouds her face. In short order, she resumes her rocking and instinctively places her arms protectively around Shaka, who responds by resting head upon her bosom. When she does finally respond, she speaks slowly and deliberately, choosing her words carefully, mindful of earlier times when she had said exactly what was on her mind.

"You's the one who birthed this child, and there ain't another woman in this world who could ever take your place. I just consider myself lucky and blessed to have such a fine young lady living here in my home and allowing me to be a part of her life and a part of this baby's life. You should be very proud. God done blessed you, for sure."

"Yeah, well...What's to eat?" Jamela's mother yells, backing down now and shifting gears, after seeing that she could not get the intended rise out of the old woman. "Y'all serving any food here tonight?"

"We're gonna be serving ice cream and cake a little later, but there's some hors d'oeuvres over on the table," Jamela offers.

"Yeah? Y'all serving hors d'oeuvres?" her mother asks, obviously impressed.

"Of course!" Jamela answers proudly.

"What 'cha got?"

"Pretzels and chips."

"Pretzels and chips?!? Honey, I just got off work and I need some real food, not some damn pretzels and potato chips!" she says, snorting and fumbling around in her purse until she finds her cigarette pack. She pulls out a cigarette and automatically places it between her lips, then remembering the conversation she had with Jamela just moments before, removes the cigarette from her mouth and stuffs it back into its pack, snapping it in half in the process.

"I've got a pot of pinto beans on the stove, and a pan of cornbread that should still be warm." Miz Mattie offers. "Jamela, go on across the hall and fix your momma a plate. Sorry I don't have no meat to offer you, but..."

"No. Forget it!" Jamela's mother states abruptly, cutting the old woman off mid-sentence.

"Don't bother. I'll just have the pretzels and chips. Where are they?"

"They're right over there on the table next to where Clyde is standing, you passed them on the way in. Momma, did you say hello to Clyde?"

"Oh. Is that who that is? Huh. No, we haven't exchanged pleasantries yet, but I'll be certain to do so," she says as she heads toward the living room.

Jamela looks down at Miz Mattie, who is still cradling Shaka on her lap. "I'm sorry," she says, embarrassed by her mother's rude behavior.

"No need to apologize, baby," Miz Mattie quietly states, "You are not your mother. Now lift your head back up and go on over there and put on some more of that snappy music. This still a party, right?"

"Yes, ma'am," Jamela says, and heads across the room, with her dress swaying, and her locs swinging.

"So, Clyde, your baby's two today," Jamela's mother states, sallying up to the table next to him and grabbing a handful of pretzels.

"Yes Ma'am," he replies proudly.

"Well it looks like Jamela's doing a pretty good job raising him alone. It's a damn shame, the way you men run off after you've had your fun and planted your seed," she says spitefully.

"Excuse me, Ms. Taylor, but you are obviously misinformed. And forgive me if I question the sincerity of your concern about us no longer being together, but if I recall correctly, you are one of the main reasons, if not *the* reason, that we're not together today," he says in a non-apologetic, matter-of-fact tone.

"Now you listen here, young man!"

The 'young man' was all of the conversation that Jamela heard, but the volume and tone of those two words caused her ears to prick up and her body to involuntarily turn in the direction of her mother's voice in time to see her head rocking and finger wagging, while Clyde stood by with his arms folded across his chest and his jaw tightly clenched. Even without knowing the story, Jamela knew that it was her mother who had initiated the disruption - she was an instigator, plan and simple. *Damn her!* she thinks as she races to the next room.

"Momma, please!" Jamela implores, "It's Shaka's birthday!"

"Can't you be civil for just two hours? I don't ask much of you, but I'm beggin' you, please! If not for me, then do it for your grandchild!"

"I'm sorry, Jamela," Clyde begins, "I had hoped nothing like this would happen.

"I was just standing here grooving to the music…" he says, motioning helplessly with his hands.

"Maybe I should go, you know?" he offers, "to help keep the peace."

From the corner of her eye, Jamela sees a wicked, twisted grin creep across her mother's face.

"No! You're his father. You should be here!"

"Then I'll go!" her mother offers.

Jamela turns sharply on her heels, "You're his grandmother. He's your only grandchild. You should be here too. Come on, mom, please don't do this!" she pleads, her voice cracking. Her mother responds with an audible smirk then turns her back on them and begins stuffing her mouth with potato chips. Jamela lifts her eyes toward the heavens, takes Clyde by the arm and hurriedly ushers him out of the room.

"Sorry you got cornered by my mom," she says with a sad shrug of her shoulders. "What can I say?"

"That was wacked!" Clyde replies.

"I know, but we can't let her ruin this day."

"Come on. I want you to meet someone," she says, and she takes him by the hand and leads him into the dining room.

"Clyde, this is Miz Mattie. She's my adopted grandmother."

"Hello, Miz Mattie," he says extending his hand, "It's a pleasure to meet you."

"Pleased to meet you, young man. You've got yourself one special little boy here."

"Thank you. I couldn't agree with you more."

"He thinks you're pretty special too," Miz Mattie continues.

"Yeah?" Clyde says, in a surprised tone, and Jamela watches as a grin once again spreads across his beautiful face. "That's good to hear."

"So does Jamela," Miz Mattie continues, instantly mortified that the words had not stayed inside her head where she intended them to.

"Miz Mattie!" Jamela yells, looking at her wide-eyed and crazy.

"Come on!" Jamela says, grabbing Clyde's hand and steering him away from Miz Mattie, "Let's get ready to cut the cake."

"Cake! Cake!" Shaka yells, jumping down from Miz Mattie's lap and running to the table, almost knocking his grandma down in the process. Jamela places Shaka in a chair while she prepares to light the candles, with Clyde standing ready with the camera. She lights the candle and everyone sings a loud, and severely off-key rendition of Happy Birthday, as Shaka's little face glows in the light of the two candles.

"Make a wish, baby," she whispers in his ear, then closes her eyes and makes one on his behalf, as he blows out the candles amidst cheers of encouragement.

"Cut the cake, child, I'm starving!" Jamela's mother yells.

"Y'all know Jamela baked the birthday cake herself." Miz Mattie comments proudly.

"Miz Mattie!"

"What?" Miz Mattie asks, "You should be proud of yourself, baby."

"Let's hold off on the compliments until after we taste it," Jamela's mom chimes in, "'Cause if we're just judging from looks, then I can understand why she wouldn't want us to know that she baked it."

"Clyde, would you please cut the cake while I go and get the ice cream," Jamela asks, and turns and hands him the knife and looks on lovingly as Shaka delicately swipes a finger across the frosted cake. She smiles as he smacks his lips appreciatively, and doesn't restrain him as he goes back in for seconds. But Shaka apparently has bigger ideas, and this time, he plunges his whole hand into the side of the cake and pulls out a sizable chunk."

"Noooo!" Jamela screams, "My cake!"

"Well, it is *his* party," Clyde replies, laughing and clicking away with his camera, "So technically, that would make this *his* cake!"

"Would somebody hurry up and cut the cake before the boy completely destroys it?" Jamela's mom demands loudly.

"Here," Miz Mattie comes forward to offer her assistance, "You take the pictures, and I'll cut the cake. Jamela, go on and get the ice cream, baby."

"Sounds like a plan," Clyde says, as he willingly hands the knife over to Miz Mattie.

When Jamela returns with the carton of ice cream, everyone is busy eating birthday cake. No one stops or even slows down as she goes from plate to plate dispensing generous globs of vanilla bean flecked ice cream next to the quickly disappearing cake. She takes her plate and sits down next to Shaka and looks across the table in amazement at the unyielding motion of forks, accompanied by the low hum of satisfaction. She has not yet taken a bite of her cake, but sits patiently waiting for someone, anyone to comment on it. Miz Mattie finally looks up at her with a wink and a grin.

"Cut me another slice of that cake, Jamela," her mother yells across the table.

"I'll take another slice too, please," Clyde adds.

"Well, honey, I gotta give it to you. The cake is good. It looks a little funky, but it tastes really good," her mother compliments her in her offbeat way.

"It's good, Jamela," Clyde offers sincerely, pausing briefly from eating to look deeply into her eyes, "I gotta say, I'm impressed. You know..." he continues, flashing a dimpled smile, "I've got a birthday coming up soon..."

"More!" Shaka yells, making the verdict unanimous, and making Jamela one proud and happy momma. She finally takes a bite of the cake, the edges now spongy from the melting ice cream. *Hmmm. Not bad,* she thinks, giving herself a mental pat on the back. *Not bad at all.*

After everyone has finished eating cake and ice cream, Shaka unwraps his birthday presents accompanied by a chorus of ooh's and aah's. After the last flurry of wrapping paper and ribbons, Shaka retreats to his favorite spot beneath the dining room table, where he alternately plays with his new toys and the boxes they came in. With Shaka now totally engrossed with his toys, an awkward silence falls across the room. Jamela hurries over to the stereo and pops in a cassette tape of various Motown artists - guaranteed to have something to please everyone. Sure enough, in no time at all, everybody's either got a finger popping or a foot tapping or, in the case of her mother, a booty shaking. Two slices of cake and a heaping pile of ice cream had apparently given her energy level a little boost, but her mood as well, and now suddenly she's the life of the party. Right about this time Shaka makes the mistake of peeking out from beneath the table.

"Come on, little man, dance with your grandma!" she says as she pries the toy from his hands and lifts him up into her arms and swoops, twirls and turns to the music with Shaka tightly clutching her sweater and howling with delight. Miz Mattie sits happily watching from her chair as everyone allows the music to set their body free. The compilation Motown tape was one of Jamela's favorites, and had become one of her favorites too. She feels tempted to get up out of her chair and, as the young folks say, bust a move. But she has not danced in so long, she fears her body may not comply. Plus, she has never before danced in the presence of others. When she lived at home with her folks, the only type of dancing her parents allowed was the Holy dance. After she married and moved north with Charlie, new music suggested new ways of moving. But since Charlie was not a dancing kind of man, she was left to explore this new form of expression alone. What resulted was a style of dance that was uniquely her own, one that she was not so certain others could appreciate. So tonight she consoles herself with sitting on the sideline, clapping and cheering, and adding words of encouragement as Shaka, now down on the floor, throws his little arms over his head and twists and turns to the music. Everyone's having such a great time that no one even hears the front door open, or sees the arrival of a new, uninvited guest.

~~~

The music greets her from the street. After entering the apartment, the first thing she does is to peek her head into the parlor. A quick glance around the room reveals the usual occupants, plus a few unfamiliar faces. Her eyes land on the remaining cake in the center of the table and she quickly makes a beeline for it. Dropping her leather briefcase into the closest chair, she waves a hello to no one in particular, then cuts herself a large slice of the cake and quickly devours it while still standing at the table in her overcoat. She hungrily eyes the cake once again, remembering that she had not eaten since breakfast, and keenly aware that there was not much of anything to eat in her apartment, she cuts herself another slice of cake and adds a handful of chips to the side for good measure. *I guess they forgot to tell me about the party,* she thinks, as she finally removes her coat and takes a seat. *Either they forgot to tell me about it, or they told me about it and I forgot.* She's been having a tough time remembering stuff lately. Been forgetting little, but significant things at work too, like remembering to return phone calls, or where she filed important documents. Last week she even forgot to show up for a meeting with her boss. She had lied her way out of that one, but she wasn't sure if her boss had fully bought it.

Lately, she has been feeling overworked and majorly stressed out, so she had agreed to go out with a few friends after work. After a few glasses of pinot noir, and a couple of shots of whiskey, she had come home feeling pretty good!

"Ball of Confusion!" she sings along to the Motown track loudly and off-key while wolfing down the remainder of her cake.

Miz Mattie's starting to get the hang of this party thing. I see she even added a little decorations this time, and no gospel or blues but Motown. Hey! We've even got some chips and mints. All we need now is a bar, but even without it, this is alright!

Bobbing her head and swiveling her hips to the beat, she heads into the dining room where most of the guests have gathered. With a sexy pout on her brightly painted lips, and her eyes bright and glassy, she goes over to where Clyde is standing and pulls him hard by the hand, catching him completely off guard causing him to stumble into her before bouncing off of her full breasts. She says nothing, but starts to dance, doing a sexy little bump and grind number. She dances the entire track with Clyde, and seems intent on keeping her same dancing partner as the next song starts up. With eyes slightly parted, and a few wisps of hair clinging to her moist face, her tongue darts suggestively out from between her lips, and her subtle bumps become slightly more urgent, and it looks as if she's one thrust away from an orgasm. Everyone, aside from Shaka, has stopped their dancing and chattering, and they all stand looking at Vamp with their mouths gaped open.

"Who's that hussy!?" Jamela's mom whispers loudly, "and why the hell are you letting her dance with your man like that?"

"He's not my man," Jamela responds angrily through clenched teeth, the tips of her ears on fire, "And that hussy is my neighbor, Vamp."

Clyde makes several unsuccessful attempts to move away from Vamp, but each time she just follows up behind him, moving in close - cha, cha, cha, bump! - before sashaying away again. As Clyde makes yet another attempt to move beyond Vamp's reach, Jamela notices the flustered grin on his face. *Hell, who can blame him? Vamp's undeniable beautiful, and tonight she's also apparently in heat. Beautiful and hot - a combination few men can resist. Even so, she's not gonna bring her ass up in her and ruin my baby's party! Who the hell invited her anyway?!*

"Vamp!" Jamela shouts, grabbing her roughly by the arm, just as she is attempting to give Clyde's retreating buns another thrust with her pelvis, "Come on! I need help clearing the table!" She loads a bowl of chips and a dripping ice cream carton into Vamp's arms and pushes her through the invited guests back toward the kitchen.

"Man! This is some party Miz Mattie's got going tonight!" Vamp comments, with a slight slur.

"Are we getting new neighbors?" she asks, as she leans in

close and whispers loudly, "Did you check out the guy? Nice ass, huh?"

For the first time that night, Jamela smells the alcohol on Vamp's breath. *She's drunk!* She had never before seen Vamp out of control like this, hadn't thought it was possible. *It's amazing what a little alcohol can do,* she thinks while she watches as Vamp reels back on her heels and nearly topples over.

"I wouldn't mind having him as my new neighbor," Vamp says with a wink, "Just don't make direct eye contact with him though," she continues, "He's got a crazy eye."

"And who's the old broad he's with?" she asks, never pausing for an answer.

"She seems too old to be his woman, but too young to be his mother. And if it is his momma, then I say she ought to be ashamed for dressing like that," she comments, laughing maliciously. "And, if it's his woman..." she pauses, struggling to contain her laughter long enough to finish the sentence, "...then I still say, she ought to be ashamed for dressing like that!" Her face is contorted with tears and laughter, and her sides ache from laughing so hard.

Oh, naw! Oh, hell naw! You come in here and disrupt my party. Diss me, diss my baby, my baby's daddy, and my momma all in one night! This time, girlfriend, you've gone too far! And since your ass is trying so hard to be white, let me just help you out!

She pushes up her sleeves, and is about to grab a fistful of Vamp's hair and direct her face into the open container of vanilla ice cream, when Miz Mattie suddenly appears at the door.

"Everything okay, baby?" she asks in her slow drawl, directing her question to Jamela. With one quick glance, she sizes up the scene and correctly concludes that she had arrived just in the nick of time.

"Everything okay?" she repeats, waiting to make eye contact with Jamela for assurance that everything was, in fact, okay.

"Yes ma'am," Jamela finally answers, looking up at Miz Mattie through eyes glistening with tears. Miz Mattie directs a stern gaze down at Vamp, who is still bent over laughing, and is about to seriously take her to task for her inappropriate behavior, when suddenly Vamp's laughter turns to groans, and she goes from holding her sides to clutching her stomach.

"Ugh, I don't feel good," she moans, and cupping her hand to her mouth, races through the apartment and departs just as abruptly as she had arrived.

~~~

The next day when Vamp returns to the parlor to retrieve her briefcase and coat, she learns from Miz Mattie that what she had assumed was another tea party had, in fact, been Shaka's second birthday party. Further, the man and woman there last night were not prospective tenants, but Shaka's dad and Jamela's mother. What's more, Vamp had learned that she had made a true spectacle of herself (*a damn fool*, was the actual term used).

"Oh, shit!" she gasps, as she climbs the stairs, suddenly remembering a comment she had made about the woman she now knew to be Jamela's mother.

I may not be a fan of Jamela's, she thinks, *but everyone knows you don't go around dissing a person's momma… at least not to her face.*

CHAPTER 20

Vamp opens the doors to her armoire and looks inside at her spring/summer wardrobe. Even though it was still crisp and cool outside, she was happy that spring had finally officially arrived and would soon melt away the remaining gray snow and usher in of new, budding life. It was a season of new beginnings, a time for new shoes. She loved making the transition from bulky sweaters, pants, wool and gabardine suits to clingy dresses and breezy skirts worn with nude legs or sheer stockings and strappy high heels.

Another thing she loved about spring was her ritual jog along the lakefront on the first warm day of the season. Given her aversion to the sun's propensity to darken her skin, she normally jogged on an indoor track. Similarly, indoor pools were always favored over outdoor ones. Ditto for tennis courts.

But her yearly jog along the lakefront was her one exception to her rule. Dressed in the latest running gear, as she ran the two mile distance, which she referred to as 'The Winner's Lap,' in her mind she silently proclaimed, *Look at me, world! The first warm day of the season and not one ounce of body fat anywhere!* She would jog at a leisurely pace, careful not to break a sweat, and occasionally slow down to allow the good looking brothers a better view, or effortlessly sprint past women who wore thick sweat suits to conceal, and hopefully help melt away, the fat on their rubbing thighs. *You'd better get yourself a real man and leave Ben and Jerry alone,* she was tempted to call out as she sped by.

And while she favored soft flowing pastels for the spring, summer was dedicated to wearing white. She wore white every chance she got, even though with her irregular period, it was always somewhat of a risk, but a risk well worth taking because she thought that there was nothing more intoxicatingly sexy than stark white clothes against dark skin; the darker the skin, the sexier. In her mind, this was the only advantage the darker sisters had over her, yet she didn't think it *so* great that she would allow her own pale skin to tan. What if it didn't completely fade after summer was over and all the white clothes had been returned to storage? Nope, she couldn't risk it; they could keep their one advantage. After all, who was she to deny them that.

CHAPTER 21

Monday morning. The familiar and welcome aroma of strong Columbia coffee makes its way to her room, giving her at least one good reason to get out of bed. As she showers, she can't help thinking about how Cat seemed so willing to simply throw their relationship away without so much as a backward glance. Vamp was certain that Danny was part of the reason why. She could practically hear him now, badmouthing her to Cat, 'You got me now, baby. What 'cha wanna keep messing around with that troubled woman for. Kick her to the curb, baby, she ain't no good for you.' But after much pleading, she had finally gotten Cat to agree to meet her for lunch next week. She wonders if she should write her thoughts out on index cards to be better prepared, or just wing it and hope for the best.

Wiping the water from the face of her wristwatch, she realizes that she has been in the shower way too long. She gets out and hurriedly puts on matching silk panties and bra, and looks down critically at her bulging belly. "Another day in the life of the losing battle against PMS," she says with a weary moan. Waiting for her period to start was always the worst. It was only after Aunt Flo's arrival that the cramps and bloating would finally subside. As she contemplates what to wear, the smooth, silky voice of the deejay announcing the time jolts her back to the present. She quickly decides on a lightweight ivory cashmere sweater from her fall/winter collection, and black pants from her spring/summer collection. After pulling on the sweater, she takes a seat at her vanity table to do her hair and make up. Since she is running so far behind schedule, she makes do with her trusty French twist, and limits herself to no more than fifteen minutes for make-up.

She skillfully applies a copper shade of eye shadow to both eyelids, and then using her fingertip, smudges a deep charcoal powder into the outer creases of each lid, creating the illusion of depth. Two coats of mascara, a quick dab with a cover stick to conceal two errant pimples, following by bronzer applied with a large bristled brush to her cheekbones, temples and chin, she finishes with a swipe of vibrant, red lipstick, and still has two minutes to spare. Sitting on the side of her bed, she slips both legs into her black tailored pants and stands to pull them over her hips. They stop at her upper thighs. "What the hell," she says in disbelief, and waddles over to the full-length mirror, the pants still compressing her thighs, and turns her back to the mirror to get a good view of her rear. "Damn!" she yells, cupping her cheeks in both hands.

"When the hell did this happen, and why the hell didn't anybody tell me!

"Now, I have always envied the sistas for what the brothers refer to as 'The Power of The Booty,' but damn!" she can't help saying again. She quickly grabs another pair of pants from the closet. These don not even make it to her thighs, but concedes and cry 'uncle' at her knees. Out of time now and starting to feel panicky and desperate, she grabs a pair of black leggings from the back of a chair and pulls them on. These pants she deemed suitable for lounging around the house in, maybe walking the dog, if she had a dog, but definitely not for wearing to work. She was an account executive at a major pharmaceutical company, and she felt that her image was as important as her knowledge. As a last ditched effort to redeem her outfit, she pulls on a red cardigan that she hopes will help camouflage her bottom, then runs out of the door feeling disheveled and distraught at being late again.

As she hurriedly locks the door to her apartment, her keys fall from her hand.

When she stoops to retrieve them, her purse slips from her shoulder and upon impact, spits its contents across the floor.

"Damn it!" Vamp cries, as she feels her resolve starting to crumble as she drops to the ground, quickly scooping up her personal items and stuffing them back into her purse, while trying hard to hold it together. As she reaches for the last couple of items, a lipstick and a tampon, a pair of scuffed, worn boots that could only belong to one person, suddenly appear before her. Since the birthday party, Vamp had done a good job of avoiding Jamela, but had always known that an encounter was inevitable. Why not today, she thinks. With the way this day is already going, why the hell not.

"Hey!" Jamela directs a gruff greeting toward the figure at her feet, looking down at Vamp's red sweater flared out over her backside.

"Hey, back." Vamp quietly replies, zipping up her bag and slowly rising to her feet.

The sight of Vamp's face catches Jamela off guard: twin streams of black goo are trailing down both cheeks and dripping onto her creamy white sweater.

"Ohhh girl. You look like shit!" she can't resist saying, "What's up with you?"

"Well, if it isn't already obvious, I'm having a bad day, okay!

"I'm late for work. All of the crap just spilled from my purse. My clothes don't fit from all

those damn cookies and cake I've been eating, so now I have to wear these hideous stretch pants. Oh, yeah, and to top it all off, now my makeup is ruined, which means I have to go back inside and wash my face and reapply my make up, which means that I'll be even later for work than I already am, and my boss will undoubtedly throw a fit…"

"Whoa, Nelly, slow down!" Jamela says, "That was a rhetorical question. I didn't really want all of the specifics.

"But, you know," she continues in a smug, satisfied voice,

"Since you brought it up, while you were crawling around on the floor just now, I couldn't help but notice how wide your butt has gotten.

"Now, I'm not a gambling woman but if I was, I'd put my money on sometime in late September, early October."

"Late September for what?"

"The baby. It's a girl, by the way."

"What baby?"

"Your baby."

"I don't have a baby."

"Not yet, you don't."

"What the hell are you talking about? And can you please stop talking in circles!" Vamp asks, feeling agitated and a little angry.

"Girl, you're pregnant! There, is that easy enough for you to understand?"

"Shut up with your stupid lies, Jamela," Vamp states, her chest heaving as her duel black lines begin to flow anew.

"What the hell have you got against me? I'm sorry about your little party. How could I have known that was your man and your mother?"

"I ain't got nothing against you, and he ain't my man, he's Shaka's daddy, and you wouldn't have known that, didn't need to know that, because you weren't invited to the party!" Jamela states, starting to get flustered and angry herself.

"Besides, why are we even talking about the party? We're talking about your big butt, and the fact that you can't fit it into all those pretty little clothes of yours."

"Why are you saying all these mean things to me? I told you I was sorry!" Vamp sobs, pressing her purse to her chest, which feels like it's been struck by a fist.

"Why are you crying now? Wasn't it you who just a few days ago was looking down your nose at me and mine? I know your type, girl: college graduate, corporate climbing, white girl wannabe! Well, girlfriend, I got news for you. Your ass is Black, okay! It might not be as black as mine, but you're Black! And I may not have a college education or fancy clothes and car, but I'm a good mother. I do have that. You'd just better hope that you can rise to the challenge when your time comes, 'cause if you screw your kid up, all those pretty clothes and fancy car won't mean a damn thing!"

"Stop it!" Vamp screams, and her hand goes out to push Jamela aside. Not wanting to be touched by Vamp, Jamela takes a big step backward, causing Vamp to stumble and fall back to the floor with a hard thud and a pain filled grunt.

"Oh, get the fuck up, girl. You ain't hurt," Jamela says as she reaches down and takes hold of Vamp's arm to try and pull her to her feet. Vamp looks up into Jamela's eyes, her face etched with a mixture of pain, vulnerability and perhaps...fear. And for the first time, Jamela feels the slightest tinge of guilt and sympathy at the sight of Vamp's questioning, wounded eyes.

"Come on, girl. You're gonna be..." and before she could get the word 'okay' out of her mouth, a torrent of greet vomit spews from Vamp's mouth and lands on Jamela's boots.

"Fuuuck!!" Jamela yells as she jumps back, seconds too late.

"What the fuck you go and do that for!" she screams, retreating back into her apartment and slamming the door behind her.

Back in the safety of her own apartment, Vamp takes her second shower of the morning, then fixes herself a cup of tea, adding a thimble of whiskey to help soothe her nerves. She sits on the side of her bed and picks up the phone. When no one answers, and her call is transferred to her manager's mailbox, at the last minute she changes her mind and instead of leaving a message saying that she will be in late, she leaves a message saying that she is sick and will not be in at all today. Then she crawls back into bed, pulls the covers up beneath her chin, and falls asleep while thinking, *This is one of those days when I should have just kept my black ass in bed.*

CHAPTER 22

She wakes up around noon with an urgent need to pee, and is greeted by the stench of something dead or dying. The 'something' turns out to be a pile of clothes on the bathroom floor, crusted over with what looks like dried lentils. Squeezing her nostrils shut with the thumb and index finger of one hand, with the thumb and index finger of the other hand she carefully lifts the soiled garments from the floor, examining them to determine whether or not they were worth salvaging, or if she should just toss the suckers out and call it a day.

"Oh my God!" she says, suddenly remembering the mess in the hallway, "I can't leave that crap out there for Miz Mattie to find!" She is embarrassed and absolutely stupefied that she had left it out there in the first place. She was not so irrational as to think that a fairy janitor was going to whisk in and sprinkle magic sawdust, leaving everything all nice and sparkly.

Tightening her robe around her middle, she grabs a bucket and fills it with hot water, a generous splash of disinfectant, and a large sponge, and then dons a pair of yellow rubber gloves that come up to her elbows. Back down on her hand and knees, with the large sponge she applies a healthy amount of sudsy water to the wooden floor and wipes in quick, broad swipes. After a moment or two at this, she jumps up and runs back inside and retrieves a scrub brush then commences scrubbing hard and furious while thinking, *Note to self: If, God forbid, I ever again find myself in a situation where I have to clean up vomit, do so before the shit dries!*

"Vanessa? Hi baby, it's me," Miz Mattie says, slowly advancing up the staircase then stopping and leaning against the railing, breathing audibly.

"Jamela told me you were sick this morning," she continues between labored breaths, "You feeling better?"

Oh, shit! Vamp thinks, but replies, "Yes, I am. Thank you for asking."

"I just wanted to be certain you're okay."

"I'm okay."

"Do you need anything?"

"No, ma'am."

"Okay, dear. I'm going back inside then. But if there's anything I can get for you, just let me know."

"I will. Thank you."

Damn that Jamela! I bet she ran downstairs and told Miz Mattie I had morning sickness and vomited all over her nice floors. That's just how rumors get started, people going around spreading lies.

Suddenly, her vigorous scrubbing of the floorboards slows down as her mind pushes to the forefront all of the seemingly unimportant and inconsequential stuff that she had kept forcing to the rear.

I have been feeling pretty lousy lately, but I always feel crappy right before my period starts. Speaking of which… when did I have my period last? The scrubbing comes to a complete halt. *I keep forgetting things, and I'm always losing things, which I never do. And lately I feel so awfully tired. Oh my God! Could I be pregnant?*

The thought of that now being a possibility washes over Vamp and settles in the pit of her stomach like a smoldering lead ball, when she suddenly feels the need to pee again. She quickly dries the floor, grabs the bucket and runs back inside her apartment, pausing just long enough to press the 'Play' button on her answering machine, before continuing on to the bathroom where, elbows on knees, head in hands, she finds relief.

This day could not possibly get any worse, she thinks, as she listens to the soft whirl of the answering machine.

...Beep...

"Nessa, it's mom. Give me a call, honey. Daddy and I want to know if you'd like to come for dinner on Saturday."

"I don't think so."

...Beep...

"Hey, Van, it's Marc. Listen, I'm running a little short on cash. Can you spot me a bill till I get paid next week? Call me when you get this."

"Right! The only time I hear from you, little brother, is when you need something. Jerk!"

...Beep...

"Vanessa. Hello? Hello? Well, all right. Vanessa, this is Susan, Susan Cartwright. I'm calling to let you know that due to your progressively deteriorating attendance and poor performance, which you and I talked about just last month, I'm sorry to say that we're going to have to let you go. There won't be a need for you to return to the office, but I do need for you to give me a call later today. Thank you. I'm sorry, Vanessa. Good-bye."

"What! Did that bitch just fire me?" Vamp cries, leaping from the toilet and stumbling and tripping back to her bedroom with droplets of pee running down her bare thighs. She rewinds the tape, and hits the 'Play' button.

"...won't be a need for you to return to the office, but I do need for you to give me a call..."

Rewind.

Play.

"... which you and I talked about just last month, I'm sorry to say that we're going to have to let you go. There won't be a need for you to return..."

Rewind.

Play.

"... Susan Cartwright. I'm calling to let you know that due to your progressively deteriorating attendance, which you and I talked about just last month, I'm sorry to say that we're going to have to let you go."

Despite what she had thought earlier, her day had just gotten worse.

CHAPTER 23

She had never felt so alone. She picks up the phone to call her mother, but Pride convinces her to put it back down. Just as she is about to hang up, Desperation orders her to call Cat. She dials. No answer.

"Cat, it's Vamp. I need to talk to you, girl. Please call me as soon as you get this message. It is urgent. Call me. Please!" Hanging up the phone, she feels like she is having an out of body experience. She sees herself standing in the middle of her bedroom, bathrobe hanging open, looking dejected and confused, not sure if she's coming or going. She struggles to maintain her composure, while forcing herself to stare down the cold realities of her life.

"Oh, man…I've lost my home, my job, and my relationship with my best friend is in the dumps, and…drumroll, please…I might be pregnant! Dear, God! Could things get any worse?

"No! Don't answer that!" she yells, knowing as she now does that just when you think things can't possibly get any worse, something happens to assure you that, indeed, they can.

"I feel so alone and abandoned. Why is this happening to me? " she asks, directing her question up toward the ceiling.

I will never forsaken you.

The voice, which sounds very much like her own voice,

seems to be coming from inside her head. She pulls her eyes away from the ceiling, and looks around the room warily.

"I so want to believe," she says wearily, "If only I could see you."

I am in everything you cast your eyes upon, everything that you touch. I am everything that you are.

"My life is so screwed up! I don't know how it got to this point, and what's worse, I don't know how to begin to try and fix it," she cries.

Trust your heart to guide you.

"God, if you truly love me, please don't let me be pregnant. Okay? Thank you. Amen," she says, feeling simultaneously relieved and intrigued, yet a bit concerned that she might have temporarily misplaced a few cards from her deck.

The ringing phone interrupts her conversation.

"Hello?"

"Hey, what's up with the intense message you left on my phone?"

"Cat! Oh, girl thanks for calling back. I really need to talk, can you come over?"

"Aren't we having lunch next week?"

"Forget next week. Forget lunch. I need to talk to you today…now! Can you come over, please!?"

"Now? I'm at work. Are you okay?" Cat asks.

"Yeah, I'm okay…What the hell am I saying! No. No I'm not okay!"

"What's up, girl?"

"I really can't go into it over the phone, that's why I need you to come by."

"You didn't even sound like yourself when you answered the phone. What were you doing?"

"Just now? Oh, I was just sitting here talking"

"Talking to who?"

"Um…myself."

"Talking to yourself? Okay… I just hope like hell you weren't answering back.

"You're sounding pretty weird; you're not about to do

anything stupid, are you?"

"No, of course not," Vamp replies, feeling grateful for her concern, yet annoyed that Cat might think that in her absence she had become completely unhinged.

"Well, I just need to return a phone call, then I'll head right over. But before I go, tell me…you weren't, were you?"

"Weren't what?"

"Answering yourself."

"What? Girl, no!" Vamp says with a nervous laugh.

~~~

After hanging up the phone, Vamp's mind automatically summons up her usual coping mechanism. It was a guaranteed cure (albeit a short lived one) for everything from a broken nail to a broken heart. As she waits for Cat to arrive, she is forced to try and quiet the dueling factions of her monkey mind, one half urging her to *Drink! Don't Think!* While the other half pleads, *Think! Don't Drink!* "Who the hell am I kidding?" she says, as she unceremoniously pours a splash of whiskey into a glass. She takes the first swallow and breathes a sigh of gratitude at the small satisfying burn that radiates throughout her body. She takes another small sip and feels the jagged edges of her world start to soften a bit, just enough to allow her to sit patiently and wait for Cat's arrival.

CHAPTER 24

"Girl, go on and pee on the stick! I'm sure you've done this countless times before."

"Actually, I've only done it once before."

"Oh? All right. Well, *I've* done it countless times before," Cat says as she rips away the cellophane paper and hastily empties the contents of the box out onto the dresser top. She hands Vamp the indicator stick, "Here, there's really nothing to it," she says, as she unfolds the instruction sheet.

"The test is simple, I know," Vamp says, "It's the results I'm afraid of."

"Go on, girl, it's gonna be okay."

"Are you sure?" Vamp asks, the question comes out shaky and barely audible.

"Yeah, sure. Now, go on!"

"Okay," Vamp replies without much conviction, and picks up the plastic cup and closes the bathroom door behind her.

~~~

As soon as Cat had showed up at her apartment, Vamp had spilled out her problems in one unyielding stream: She was feuding with her neighbor, had just lost her job and, to top it off, she might be pregnant. Cat, who had quite literally, only gotten one foot in the door, insisted on going right back out to find a neighborhood drug store and pick up a pregnancy kit.

"They say that curiosity killed the cat," she said, as she clutched the steering wheel and glanced around quickly to make sure all the car doors are locked, "but satisfaction sho' brought him back!"

~~~

"Okay," Cat calls through the closed door. "It says here to dip the stick in the cup of piss and wait 15 minutes. If it's blank – hallelujah! If it's pink, well, I guess it's time to start picking out names."

"Okay." Awkward silence. "How long does it say I have to wait, again?"

"Fifteen minutes."

"Umm...okay."

More silence.

"You're not planning on sitting in there the whole time and leaving me out here by myself, are you? Girl, get you ass out here! Come on. We can sit and talk while we wait. It'll make the time go by faster."

Vamp cracks the door open, steps out and closes the door behind her. Cat couldn't recall a time when she's seen Vamp look like this. Her face is free of makeup and her skin looks shallow and blotchy, and the chipped red nail polish on her ashy bare feet confirms to Cat that Vamp is not her usual self.

"Thanks for coming over, Cat" she says, her eyes glassy with tears, "I really appreciate it. I didn't know who else to call."

"Glad I could help!" Cat answers a little too brightly. "So, what have you been up to lately?

"Oops, sorry!" Cat says with a small grimace, "Umm...let's see. Why don't I just tell you what's been going on with me. There's been so much, where should I begin..." she says, rubbing her hands together like a greedy slumlord.

"Well, shortly after you moved out, Danny – surprise – moved in. He said he felt he needed to be close by to make sure I was okay. I tried to tell him that he didn't have to, that I was all right, but he insisted. Anyway, it's working out okay," she says, not at all convincingly.

"Oh, I got the promotion! Yeah, that Vegas trip apparently helped cinch the deal. So, say hello to Ms. Assistant Director! It's a cool gig, but it keeps me crazy busy with meetings and traveling. You know how it is, girl, smoozing with the right people is a major part of the job."

"Wow, you got it! I know you really worked hard for it, so congratulations, Cat." Vamp says, trying desperately to sound happy for her friend, yet feeling that all her friend's good news was not doing much to help her current state of mind.

"So, of course I had to go out and buy some new clothes, and I've been shopping around for a new car. I'm thinking about maybe getting a convertible. Girl, you know how it is, gotta look the part!" she says, running her French-tipped acrylic fingernails through her long synthetic weave.

"How many more minutes?" Vamp asks, anything to disrupt Cat's gloating.

"Oh shit! It's been over 20 minutes! Girl, you know me, sometimes I get to talking and can't stop. Are you ready?"

Vamp nods her head yes.

"Okay, here goes."

Vamp remains glued to her spot on the side of the bed, twisting a used tissue round her index finger and digging her toes into the faux leopard skin rug beside her bed.

"Come on. We'll go in together." Cat offers.

Vamp reaches out her hand and Cat takes it, gives it a gentle tug, and pulls Vamp up off the bed. Hand in hand, they silently cross the room and come to a stop outside the bathroom door. Vamp puts her hand on the doorknob, Cat places her hand securely over Vamp's, and together they turn the knob and push the door open.

From her spot at the door, Vamp can clearly see the indicator stick that has been placed across the top of the specimen cup. Her body slides down the doorframe, and she sits with her knees pulled up to her chest with her arms wrapped tightly around her legs, feeling as if she had just fallen down the proverbial rabbit hole. She offers no resistance as she feels her body topple over, leaving her lying across the threshold of the bathroom door in a fetal position. Her hair falls forward concealing her face, but from the quaking motions of her upper body, Cat can tell that she is crying. Cat steps across Vamp to enter the bathroom, picks up the stick, then sets it back down.

"Oh, girl!" Cat says as she kneels down and puts her arms around Vamp's heaving shoulders.

"Oh my God, Vamp," she says again, while silently thinking about all the complex, far reaching, life altering consequences represented by that little pink-tipped stick.

"What are you gonna do? How are you going to take care of a baby with no job? What's your momma gonna say? What's the daddy gonna say? By the way…who *is* the daddy?"

Vamp doesn't respond. Although her eyes are tightly shut, it doesn't curb the flow of tears streaming from them.

"Come on, girl. Don't cry. Get up. Come on. Why don't you get in bed," Cat asks while half heartedly making an attempt to pull Vamp up from the floor. Vamp remains tightly glued to her spot.

"You know what, girl? We need a good stiff drink. Oh, damn, girl. Sorry. You shouldn't be drinking. Okay, I'll make a pot of coffee," Cat offers, turning toward the kitchen before stopping in her tracks, "I don't suppose you should be drinking coffee, either.

"I know!" she says cheerfully, "Milk. That's it, a cup of warm milk. It'll relax you and help calm your nerves. Don't move. I'll be right back. I mean, it's okay if you move, but I'll be right back." She returns a few moments later.

"Damn, girl, when was the last time you shopped for food? There wasn't any milk, so I brought you a glass of water."

Vamp sits up, pushes her hair off of her damp face, and takes a small sip of the water.

"Thank you," she manages in a small, pitiful voice.

"Come on, let me help you up," Cat offers again, taking

Vamp by the arm and helping to pull her to her feet, then ushering her back to her bed. Vamp sits down on the side of the bed, apparently oblivious to the snot running down her nose and pooling on her upper lip.

"Can you stay, please?" she quietly pleads to Cat, "I don't want to be alone."

"Girl, you know I wish I could," Cat replies as she turns away, repulsed at the sight of the snot creeping between Vamp's quivering lips, "but I've got to return to work to prepare for a meeting I've got first thing in the morning.

"But listen. Tomorrow, as soon as my meeting's over, I'll give you a call, okay?" she states, grabbing her jacket and purse and heading for the door.

"Don't get up!" she calls out, "I can find my way out."

Spying a box of tissues on Vamp's dresser, she tosses the box onto the bed next to Vamp.

"Heads up! Looks like you could use a few of these," she says as she departs, closing the door behind her.

"Man, oh, man!" she says as she runs down the stairs and jumps back into her car.

"Talk about the chickens coming home to roost! Wait till I tell Danny!"

CHAPTER 25

Vamp spends the remainder of the day and the entire night sitting on the side of her bed in the exact same spot where Cat had left her, alternately crying, praying, pleading with God, and staring at the walls. She was hurt and disappointed that Cat had not agreed to stay with her through the night, given her delicate state of mind. But she soon comes to realize that Cat's insensitivity was the least of her worries. The following morning at 8:00 a.m., she finally abandons her spot on the side of the bed and telephones her gynecologist.

"Hi, this is Vanessa Lawson. I'd like to schedule an appointment to see Dr. Riley."

"Just a moment, please. Let me check the doctor's calendar for availability."

Over the counter pregnancy tests claimed a high degree of accuracy, but there was always room for error, and Vamp felt she needed professional advice.

Was I supposed to do a 'clean catch,' or was the first flow adequate? I don't really know. I didn't actually read the instructions.

"Thank you for holding. Dr. Riley can see you at 2:30 on Friday, July 18th."

"What! July 18th? That's almost 3 months away!"

"Yes, I know. I'm sorry, but Dr. Riley is just returning from vacation, so she has a little catching up to do.

"But this is an emergency!"

"Are you a current patient of Dr. Riley's?"

"Yes, I am!"

"What is the nature of your emergency, Miss?"

"I think I might be pregnant!"

"Let me look again…Okay, the very earliest I can squeeze you in would be on June 10th. But unfortunately I won't be able to schedule you for a definite time; you'll need to come in when we open at 8:00 a.m., and then wait until the doctor can fit you in."

"That's still over 2 months away!"

"Yes, I'm sorry, but that's really the best that I can do. How far along do you suspect you might be?"

"I don't know."

"Have you missed more than one period?"

"Yes. Two or three, I think. I'm not too certain, I've always been irregular."

"Hmmm. Well in that case, I would suggest that you meet with another doctor who can see you immediately to confirm whether or not you are pregnant. And if you are, to get you started immediately with your prenatal care. But what I'd like to do is still put you down for the July 18th appointment at 2:30 p.m. That way, if you find out you are pregnant and you want Dr. Riley to be your obstetrician, you'll already have a spot on her calendar. And if you find out that you're not, just call and cancel. Okay?"

"Okay. Thank you."

Vamp hangs up the phone and thumbs through the telephone directory and runs across several medical facilities offering free pregnancy tests and free counseling. By 9:00 a.m. she has showered, dressed, and is driving to the clinic for her 10:00 a.m. appointment, alone. She is relieved to find that the clinic is bright and clean. After completing a brief questionnaire about her medical history, she provides the nurse with a urine sample and is given an ultrasound. Finally, at 11:30, after sitting alone in a waiting area filled with sad-eyed young girls and their fidgeting boyfriends, she is ushered into an office where she is soon joined by a young Latino doctor with large, intelligent brown eyes, and straight hair that hangs to the middle of her back. She sits down on a low stool next to the table where Vamp is seated. She flashes Vamp a quick smile as she introduces herself, then without any further fanfare, opens a manila folder and reads aloud the results of the tests. "Yes," she says, "It appears that you are pregnant. And, according to the ultrasound and the date of your last period, or, as indicated here, the approximate date of your last period, that would put you at being approximately 20 weeks along, or, 4 to 4 ½ months pregnant."

Vamp's jaw drops, and it takes all of her will power to remain seated upright on the table, resisting the urge to flee or, more to her liking, to just disappear into a void of nothingness.

"So, this is good news, yes?"

Her head is reeling from the words, '20 weeks along,' unable to speak, she simply shakes her head no.

"You do understand that at this point it is too late to consider terminating the pregnancy?"

She nods her head yes.

"Have you thought about adoption as an option?"

No.

"Is that something you think you would be interested in pursuing further, giving the baby up for adoption?"

No.

"You're planning on keeping the baby?"

After staring blankly at the doctor for a long moment, Vamp finally nods her head yes.

The doctor stands and gently places her hand on Vamp's shoulders before continuing, "Take some time, Miss Lawson, and think carefully about what you need to do. Here are some very informative pamphlets for you to read. And please, if you have any questions, any at all, don't hesitate to give me a call. All right?" she adds, looking intently into Vamp's frightened eyes. Vamp climbs down from the table and stuffs the pamphlets into her purse.

As she is driving home, she finally finds her voice, "Dear, God, why! Why would you let this happen to me now, when I've got no way of even providing for myself, much less a baby! Aren't I dealing with enough already!" she screams hysterically, as she speeds down the entrance ramp onto the freeway, driving fast and feeling reckless and crazy. As her foot bears down on the accelerator, she does not care about her life, the life within her, or the lives of any of the unknown faces she passes on the expressway.

"Why!" she screams again, her heart is racing and her head feels like it could explode at any moment, and part of her wishing that it would all just end in a big climatic explosion, just like in the movies.

"I'm pregnant with a child I can't support, and I can't ask his daddy for any help because I don't know who the hell the father is! I don't fucking know who the father is," she repeats as her screams turn to sobs and her foot eases up on the accelerator. She pulls over onto the shoulder of the road and rests her forehead on the clammy steering wheel, and then, in a small, pained whisper, pleads, "God. Please, help me."

~~~

Vamp makes it home safety and encounters Miz Mattie at the front door.

"What's wrong baby? You look like you done seen Satan himself." Despite herself, Vamp gives a timid smile at the colorful and apt metaphor, while thinking, *If you only knew.* Gripping the handrail, she looks up at the stairs looming before her like a steep mountain. With one foot on the first step, and one hand gripping the railing, she bows her head and lets out an audible sigh.

"Why don't you come on in here for a moment," Miz Mattie offers, "Take a load off."

Vamp hesitates for a brief moment and then, feeling the weight of the day bearing down upon her, graciously accepts. She steps into the parlor, passes through the living room and settles herself on the sofa across from Miz Mattie's chair.

"Boo!"

She lets out a small yelp, and a grinning round head suddenly appears from behind the sofa.

"Hi, Shaka," she replies cautiously, feeling her shoulder muscles tightening.

"I think I'll come back and visit some other time," she says, slowly standing and smoothing out the invisible wrinkles in the front of her blouse while trying to concoct a plausible excuse for her abrupt departure.

"I really don't want to intrude," she continues, but what she is really thinking is that she cannot risk an encounter with Jamela today.

"Where you running off to? Go on and sit back down. It's just the three of us here. Jamela's at work. She won't be back 'til supper."

"Jamela's got a job?" Vamp asks, unable to suppress her look of surprise mixed with a tinge of envy.

"Yes, she got herself a job at the hospital down on the Boulevard working in the Dietary Department. That's where they fix food for the patients," she states proudly, assuming that like her, Vamp would need an explanation of what the folks in a dietary department actually did.

"She seems to like it a lot. She gets to wear a uniform and everything."

"That's nice. Good for her," Vamp says, yet knowing, even as the words cross her lips, that she does not sincerely mean it.

"But how are you doing?" Miz Mattie asks, "I've been a little worried about you lately."

"Well, Miz Mattie, it's a long, sordid story. Let's just suffice it to say that I've made a pretty good mess of my life."

"God's sakes, chil', what's the problem?"

"Do you believe in God, Miz Mattie?"

"Why, yes, chil'. I most certainly do!"

"Well, I thought I did too, or at least I wanted to, until he turned his back on me."

"Chil', God would never forsake his chil'ren!"

"Well, he forsaked...forsook...whatever! He left me high and dry." she says wearily, leaning back into the soft cushions of the sofa.

"Yesterday, I asked God for a favor. A really big favor," she continues, "Not just your everyday run of the mill favors like, 'Can you help me buy a car?' or, 'Can you please help me get this new job?' No, this was admittedly B-I-G. But it wasn't me I was asking the favor for, so I felt confident that my prayers would be answered. But he let me down, and now my life…our lives," she says, making a circular motion around her midsection, "are ruined."

"What did you ask God for, chil'? If it ain't too personal a thing for me to ask."

"Seeing as how the whole world will soon know, there's not much point in me trying to play coy now," Vamp says, now resigned to her fate, and finally willing to admit the truth about her situation.

"The fact of the matter, dear Miz Mattie, is that I am pregnant, four and a half months pregnant, to be exact. But I asked God… I said, 'God, if you really love me, please don't let me be pregnant!

"And, Miz Mattie, this I swear to you, God answered me back. Okay, maybe it wasn't God, maybe God's too busy to have a one-on-one conversation with the likes of me. Maybe it was a guardian angel, or spirit that the elders in the church used to speak of," she pauses from her ramblings to ask, "Just what *is* Spirit anyway?"

"Well, baby, I suppose it depends on who you ask. Some people refer to their souls as Spirit. Some, when they commune with God, talk of hearing the voice of the Spirit. But what exactly did God say, baby?"

"Well, he said something along the lines of what you said, about not forsaking me, and he told me to trust my heart."

"Sounds like Spirit to me!"

"But the point I'm trying to make is that I thought I had made a real spiritual connection. I thought that once my prayers were answered, I could finally turn my life around and start living right."

"Baby, God don't work like that. You can't bargain with the creator by saying, 'If you do this, then I'll do that.'"

"I wasn't trying to bargain with God," Vamp replies sullenly, "I was simply asking for help."

"Just a second," Miz Mattie says, holding up an index finger to signal an interruption in their conversation. She bends forward and softly instructs Shaka, "Baby, run on back to your room and play with your letter blocks for a little while. Grandma needs to have a grown-up talk with Miss Vanessa," she sends him off with a little peck on the nose. Shaka obediently gathers up his toys and turns to go to his spare bedroom, then quickly turns back and wraps an arm around the old woman's neck, and plants a kiss on her nose before scampering off. Vamps watches with a pang of sadness as she contemplates the child in her womb. Miz Mattie relaxes back in her chair, her face radiating love.

"I didn't know you all were related."

"We're not blood relatives," Miz Mattie says, smiling, "We just sort of adopted one another."

"Adopted? Isn't Jamela's mother still alive? Didn't you tell me that's who that woman was at Shaka's birthday party?"

"Oh, yes, chil'. Jamela's mother is very much alive. I'm her adopted grandma. She apparently needed a grandma's love, and I needed some chil'ren to love, so now we're related," she states matter-of-factly.

"Now, let's get back to our conversation. Vanessa, forgive me for being so frank, but I'm gonna ask you a personal question. Did you engage in fornication?"

"Yes, of course I did; otherwise, we would not be having this conversation."

"Well, I assume that a woman your age knows about the birds and the bees, and how babies are made?"

"Yes, Miz Mattie. I have already been thoroughly schooled in the biological aspects of conception."

"But then you go and lay down with a man and hope that you don't wind up pregnant? God blessed you with the gift to bear children. Not all women are so lucky. I woulda imagined you'd be thrilled to death."

"Thrilled?! Why would I be thrilled? I'm not married. I'm not even in a serious relationship. Hell, I'm not in a relationship at all! And, I just lost my job and..." she looks down at her hands as the tears once again begin to flow, "....I don't know who the father is."

"Goodness, chil'! What do you mean you don't know the father. Was you meddled with without your consent?"

"What? No, it's nothing like that; I didn't say I don't know the father, I said I don't know *who* the father is."

"You have to forgive an old lady, but I'm confused. How can you know the father, but not know who the father is?"

"Well, I have these... let's call them 'episodes,' where I'll suddenly become aware of myself being some place or doing something, but can't remember exactly how I got there, or what preceded that moment in time. So far, I am aware of six 'episodes" of lost time that have spanned anywhere from 20 minutes to 4 hours. But that doesn't take into account the lost time that even I am unaware of, because I haven't missed it yet. And I won't ever miss it, until something like this happens. So, even though I'm pregnant, I don't recall doing the deed, or fornicating, as you prefer to call it, during a time that would correspond with how far along the pregnancy is."

"Have you seen a doctor about these 'episodes'?"

"Umm....no. There's really no need. I already know what causes them. They tend to occur when I've had too much to drink. But don't worry, I've been working really hard on cutting back."

"So, what you're saying," Miz Mattie says, her face scrunched up with obvious confusion, "is that one day you drank too much, blacked out, and several months later woke up pregnant?!?

"Close enough," Vamp says, wincing at hearing it stated so bluntly.

"Sweet, baby Jesus!" Miz Mattie exclaims, "Now I understand why you was praying so hard. Well for starters, you gotta stop all that drinking, and you gotta stop it now! Then you need to go and find a doctor who specializes in taking care of little unborn babies, to make certain that your little one's okay."

"Yes, ma'am," Vamp replies solemnly, and the dam of tears opens again as she's consumed with guilt. Here she was nearly halfway through the second trimester, and she had not yet seen an obstetrician.

"I don't..." she struggles to say the words, "I don't want this baby!"

"My God, chil', what are you saying? How could you not want this precious gift of life?"

"I'm not prepared to take care of a child. I can barely take care of myself, and I'm not doing such a bang up job at that. Today...this morning...I went to an abortion clinic." She chokes back her sobs and lifts her head to meet Miz Mattie's eyes. The repulsion and contempt she had braced herself to find, isn't there. Instead, she sees that Miz Mattie's eyes are filled with tears, sorrow, and compassion.

"What am I going to do with a child? I don't know what I'm going to do with a baby! You've gotta help me, Miz Mattie!" she pleads.

"Chil', you need to pray."

"I already told you, no one's listening to my prayers," Vamp sobs.

"Well, chil', Miz Mattie begins, "Let me ask you this? Do you wanna do right by this baby?"

"Yes. Yes, ma'am I do."

"And do you think you could love this chil'?"

"Yes, I know I could."

"Okay. That's a good start, but we can't do this on our own Vanessa. You need to understand that *especially* when things ain't going your way, *that's* the time when you need your faith to pull you through. Now, it seems to me like you've turned your back on the Lord. But I need you to just turn back around and say, 'Hallelujah! Thank you, Father!'"

"Okay."

"No. I want you to say it. Say the words."

"Hallelujah. Thank you, Father."

"No, Vamp. Say it like you mean it!"

"Hallelujah. Hallelujah. *Hallelujah! Hallelujah!!*" Vamp cries, as her voice starts to rise and her body quivers uncontrollably. After all those years of cowering in the church pews of her youth, her fears are finally realized, as she's overcome by the Holy Ghost.

"Thank you, Jesus! Thank you, Father! Thank you!" she cries as her fervor subsides, leaving her physically, emotionally and spiritually spent.

"Hallelujah, dear chil', Hallelujah!" Miz Mattie cries, and clasping Vamp's hands tightly between her own, solemnly proclaims: "Then with God's help, we gone raise us a baby!"

CHAPTER 26

As Vamp climbs the stairs finally heading home, she feels as if a heavy weight had been lifted from her shoulders. Yet, the ache in her solar plexus remains, due in part to the fact that there was still one crucial piece of information missing: the name of the man whose child she was carrying. One thing she was absolutely certain of, and that was that she had not had sex since moving to Ravenswood. The last sexual encounter she remembered having had been back in October. But if she were to place any credence in the doctor's findings, conception would have had to occur sometime during mid to late December. *I suppose it makes sense*, she thinks, remembering the back-to-back celebrations Cat had hosted at their apartment.

First, there were the weekly pre-Christmas parties comprised mainly of Cat's friends, for which Vamp had felt no need or desire to do anything more than put in a brief, perfunctory appearance. Then, there was the actual Christmas party. And what a party *it* was! Girlfriend had pulled out all the stops for that one. Even though when it came to cooking, Cat could seriously throw down, for the Christmas party she had hired a caterer to serve up spicy Cajun cuisine, coupled with a bartender who served Dirty Cajun Martinis, and a kick-ass DJ who kept the joint a jumpin'!

The Christmas party started at 11:59 p.m. on Christmas Eve, and lasted until around 12:00 noon on Christmas day, leaving just enough time for everyone to stagger home and grab some much needed, but not nearly enough, shut eye before rolling out of bed and showing up still partly inebriated, for a sobering dinner with family. Vamp had been present for the Christmas party, but had missed out on what she was certain had been a fun and memorable New Year's Eve celebration. Still reeling from her sudden uprooting, Vamp had been strangely content to sit home alone watching Dick Clark and the thousands of brave revelers who had packed into Times Square to watch the crystal ball drop, as they counted down in unison the start of a new year.

Suddenly, an image of her nude body reflected back to her in the mirror at the foot of her bed flashes before Vamp's eyes, causing her heart to lurch, followed by a sinking feeling in the pit of her stomach. Typically, memories from lost 'episodes' were lost forever, but as she sits alone in her apartment thinking back to her last whirl of parties at the apartment she shared with Cat, images of what could only be fragments of her forgotten past suddenly come flooding back. She sees herself alone in bed between rumpled satin sheets...Now she is dancing before the full length mirror, champagne glass in hand...The image of a man's broad shoulders and back, tapering down to exquisitely chiseled buttocks. She inhales sharply at the next image, a hand appears from behind her reclining body, caressing her thighs, her breasts, now tilting her head backward and covering her mouth with a hot, smoke filled kiss.

Under the circumstances, the images are painful to witness, yet she fears that if she closes her mind to them, they will vanish forever, so her mind's eye searches frantically for a face. Not just any face, but *the* face. She hears Jared's voice, the bartender who worked the Christmas party; smells Randy's cologne - her favorite, Polo; sees her friend, Sadie's, full, pouty red lips; and can almost feel Brandon's familiar hands, with their strong, nimble fingers expertly massaging her shoulders.

A collage of limbs, body parts, sounds and smells, but no face.

"Well, this is a fine mess you've gotten yourself into, Vamp," she stays aloud.

"But… if I had a choice in the matter…I guess I would have to pick Brandon as the father. Jared, I wouldn't recognize if I passed him on the street. As for Randy, well everyone knows that he plays on his own team. And Sadie…what the hell!

"Well, one thing's for certain," Vamp groans as she kicks her shoes off and plops down on the sofa, "The kid definitely is not hers."

~~~

After several moments of hesitation, she telephones Brandon and, trying to keep her voice sounding casual and aloof, invites him to stop by later that evening. *What harm could it be?* she reasons. Besides, it was something she had done several times in the past, asking him to come over to check out her new stereo system, or to help program her new DVD recorder, or just to kick back and watch a movie together. Brandon was what she considered a very fine specimen, with his chocolate chiseled body, decked out in his tastefully culled wardrobe. That alone was enough to catch any woman's attention. But to top it off, the brother could dance his butt off! The only reason he had never been anything more than a friend became apparent the moment he opened his mouth - he had an unusually soft and effeminate voice which, even though they had been friends for more than six years, still caused her to do a double take. Only once had they come close to crossing the line that separates friends from lovers.

A few years back, they had been at his apartment drinking beers and watching a movie, when he started playing footsies while tossing popcorn at her and laughing hysterically each time a piece stuck to her hair. Just as she was becoming really annoyed, he grabbed her foot and started kissing her toes. She had been startled by how good it felt, and had squirmed and squealed while lightly protesting, and half-heartedly demanding that he stop. He immediately complied with her orders to stop kissing her toes, and started gently sucking on them instead. First the baby toe, then the next one, and all the way down until he had worked his way all the way across to the big, momma toe. Holy Moly! She had never had her toes sucked before, and it was feeling pretty damn good! She thought it would be best to disengage her foot while she still had the good sense to do so, and had kicked at him playfully, yet forcibly, with her free foot. As luck would have it, her foot slid off his chest and landed on his crotch where his penis straining against his jeans revealed the she was not the only one enjoying the toe sucking. When their eyes met, he had simply shrugged, grinned sheepishly and asked, in *that* voice, "You wanna do it?"

"No!" she'd yelled, laughing while backing away to the far end of the sofa.

"No, I don't! Why'd you have to go there?"

"Hey, there's no harm in a man asking," he replied.

"You said no. And no means no." he said, standing and brushing the popcorn from his clothing.

"I've gotta run to the John. Why don't you rewind the movie a bit and grab us a couple of cold beers. I'll be back in a few." When he returned from the bathroom, they finished watching the movie as if nothing had ever occurred (although she had made a point of slipping her loafers back on as soon as he left the room). No further mention was ever made of it, and she had come to think of it as simply one of those 'guy things'. As accustomed as she had become to being propositioned by her male friends, by her girlfriends' brothers, fathers *and* boyfriends, she had begin to believe that somewhere there existed a secret handbook that young boys received after their first erection, whose leading directive stated: 'Whenever you befriend an attractive woman, you must attempt to 'hit it.' You may already know that you don't stand a snowball's chance in hell, but it is your duty to the eternal fraternity of manhood to at least ask,' or some other crazy shit to that effect.

As always, Brandon agrees to come by. When he arrives, she buzzes him in and less than a minute later, he's standing at her door holding a bottle of red wine and a little potted plant. He removes his leather jacket and gives her a hug and a kiss on the cheek. "Hey, girl, you're looking good, as usual," he says, handing her his coat. As she takes it and turns to hang it up in the closet, he adds, "Although it looks like you're packing a few more pounds," he says, playfully patting her hips, "Don't worry, it looks good on you," he says with a twinkle in his eye, and extends the bottle of wine and potted plant before she could reply.

"Yeah, right!" she comments, "Would you like a glass of wine?"

"Of course."

"Okay. I'll be right back. Make yourself at home."

He leisurely strolls about looking around, as she goes to the kitchen for a corkscrew and a wine glass.

"So, this is your new home," he asks rhetorically.

"Yep. This is it."

"Nice. Different - not what I'd expect from an uptown girl such as yourself, but I like it," he says, nodding his head in approval.

"Thanks."

"How long you've been here?"

"Since the end of December."

"December! And you're just now inviting me over!" he says with a mock frown.

"Yeah, well, things have been a bit..." she searches for the right word, "...complicated."

"How's Cat? You two still best buds?"

"Cat's fine. We're still friends; she was just here yesterday," she says, handing him the glass as she prepares to pour from the bottle.

"Only one glass? What, none for you? Oh, I see, what's your guilty pleasure tonight? Whiskey, or maybe something of the rolled variety?"

"No wine. No whiskey. No Mary Jane."

"What? Are you sick?"

"Not sick, just pregnant."

"Pregnant!" The red wine sloshes out of his glass and spills down the front of his shirt. "Oh, hell!" he groans, then less dramatically, "Sorry, but you startled me. I thought you said you were pregnant!"

"I did. Here, take that off. Let me blot it for you before the stain sets in," she says, setting the bottle down and reaching for the shirt as he unbuttons and removes it, exposing a solid six pack. His jeans ride just low enough on his hips to reveal the waistband of his designer underwear. Automatically, she wonders, boxers or briefs? He catches her staring at him and covers his chest in false modesty.

"Why are you trying to act shy with me? I've seen your precious jewels before," she states boldly, hoping to draw him in with that lead.

"Right! The Christmas party! So typical of you women, you tell me you love me so that you can sleep with me, and then months go by before I hear from you again," he says, feigning heartbreak.

"Mama always warned me about women like you. She always said, 'If you give them the beef, baby, what's gonna make them want to buy the cow,' " he says, grinning.

Armed with the knowledge that she actually did have sex with Brandon the night of the Christmas party, Vamp is determined to finally put the "Case of the Unknown Daddy" to rest.

"Was it good for you?" Vamp asks.

"As good as I always knew it would be."

"Well, I'm glad," she says, choosing her words carefully, wanting to break it to him gently, then quickly abandons that approach in favor of cutting straight to the chase, "I'm glad it was good," she continues, "hopefully, that will make it easier for you to step up to your responsibility."

"My responsibility?" he asks, his brow furrowed in confusion. Vamp stares intently at him, and she swore she actually witnessed the exact moment of his comprehension, evidenced by a shooting flicker of light in his eyes.

"Oh, no! Hell no! You're not trying to tell me that this kid is mine, are you?!" he asks incredulously.

"I'm 4 ½ months pregnant. We had sex exactly 4 ½ months ago at Cat's Christmas party, Brandon. Do the math."

"Okay, so now I get it. After being MIA for months, you decide to call me up when you discover that you're pregnant and need a father for your kid?" he asks, practically spitting the words out at her. Even in her fragile and desperate mental state, she can't help but notice that his words come out in a deep rumbling baritone.

"Vamp, you know you're my girl and all, but I just can't stand here and let you railroad me like this," he continues.

"Railroad you? What the hell are you talking about?!"

"What proof do you have that this baby is mine?"

"We fucked in December! What more proof do you need!" she yells.

"Granted, I had sex with you," he says, softening his tone and motioning with his hands for her to calm down and turn down the volume. The vein that had suddenly jumped out in the center of her forehead had freaked him out, "but I was careful to use a condom, both for my protection as well as yours."

"Your protection?" she asks, hands on hips.

"Forgive my frankness, Vamp, but you haven't exactly earned a reputation for being particularly chaste. Besides, I know for a fact that there were other guys besides me in your room that night. What were you all doing, playing Monopoly? It's possible, I suppose."

"Are you implying that I slept with someone else in addition to you that night?!"

"All I'm saying is that I personally witnessed the bartender guy entering, and Randy exiting your room that night. Now you know for a fact that I never kiss and tell. Unfortunately, not everyone is as discreet as I am."

"You heard somebody talking about me!?" she asks, fire raging in her eyes.

"I heard a few words exchanged between Randy and some other fella."

"What the hell did he say?" she demands.

"Actually, I don't know; didn't care to stick around to hear the details."

"So, you're telling me that you slept with me anyway knowing, or suspecting, that I may have already slept with someone else that night?"

"Yeah. What can I say?" he asks, shrugging his shoulders by way of explanation, looking like a big kid who had been caught with his hand in the cookie jar.

"You know that I've been lusting after you forever. I figured that that might be my one and only chance. So, I put a little raincoat on the big guy and took a walk on the wild side."

"A walk on the wild side," she repeats, "that's how you view making love to me, 'a walk on the wild side.' "

"Well, you gotta admit, there was an element of risk involved." he replies.

"Well, for that matter there's risk involved every time you walk out of your front door! Hell, you could get hit in the head by a falling tree branch. Now you wouldn't ordinarily think of a tree branch as being deadly, but let that sucker fall and hit you the wrong way and you could lose an eye, or worse, suffer brain damage!"

"True that, true that!" Brandon laughs, amused by the absurdity of Vamp's argument, yet also saddened by his friend's dilemma.

"Look here, girl. You know I'm crazy about your ass," he says tenderly in his normal, falsetto voice, "but I'm pretty certain the kid's not mine."

"Come here, darling," he says, arms outstretched. Vamp collapses into his arms, her defenses now totally down, and bathes his bare chest with salty tears as he gently strokes her hair and softly murmurs, "Dear, Vamp. My dear, sweet Vamp." He waits until her tears have subsided before speaking again, "You know, I'm actually kind of flattered that you picked me; unfortunately, I'm just not ready to be anyone's daddy just yet."

Later that night, long after Brandon had tucked her into

bed and departed, she lay in bed thinking about what Brandon had said about not being the only man in her room that night. "Maybe I'll just tell the kid that his daddy came from a sperm bank. Either that, or that he abandoned us. Either way, it's a rotten deal for the little bastard, but at least it'll keep folks from speculating about my business, and having the kid growing up thinking that his daddy's name is 'Anybody's Guess,' she says wearily, before falling into a restless sleep.

CHAPTER 27

The flame beneath the pot of tomatoes is turned to a slow simmer. The added sugar and butter thickens the juices of the coarsely diced red fruit, transforming them into a dish that is both savory and sweet. Miz Mattie stands at the stove flipping for one final time, the golden pan-fried salmon croquettes. Jamela checks on the pan of biscuits browning in the oven, then gives Shaka a peck on the forehead as she takes a seat beside him at the kitchen table. Shaka finishes cutting out his pan of biscuits, fashioned out of red and yellow Play-Doh.

"Thanks for inviting us for lunch. I'm starving," says Jamela. "It smells so good in here. I can't wait to try everything."

"The stewed tomatoes and the salmon are done," Miz Mattie says, removing the salmon patties from the skillet and placing them on a paper towel covered plate.

"And from the smell of the biscuits, I'd say they need 2 to 3 minutes more."

"That's amazing!" Jamela proclaims.

"What's amazing?"

"That you can tell how much longer the biscuits need to cook just by the way they smell."

"Well, when you've been cooking for as long as I have, it

becomes second nature. Okay, let's get them biscuits out of the oven and sit on down and bless this food."

Today they eat in silence, long past the point where they feel inclined to fill every gap with idle chatter. Miz Mattie sits quietly eating as she listens to the gospel music that drifts in from the dining room. With an amused smile on her face, she observes Jamela using a teaspoon to eat her stewed tomatoes, and sandwiching her salmon patty between the two biscuit halves. Miz Mattie was accustomed to seeing the meal eaten the old-school, down home way of sopping up the sweet, buttery broth and tomato bits with a biscuit halve, and eating the salmon separately.

"That hit the spot!" Jamela states, unfastening the top button of her jeans and patting her belly contentedly, "I could really go for a nap," she grins. "I even dug the tomatoes. Who woulda ever thought of putting sugar in tomatoes?"

"I don't know, darlin'. That's just the way we cooked 'em back home."

"And those salmon patties weren't bad either. When I was pregnant with Shaka, just the mere smell of fish would make me want to hurl. Women used to tell me that once you develop an aversion for a food while you're pregnant, you can just forget about it. Lucky for me, that wasn't the case, since I don't eat pork or beef. And there's only so many ways you can cook a chicken."

"Yes, Lawd! I know what you mean!" Miz Mattie says, laughing. "I eat a lot of fish and chicken too. Back when Charlie was alive, every now and again, I'd cook us up some steaks in butter and onions. Ooh, wee! That made for one good meal, to be sure! But that was back when I had my own teeth," she says, grinning bashfully.

"Hey!" Jamela says, suddenly, "That reminds me of something I've been meaning to tell you. Remember last week, when Vamp threw up in the hall?"

"Yes."

"And remember at Shaka's birthday party, when she got sick and ran out?"

"Hmmm."

"And, have you noticed how big her butt's gotten lately?"

"No. I can't say that I have. Where, exactly, are you going with this?"

"I betcha anything she's pregnant!" Jamela announces gleefully.

"Wouldn't that be a hoot! I still remember how she reacted that time Shaka tried to hug her. Acted like my baby had head lice. Made me so mad! But can you picture *her* with a little crying, pooping baby spitting up everywhere? It would be just what she needs to knock her off of that high horse she rode in on. Then, we'll have a chance to see just what our little vampire is made of."

"Hmm," Miz Mattie says thoughtfully, a little surprised at witnessing this unflattering side of Jamela.

"You don't even know for certain that Vanessa is pregnant, yet you already got it all figured out what kind of a mother she'll be? For the sake of this argument, let's just say that she is pregnant. Don't you think that what she'll need most is some kindness and compassion? It can't be easy raising a chil' alone. You, of all people, should know that."

"I do know. And, no, it ain't easy."

"In that case, wouldn't you want to help her out? Teach her some of the things you've learned, instead of waiting to see her fall on her face, or off her high horse, as you put it."

"Why should I help her? She's never had a kind word to say to me since she got here. In fact, she's been a real shit!"

"Watch your mouth, baby."

"Excuse me, Miz Mattie. I didn't mean no disrespect, but every since she moved in here she's been giving me nothing but attitude. I, on the other hand, have done nothing but tried to be righteous toward her, seeing as how she is our neighbor, and all. But I'm sick of people like her treating me like a second-class citizen just because my skin's dark and I prefer my hair naturally nappy. It's no secret that I don't own a fancy car or expensive clothes and things. Heck, I ain't never even been inside of a college, but that still don't make her better than me. So to be honest with you, Miz Mattie, if she did fall flat on her face, she would be getting exactly what she deserves. Now, I'm not saying that I'm gonna push her, or nothing. I'm just saying that I won't bother to try and break her fall."

"Baby, God don't like ugly. Besides, there are always things about a person that we don't know, couldn't know, in the brief time we spend together. So for that reason alone, we should try not to judge. Most of what we get to see of people is just their little hurt selves all polished up, trying to project a brave front to the world."

"Why are you taking her side?" Jamela asks, accusingly.

"I'm not taking anybody's side, baby. I'm just saying that sometimes people are confused about life. They be heading down the wrong path, and the thing that helps them to stop and turn back in the right direction, is usually just a little kindness."

"Well, can't everybody be the saint that you are, Miz Mattie." Jamela states, sullenly.

"Chil', I'm an old woman now, but there was a time when I was young too. And I'm no saint, but I am a chil' of God. And all of God's chil'ren make mistakes from time to time."

"I'm sorry, Miz Mattie, I just don't think you fully understand. I'm sick of her walking around here with all that talk about not wanting to go out in the sun because she's trying to preserve her precious light skin! What kind of crap is that!? I mean, look at you! Even thought you don't do much with your hair, I can still tell that the texture is more like White folks hair than Blacks, but I bet you never went around believing that you could walk on water because of it!"

"Like I said before, chil', I've done a lot of livin' in my time on this here Earth, and some of the roads I've travelled down should have been barricaded with yellow tape and flashing lights. But now that I'm older, I understand that sometimes it's necessary to travel down a broken road or two. But hopefully, when you're trying to make your way back onto the paved path, there'll be an outstretched hand to help you over the rubble."

"Yeah, well, I'll think about what you've said, but right now I'm going to get busy washing these dishes."

"Oh, baby, just leave them. I'll get to them later."

"Are you sure?"

"Yes, I'm sure."

"Okay. Well in that case, I think I will go upstairs and have myself a little nap. I was tired before, but now I feel exhausted. Come on sweetheart, it's nap time," she says, taking Shaka by the hand, who waves goodbye to Miz Mattie as they depart.

"Yes chil'," Miz Mattie says, waving back to Shaka as she settles into her rocker lounger with a full belly and heavy lids, "You'd best believe me when I say, I've done a whole lot of living..."

CHAPTER 28

To the people in the small Southern town where she grew up, Mattie was considered an anomaly. Even among the townsfolk who knew her by name, most still insisted on calling her, The little blue-black gal with white folks hair. While not exactly rare, it was a combination that occurred infrequently enough that folks felt the need to make a fuss over it; much in the same way they did when a calf was born with three legs. But unlike the calf, which was put down instantly, Mattie had to learn to endure being perceived as different.

All heads would swivel as she skipped down the street with her thick, shiny plaits bouncing on her shoulders. Wherever she went, folks gathered around and commented on how beautiful she was. What they really meant, even she was not too naive to realize, was how beautiful her hair was. During the times that she grew up in, dark skin and kinky hair were not the standard of beauty; not even to her own people who, ironically, had dark skin and kinky hair. Despite her young age, she fully understood that her 'good' hair spared her the pain of being teased and bullied by her classmates, and diminished and ignored by her elders. So she made a point of never refusing anyone who reached out with eager fingers and curious hands, the chance to caress her hair, while she simply stood by and smiled her little Mona Lisa smile.

As she grew from child to teen, little Mattie lost some of her old admirers. Those who now despised her did so for precisely the same reason they had once admired her. And they no longer referred to her by the too long nickname that she secretly loathed, but had somehow managed to come up with a grouping of even worse monikers: Darkie, Blackie, and Sambo, that they viciously spat in her direction. The group that no longer liked Mattie, not surprisingly consisted of other teenaged girls who were just beginning to discover that there were not enough cute teenaged boys to go around, but there were also some older women who scrunched their noses up like they smelled something that stank, whenever Mattie walked by. These were the married women who had lots of little babies who had suckled away their youthful beauty and the fullness of their breasts, and whose husbands had taken to going into town every Saturday morning to get their shoes shined or their hair trimmed, under the pretense of preparing for church on Sunday morning, all the while knowing full well (and their wives knew it too) that they had no intention on setting foot inside anybody's church, come Sunday. But Saturday was market day. A day when the older girls ventured into town on their own, away from the watchful eyes of their mothers, to buy provisions for the family. And Mattie, who was just beginning to develop little buds on her chest and soft curves at her hips, along with the other blossoming maidens, would sashay down the main dirt road as if they were participants in a parade. And the teenaged boys, such appreciative spectators, would gather in clumps around the shoeshine stand, or lean against the barbershop pole and smile and nod good morning as the girls passed by, while the married men would take pause from their shaves or haircuts to lean out of the barber's chair and leer lustfully out the window.

Mattie knew that many of the boys lining the streets looking like tall, overgrown weeds, were there to see her, and she smiled her little smile and secretly vowed to use the one thing that had even gotten her any position attention, to help her get what she desired in life. And at the tender age of 15, all that she desired came wrapped in a 17 year old muscle-bound package and possessed a smile capable of lifting the sun into the sky, and answered to the name of Jimmy.

CHAPTER 29

Mattie's folks were devout Christians who looked forward to the start of each new week when they could enter His house to praise His name. And today, they felt extra blessed because their little modest country church had been chosen to host members of a visiting church from up north. No one they personally knew had ever been north, but stories of the Northerners' grandeur and sophistication had filtered back to their ears through various sources. To make certain that her family was not going to be viewed as back-woods country bumpkins, Mattie's mother had stayed up late into the night painstakingly preparing their Sunday finest.

Seated at the kitchen table, Mattie watches quietly as her mother stands hunched over the ironing board, dabbing at the thin streams of sweat that escape from beneath her headscarf with the collar of her housedress. Earlier in the day, Mattie had sat in the exact same spot and watched while her mother had prepared the clothes for ironing by lightly showering each item of clothing with water from an old vinegar bottle that she had made into a sprinkler bottle by punching holes into the little metal cap. Each garment was then rolled into a tight, little ball and set aside to allow the moisture to soften the fibers, which had been stiffened by the wind and sun. It is these garments that her mother now shakes out, one by one, and applies the hot iron to steam out wrinkles, smooth down collars, and press in pleats, while her father sits nearby, hunched low on a stool, giving his shoes a serious spit shine.

~~~

The next morning as her mother attempts to rouse her from her sleep, Mattie rolls over but makes no effort to get up. With sad eyes and a pained whisper, she complains of severe stomach cramps and aching legs, and pleads with her mother to let her remain home in bed. Her mother nods knowingly and caresses Mattie's cheek with cool, strong fingers before hurrying off to prepare breakfast. As Mattie lie quietly listening and waiting with bated breath for her parents to depart, she mentally prepares for the day ahead.

Finally rising from the well-worn couch that doubles as her bed, Mattie pulls back the room divider - a sheet threaded across a length of clothesline and tacked to opposite ends of the room. She quickly folds her sheet and blanket and places them, along with her pillow, in the trunk alongside the wall that houses all of her personal belongings, before heading for the bathroom. Stepping out of her nightgown, she plugs the hole in the sink with a rubber stopper and turns on the water. As she waits for the sink to fill with water, she casually observes her naked body in the cracked mirror over the basin. The cracks in the mirror cut an ugly, jagged line down between her breasts, before veering off across her right hipbone. This distorted view of her body, the only view of her body she has ever seen, has left Mattie with a distorted view of herself. As she searches for a pair of hole-free cotton panties, Mattie recalls the day when she had discovered blood in her panties. She thought something was seriously wrong with her until her mother gruffly stated, "Girl, you ain't hurt; you's just menstrating!" Afterwards, her mother unceremoniously presented Mattie with a large box of brick shaped sanitary pads, along with an elastic belt with clasps in the front and back, and informed her that she would get a new box of pads each month, and when the box was empty, there was a bushel basket of rags in the closet that she was to use. There had never been any further discussions about what was happening to her body, how long it was going to last, or what any of it meant.

Returning to the living room, Mattie carefully lifts her favorite dress from the trunk. She is always careful to keep the dress on top of her pile of belongings to prevent it from getting crushed. Despite her care, today the dress looks like it could stand a little pressing. Mattie goes and reheats the iron on the stove and, standing in the exact same spot where her mother had stood the night before, gingerly applies the hot iron to the thin fabric of the dress, being especially careful not the scorch the pink, satiny ribbons that tie at each shoulder. The dress, along with all of Mattie's clothing, had been purchased at the Salvation Army in the next town over. This particular dress was the prettiest that Mattie had ever owned, and she felt extremely lucky that her mother had plucked it from one of the many boxes of used and discarded clothing before someone else had discovered it. Mattie carefully steps into the dress and ties the ribbons into two perfect bows, and then carefully brushes her hair so that it cascades softly down her back. Satisfied with her fragmented image smiling back at her from the cracked mirror, Mattie goes outside and sits on the porch swing, looking ever so demure with her legs crossed at the ankles and her hands folded daintily upon her lap, to await her beau's arrival.

From the first time Mattie had laid eyes on Jimmy's honey-colored face, she instantly knew that he was the boy that she would marry and have babies with. He was tall and handsome with nice, strong teeth. And his skin was light enough to dilute the darkness of her own. Today, on the eve of her 16th birthday, she plans to make him all hers, and she watches with smiling eyes as his lopes across the field, all limbs and lean muscle. Although he is more than an hour late, she chooses not to make a fuss about it today, but makes a mental note that punctuality is something she will have to work on with him later. He greets her with a smile and an exaggerated bow, and then at her instruction, picks up the picnic basket at the foot of the steps, and follows her up the hill to her sacred spot - a weeping willow tree whose branches sweep low to the ground, exchanging stories between the heavens and the earth. They nestle beneath the tree on a blanket she had laid out for them, and silently arranges the food before him - an offering to her king. He picks up a chicken leg and hungrily sinks his teeth into it. He eats with the veracity of a starving man, never pausing to say grace, or to wait for her to commence eating. When it soon becomes apparent that there is not enough food for two, she tells him that she has already eaten, and for him to help himself to the plate of fried chicken, spaghetti, and potato salad that her mother had prepared for the visiting congregation, and left behind a heaping plate of food for Mattie's lunch. Even though her stomach emits an occasional low growl, Mattie is old enough to know that love sometimes requires sacrifice.

After the meal, Jimmy becomes animated and playful, lightly tickling her ribs and tugging at her earlobes, all the while flashing his big, pretty smile. Mattie sits with her limbs crossed and a slight scowl on her face. She hates being tickled. Not to mention the fact that Jimmy has yet to compliment her on her hair, her dress, or to even to thank her for the meal. Mattie suddenly finds herself becoming increasingly annoyed that her pretty boy lacks such basic manners. Just as she is about to gather everything up in the blanket and tug it back down the hill, the tickling and ear tugs turn into kisses as soft as whispers that cover her neck and shoulders, making her feel warm and tingly in her private region, reminding her of a sensation she had experienced once before while waiting to use the solitary bathroom, as she sat with her thighs pressed tightly together. His breath is hot in her ear as he finally tells her again and again how pretty she looks. She feels her agitation and annoyance melting away, and offers no resistance as he gently pushes her back onto the blanket, flashes her a bright, reassuring smile while managing to lower the bodice of her dress without untying either of the bows at her shoulders. And there in the alcove beneath the curtain of leaves, as the penetrating rays of the sun create a kaleidoscope of light and shadows, she holds her breath as he runs his moist tongue in the crevice between her breasts before coming to rest on the first chocolate peak. She feels as if tiny light bulbs are exploding inside her head, and that if he does not soon stop, she will ascend up through the curtain of leaves and disappear among the clouds. When Jimmy attempts to tug the bodice of her dress down further, Mattie assists by untying the bows at her shoulders and allowing Jimmy to apply hot, wet kisses to her stomach, along the sides of her ribcage, and her navel. He then lifts his hard, damp body gently onto her moist, outstretched one, and kisses her for the first time squarely on her mouth. The soft, feathery kisses quickly give way to probing, urgent kisses, and she offers no resistance when she feels his hand slide up her dress and caress her thigh with long, sure strokes.

The little that Mattie knows about sex had been gleaned from snippets of conversations overheard during market day. In her limited understanding, sex occurred when a man lay on top of a woman and they rub their bodies together. She is giddy with the thought of having now left the innocent world of childhood and finally becoming a woman – Jimmy's woman. She can hardly wait until next weekend when she can share this significant event with the other women. Will she look differently? Act differently? Will her face have 'the glow' that she's heard women talk about? So caught up in the details of how she will share her story of becoming a woman, that she barely notices when Jimmy starts poking her down there with his private thing. Panicked, Mattie pushes at Jimmy's chest, "What are you doing!"

He looks down at her with his big, gorgeous eyes and pleads, "Let me put it in you."

"No! Are you crazy?"

"Please, baby."

"No!"

"You'll like it, I promise," he says, as he covers her mouth and eyes with kisses.

"No, Jimmy. My folks will kill me."

He collapses on top of her and his whispered pleas turn into a continuous tortured moaning of her name. Mattie's panic slowly subsides and gives way to an unfamiliar sense of power as she becomes intrigued by the transformation that has come over this strong boy of hers. She is both curious and a little frightened about what could happen next, but she bites her lip and murmurs, "Oh, Jimmy!" and willingly surrenders. As Jimmy climbs back on top of her, he smothers her face with moist kisses while whispering, "Oh, thank you, baby! Thank you! Thank you, my sweet Mattie."

Mattie has never had anyone behave so appreciatively toward her, and she is starting to feel pretty happy about this magical hold she has over him, until she feels the rupture of her innocence. She cries out at the sudden, unexpected pain, and hears her mother's voice giving her the only, but oft-repeated warning about her privates, "That's yo' pocketbook, all you need to know about it is to keep it shut!" As she lay sprawled beneath her favorite tree with her prized dress bunched up around her torso, she finds herself wondering about the women at market who had giggled as they spoke in tantalizing whispers about sex. *Is this what they were doing, and did they know about the pain? Surely, someone had to have known about the pain.*

CHAPTER 30

Tired and sore, Mattie slowly walks the short distance down the hill back to her home while trying to figure out what the white stuff is that has got the front of her dress sticking to her thighs. She strips out of her soiled clothes, rolls the dress into a tight ball and tucks it beneath the cushion of the sofa, before sinking down upon it and falling into a deep, satisfying slumber.

Later that evening the sound of people moving about rouses her from her sleep, and when she opens her eyes, she sees something white floating above her head. She shuts her eyes tightly, then opens them again, and can now make out her mother's slender brown arm and what appears to be a piece of cloth dangling from her crooked index finger.

"What is this!" her mother demands. Mattie blinks her eyes again and her underpants suddenly zoom into focus. *Oh my God! How could I be so stupid!* The last thing she remembered was kicking off her underpants as she pulled on her nightgown, something she did every night. Only today, of all days, she had forgotten to pick them up from the floor and place them in the dirty clothes bag. Weary from spending the week working to show the visiting congregation that God was alive in small, modestly adorned temples too, Mattie's mother wants nothing more than to rest her aching feet. Instead, she must give her child another lecture about the responsibilities of a young lady to properly care for her private undergarments, and not leave them lying around in plain sight.

As her mother stands waiting for an answer, the underpants swing back and forth like a pendulum over Mattie's head, who becomes alarmed when she sees that the crotch of her underpants is caked with blood. Suddenly, the young lady who had gone to bed feeling like a bona fide grown woman, suddenly dissolves into a scared little girl.

"Oh momma, I'm hurt!" she cries, hands still clamped between her legs.

"What's wrong, baby!" her momma asks, her heart suddenly pounding as her body absorbs the fear she sees etched in her child's face.

"He didn't mean to hurt me, momma. I swear he didn't mean to..."

"What are you talking about, chil'!?"

"He loves me, momma. I know he does. We were foolin' around and we did some things I know I shouldn't have done, and I got hurt down there. But he's gonna do the right thing and marry me once he finds out I'm pregnant. I'm sure of it, momma!"

When she hears the word, 'pregnant,' Mattie's mother lets out a pained wail and runs from the room, dropping the underpants from her grasp, where they land squarely on Mattie's face.

~~~

As soon as the sun completes its ascent into the early morning sky, Mattie's father, still in his Sunday clothes, beats a hasty down the dusty road to Jimmy's house. He returns a short while later, with the shine gone from his shoes, and a deep furrow etched in his brow. Never one much for words, today is no exception as he stands alone on the porch waiting for the young man to arrive, much like his daughter had waited the morning prior. A short time later, Jimmy returns to

Mattie's home, but this time with his parents in tow. Mattie quietly watches from the kitchen window as the trio climbs the creaky steps up to the front porch. Jimmy's mother gently raps at the window, and is ushered in by Mattie's mother, who leads her into the kitchen where they stand over the kitchen sink, heads together, speaking in hushed tones. Mattie sits alone at the kitchen table, perched on a wooden stool, back erect, eyes unblinking as she stares past the bent heads of the women and out the window to the men folk gathered on the porch. She silently watches as her beau nervously shifts his weight from one foot to the other, head bowed and hands jammed deep in the front pockets of his overalls. Today as he stands between the two older men on the sun-bleached porch in the early morning light, her strong, confident Jimmy of yesterday, looks more boy than man.

When she hears her father's booming voice ordering her out onto the porch, she slides down from the stool and heads to the door, pausing just long enough to carefully run her hands over her hair, while the two women fall in step, nervously bringing up the rear. Mattie fully understood her father's intentions, and has to will herself to walk slowly and portray a somber mood consistent with that of the adults gathered on the porch, and not to skip out giddily, as her heart would have her do. Mattie goes and stands next to her beloved and realizing that he is trembling ever so slightly, slides her arm through his in a gesture of love and reassurance. Her father wastes no time with pleasantries or formalities, but gets right down to the business at hand. "I'm gonna ask you again, son. This time in the presence of the women folk," her father booms in a tightly controlled voice, "Are you the father of the child that my little girl here is carrying?"

"Son?" Jimmy's father chimes in, stretching the single syllable into two. With both hands still jammed deep into his pockets, he turns and glances briefly at Mattie. And as she tries to decipher the puzzled expression in his eyes, Jimmy abruptly turns back to face her father and answers in a small, but clear voice, "No, sir. I am not."

Mattie could not recall who said what next, or how she had managed to get her arm out of his, put one foot in front of the other, and make it back inside the house. She could not have known it at the time, but that was also the last time she would ever cast her eyes upon her beloved's face. The following week, word quickly spread that Jimmy had left town to help out his mother's sick brother, leaving Mattie to steadily grow with child, and face her shame alone.

After Jimmy's departure, Mattie's parents quickly sought to come up with a solution to their dilemma, and began discretely combing the town in search of their savior - a decent man who would be willing to marry Mattie, in spite of her indiscretions. The man chosen was a quiet, hard workingman by the name of Charlie, who solemnly swore to take good care of their Mattie. Not much was known about Charlie except that he kept out of trouble, had never been married, owned some land and didn't drink. Her parents made it clear to Mattie's husband-to-be that his main obligations would be to care for Mattie and help raise her yet-to-be-born child. In return, he was getting a strong, hard working partner with limited book smarts, but whose hair was legendary about town. Charlie had no qualms with the terms of the marriage. And, in fact, accepted them quite willingly. Although handsome in a rugged kind of way, Charlie's self esteem was as withered as the leg he had been born with. And while his withered leg did not keep him from working his land and making a good living, it did prevent him from having the courage to find a mate to share his life with. For the past 10 years, Charlie had been hoping and praying for a miracle. So when Mattie's parents approached him and presented him with the proposition of marrying their daughter, Charlie felt that his prayers had been answered.

In the days leading up to the wedding, Charlie starting thinking about the kind of life he and Mattie could build together. In the small town where they lived, he knew that they would be the subject of constant speculation. He was personally used to folks whispering about him behind his back, when they mistakenly thought that he was out of ear-shot, but he did not want his new bride, nor his child, to have to live with that kind of quiet, suffocating pain. So with the blessings of Mattie's parents, Charlie made preparations to move his new family north, immediately following the wedding ceremony. He had worked his land practically by himself for over 15 years, and he was eager to try a new way of living. His horse and his chickens he gave to Mattie's parents, and then he sold his land and used the proceeds to purchase a house up north for his new bride.

The day that Jimmy stood on her porch and denied his child, left Mattie's heart broken and her spirit crushed. And although she heard the chatter of others planning her future, she offered no protest and no resistance. And exactly two weeks from that fated day, beneath the same weeping willow tree where she had lain with the man she had chosen to be her husband, Mattie spoke her vows to a man twice her age, *for better and for worse*, that united her in the bonds of Holy Matrimony to Charlie Kincaid, *from this day forward*, a man she neither loved nor desired.

Following the brief wedding ceremony, which was witnessed only by Mattie's parents and the local preacher, Mattie sat alone in the loaded car waiting to begin the long road trip north, while Charlie stood off to the side of the road deep in conversation with his new father-in-law, presumably receiving the last of his instructions, when Mattie's mother suddenly appears alongside the car and presents Mattie with her one and only wedding gift. She places the large white box very gingerly onto Mattie's lap, and thrusts a bunch of wilting daisies into her hand. She gives Mattie one final teary hug good-bye, while whispering into her ear, "God's always with you, chil', don't ever forget that!" Mattie stares stoically ahead, feeling hurt, angry, confused and betrayed, yet determined not to cry.

"Is there anything else I can get for you, baby? Anything...anything at all?" her mother begs.

Mattie stares blankly at her mother for a long minute, then replies, "Yes, momma. Can you go and fetch me some scissors?"

Her mother scurries across the dirt path and disappears into the crooked little house, and then quickly reappears and scurries back to the car carrying the scissors. She eagerly hands them to Mattie, excitedly anticipating the look of joy on Mattie's face when she cuts away the string and reveal the contents of the white box. But instead of cutting the string from the box, Mattie gathers up her soft loose curls in one angry fist, and in one swift, defiant motion, clamps down hard with the sewing scissors.

"Here, momma," she says, with a triumphant glint in her eye, handing her mother both the scissors and the fistful of hair, "Now you have something to remember me by."

"Oh, sweet Jesus, have mercy!" her mother cries out, dropping the scissors and the clump of hair to the ground and running back toward the house sobbing loudly. Mattie's father abruptly ends his talk with a final, quick handshake and dutifully heads towards the house to see about his wife, shaking his head and muttering something about a *damn fool*.

Mattie gathers up what's left of her hair and tries to twist it into a plait, but the thick, bluntly cut hair refuses to stay braided. So, she takes the rubber band from around the bunch of daises, tosses the flowers out the car window into the dirt, and twists the rubber band onto the end of her braid.

Mattie was now a married woman. And although she had been powerless to stop the arranged marriage, she did possess the power to deny Charlie the one thing that she believed had made him agree to marry her in the first place, her hair, which now lay in the dirt road, covered by the wilted flowers, looking like road kill.

CHAPTER 31

For two days they travel in almost complete silence except for the occasional exchange of crucial information.

"You need to pee?"

"Yes."

"Okay."

Mattie sits in the passenger's seat gripping the white box as if her life depended on it. Never once did she look inside, but now the formerly pristine box is showing signs of her anxiety which she has tried to keep hidden – tattered corners and puckered areas where her sweaty palms has sat immobile for hours on end. Just as she is unconsciously peeling another small sliver of paper from the outer layer of the box, Charlie brings the car to a stop in front of a large, two-story, single-family house.

"This is it!" he says, his voice a mixture of excitement and fatigue, "We're home!"

"It's awfully big," Mattie says, speaking softly, almost to herself, "I wonder if any of the other families have chil'ren. It would be nice if some of the other families living here had chil'ren."

"Other families?" Charlie asks, confused as to what other families Mattie was referring to.

"Yes, the other families that live in all them rooms," she says, glancing nervously up at the windows, before bowing her head and turning her body slightly away from the large picture window, certain that unseen eyes were watching them. Charlie takes Mattie's small hands in his large ones and looks down into her anxious face. "This here's *our* home, Mattie. It's just the two of us now, but my prayer is that one day it will be overrun by children laughing and playing and running all through this big ol' house!" he says, his voice beaming and his face suddenly alive with hope.

"Come on," he says, "Let's go on inside!"

He escorts her up the front stairs and opens the large carved door with a flourish. Mattie peeks her head inside, eyes wide in disbelief. She is still unable to believe that all of this is theirs.

"I've never known anybody to live in a house this huge, not even the rich folks back home have houses this big!" she says, her voice filled with wonderment. She steps one foot inside the door, intent on running and counting every single room, when suddenly she feels a hard tug at her sleeve.

"Whoa! Slow down, not so fast!" Charlie says with a chuckle.

"What?" Mattie asks, "I thought you said this was our house."

"It is! It is! But I would be much obliged if you would grant me the honor of carrying my new bride across the threshold."

"You want to carry me?"

"Just across the entrance. It's an old custom. Don't tell me you've never heard of it."

"No! I ain't never heard of no such foolishness!" she says, looking at him suspiciously, trying to figure out the ulterior motive behind his badly told lie. Charlie fails in his gallant attempt to hide his disappointment, but his new bride's feelings are more important to him than trying to uphold some silly old tradition seeped in meaning that, truth be told, he didn't even understand, so he simple steps aside to allow Mattie to enter. The newly wed couple stand looking at each other awkwardly before Mattie finally speaks, "Well if you gone carry me inside, hurry on up before folks start staring," she says, glancing around nervously. Charlie grins and gently hoists his wife, along with her tattered box, up into his arms, and humming a little tune, takes one giant step across the threshold. "Welcome home, Mrs. Kincaid," he says, giving her a small peck on the cheek before gently lowering her back to the ground.

Mattie finally places the white box down on the large table in the dining room. When Charlie returns outside to start unloading the car, slowly and hesitantly now, she begins to explore her new home. The house is sparsely decorated with strong, sturdy pieces of furniture that although used, are still in excellent condition. It is immediately apparent to Mattie that Charlie had gone to great lengths to prepare the house for her arrival; the only thing it lacked was a woman's feminine touch. When Charlie returns from the car carrying an armload of boxes, Mattie asks to borrow his pocketknife. Slowly setting down his load, he reaches into the rear pocket of his trousers and takes out his knife. "You don't have to go cutting off any more of your hair on accounta me, Mattie. I know you think that's the reason I married you, but it ain't so. I honestly believe that we can build us a good life together. But if you think you got something more you need to prove, then here you go," he says, placing his knife in Mattie's outstretched hand.

Mattie takes the knife without uttering a word, and walks over to the table and cuts away the string from the white box. Nestled inside the box, buried in white tissue paper, is a delicate porcelain tea set, hand painted with colorful butterflies and tiny ladybugs. A small gasp escapes Mattie's lips at the luxuriousness of the gift, coupled with the realization that her parents had to have used all of their savings they kept stored in the cigar box, and possibly even sold a chicken or two, to be able to buy the gift for her. The delicate tea set loudly conveyed the message that her parents, people of few words, had been unable to say. And for the first time since leaving her parents' home, Mattie gains a sense of how difficult it must have been for them, her mother especially, to send her away in the way that they had. Never before had she given much thought to the daily negotiations of what, on the surface, appeared to be a very simple life. All she knew was that for every meal, there was food on the table. She always had clean clothes and shoes for her feet, even though at times she had to resort to walking on the backs of her canvas sneakers because her feet had outgrown them a few weeks shy of the scheduled time to purchase her autumn/winter shoes. Mattie was just now comprehending that a new life meant another mouth for her parents to feed and another body for them to clothe. The delicate, perfect little tea set was in shark contrast to the modest life they lived, and Mattie finally understood that the gift was a reflection of her parents' hope for her future - a future that they could not afford to give to her and her unborn child.

The totality of the stress from the last few weeks suddenly come crashing down on Mattie and she allows her tears to freely flow, purging from her body the expressions of love she had stubbornly withheld from her parents, even with knowledge of the uncertainty of whether or not she would ever see them again; purges the shame at attempting to ensnarl a man (a boy, really) with the weighty net of an unborn child; purges her sorrow at the plan that had gone horribly wrong, resulting in her fate now resting in the hands of a complete stranger. She blindly gropes through the house looking for a dark, quiet place where she can curl up and hide from the world, if only for a moment, when she stumbles across a furnished bedroom. She crawls into the bed fully clothed, and clutching the covers to her breasts, falls into a deep sleep where she dreams that she is safe beneath her willow tree, listening in as the sky trade stories with the earth.

CHAPTER 32

Even though her body was still weary from the long road trip, and the bed, the first real one she had ever slept in, was deliciously comfortable, she was not keen on the idea of having to share it with the stranger asleep beside her. So, at the first hint of daylight, Mattie slips out of bed, quietly dresses, and heads downstairs to prepare breakfast. Even at her young age Mattie was already a very good cook. As she slides a pan of biscuits into the oven and goes about setting the table with the lovely new tea set at its center, she observes herself experiencing something almost akin to happiness. But in those still, unoccupied moments, as she stands waiting for the pan of biscuits to brown, she glances at the beautifully set table and feels an ache in her heart, accompanied by a small voice inside her head whispering, *"If only..."*

She removes the biscuits from the oven and dutifully summons Charlie down to breakfast. Seated at opposite ends of the large wooden table, Mattie pretends to be too busy eating to engage in conversation, or to even make direct eye contact with this man who was now her legal husband. But each time Charlie bends his head to take a bite of his food, or lowers his eyes to his plate, Mattie intently scans the etches and grooves of his face for clues to the questions that have plagued her from the moment he first showed up in her life - *Why did this man agree to marry me, and what does he expect in return from me?*

Her thoughts are suddenly cut short as she watches in horror Charlie clumsily gripping the small, delicate teacup with a hand the size of a baseball mitt. Mattie is barely able to breathe, much less continue eating. So when Charlie wipes his mouth and pushes back from the table, signaling that he is done, Mattie exhales an audible sigh of relief, but catches her breath again as Charlie rises from his chair, and in two long strides is at her side of the table looming above her like the skyscrapers she saw from the expressway. Her heart beats wilding in her chest as she waits in fear for what might come next. Charlie leans forward and plants a kiss on the top of her head, thanks her for the delicious meal and begins clearing the table. Mattie sits stunned. Never before had she seen a man doing women's work. Her own father would not be caught dead lifting a spoon unless he was bringing it to his mouth. But when Mattie sees those huge mitts for hands about to grab the fragile little teapot, she literally jumps to its rescue, gently shooing Charlie away with her napkin.

Alone in the kitchen, she gathers up the tiny cups, saucers and the little teapot and carefully washes the entire set before arranging all of the pieces on a large serving tray she had discovered while rummaging through a box of assorted dishes. With the aid of a step stool, she places the serving tray on an uppermost cabinet shelf out of harm's way. "Don't want to risk ruining my one good set," she tells herself, "Gotta save it for special occasions."

CHAPTER 33

The newly married couple soon settles into a pleasant and civil routine. With the marriage not yet consummated, Charlie and Mattie make up for the lack of intimacy by working diligently together to prepare their home for the eagerly anticipated arrival of the new baby. But the continuous march of time did not perceptibly morph the little embryo into a growing fetus, Mattie's still flat stomach and linear hips confirmed the unthinkable: Charlie's new bride was not ripe with child.

Like thick molasses, the impact of this new reality seeps slowly into Mattie's consciousness. There had been no reason for her to leave the safety of her parents' home. No reason for Jimmy to run off from his home. As she thinks about all of the unnecessary plans that had been made and executed, all of the known and yet unknown ramifications of her simple little plan gone awry, the weight of it all becomes more than she can bear, and she disengages from her daily routine and starts spending her days at a nearby park, sitting beneath a maple tree with her hands folded on her lap, staring off into the distance, leaving Charlie to plan their future alone. His unspoken desire is for Mattie to remain in the city with him, and for them to give their marriage a real fighting chance. But now that Mattie no longer had any use for what he had essentially been contracted to provide, and because he knew that under normal circumstances, Mattie would have never agreed to marry him, he feels that the only decent thing to do is to take her back home and deposit her safely into the hands of her parents.

Toward the end of the second week of spending her days at the park, Mattie realizes that a decision needed to be made. She could either go back home to her folks, or she could stay with Charlie. She had no idea how her parents would receive her – returning home with no husband *and* no baby - but she sensed that her return would not be a cause for celebration. And as she tries to imagine where she would fit in among her still virginal girlfriends and the married women with children, the more it becomes clear that there was no longer a place for her there. Yet despite all of her confusion, she knew that Charlie was a good man. He was kind-hearted, honest and generous. And although he did not possess the golden smile and caramel hue of her Jimmy - he had a full set of dentures and his perpetually ashy hands were only a slight shade lighter than her own - in the short while they had been together, dear sweet Charlie had taken her tattered heart into those big ol' ashy hands of his, and stitched it back whole.

When Charlie returns home from work and once again finds dinner waiting on the table, he eyes it hungrily but warily, for fear that what he sees before him might be his proverbial Last Supper. After dinner, Charlie begins speaking in halting, broken sentences, talking of a return trip…annulment…new beginnings. When Mattie fully realizes what Charlie is trying to say, she takes his hands in hers and tenderly replies, "No, Charlie, here with you is where I belong." She speaks lovingly of having babies, promising him *his* babies, and vows that if he would still have her, she was ready and willing to fully be his wife. That day Mattie experienced another first – she got to witness a grown man cry.

Five years later, the stately house on Ravenswood still bore none of the telltale signs of children: the pitter patter of little feet, laughter echoing throughout the house, toys strewn about, and the walls and windows smudged with tiny hand prints. With gentle prodding from Charlie, Mattie finally agreed to a trip to a specialist. There she learned the life altering news that just like Charlie's leg, her womb was withered and shrunken, and would never be able to sustain life. Mattie was devastated, yet in some ways felt that this was just punishment for what had been her ugly, manipulating ways; but there was no reconciling the pain and guilt she felt for Charlie's suffering, whose only sin had been to love her. Still, they remained totally devoted and committed to one another, and about the only indicator that something was amiss was the odd ritual that Mattie developed shortly following her visit with the doctor. Early on Sunday mornings, Mattie would creep down the stairs to the kitchen and run a sink full of warm, soapy water. Climbing to carefully lift the tray down from the kitchen cabinet, she would gently submerge each piece of her delicate tea set in the warm, sudsy water and then wash each piece with tender loving care. She performed this act religiously every week, despite the fact that the tea set had been used only once.

~~~

When Charlie is called home to be with his heavenly Father, with no living relatives remaining, Mattie bravely musters on one day at a time. She occupies large portions of her days by working in her garden, painstakingly coaxing from the ground green beans, yams, collard greens, turnips and rutabagas. She keeps herself busy in the autumn months by canning all of the vegetables that she had grown during the spring and summer, which she then uses as sustenance during the long, cold winter months. Occasionally, Mattie will stop by a neighbor's home with a plate of gingerbread for them to munch on, as they sit sipping tea and bringing each other up to date on the happenings in the neighborhood. And for an occasional rare treat, Mattie will take the bus downtown to catch a matinee or eat lunch at one of the nicer department stores.

But as the years tick by and her few close friends drift away, move away, or pass away, and with the neighborhood slowly deteriorating around her, Mattie ventures out less and less. Eventually, even her prized garden is abandoned, and her world shrinks to the size of the footprint of her house. After the passing of too many years alone in her big old house, the once manageable void in Mattie's life becomes a gaping, bottomless hole that she can no longer fill. Even her weekly ritual, that curious routine of washing her tea set, which had somehow kept her tethered to an invisible strength, comes to an end too. Now, with absolutely no order or structure to her life, she spends her days in a semi-conscious haze of stifled despair. But just when it seemed like all hope was lost, on a cold, frosty day in December, Spirit told her to rise.

CHAPTER 34

Fresh from the shower, Vamp stands naked in front of the full-length mirror and slowly rubs baby oil onto her moist body. She used to love the sight of her nude body glistening with oil; the sheen enhancing the peaks and valleys of her well-toned muscles. That was before her thighs and buttocks started their slow spread, turning her once athletic and evenly proportioned body into a pear shape - a too ripe pear, small on top and large and squishy on the bottom. What had once been a pleasing part of her daily routine - self assessment bordering on self arousal - was now simply a part of her daily grooming, done quickly and without the aid of a mirror. But today as she rubs the oil on her skin, she sees her body through the lens of her mommy eyes, and instead of being repulsed by the thick thighs and the high shelf-like butt, she is amazed by the transformation that is taking place. For the very first time, she notices the deep blue veins snaking beneath the surface of her chest, and that her areolas have almost doubled in size. Gently touching a nipple, she winces at its extreme tenderness, another reminder that her breasts are changing from being a source of pleasure into a source of nourishment.

"Little brown jugs, how rich!" she says with a derisive snort, yet at the same time cannot deny feeling a sense of awe at the genius of the design: Food receptacles that automatically replenish upon demand. No batteries or attachments needed, just a few good bras to hoist those puppies up!

Her hands move down to cradle her belly. Last night she felt the baby move for the first time. And now, what appears to be an elbow is protruding freakishly from her otherwise smooth belly. One poke and the elbow disappears. She strokes her stomach in slow, concentric circles, speaking in a halting whisper to her unborn child, "Hi little one. It's me, mommy. I'm sorry I haven't done better by you…by us. But starting now, I swear I'm going to be better. And…" she continues tentatively, her voice breaking with emotion, "Miz Mattie says that everything's going to be alright, and for some reason I believe her. I have to believe her."

~~~

Vamp gets dressed and heads for the kitchen with a newfound sense of purpose, and feeling the happiest she has felt since moving to Ravenswood. Determined to keep the promise she just made to her unborn child, she plans to start by eating breakfast, a meal that she previously only ate on the Sundays when Cat cooked. Scanning the contents of her fridge, she finds a wilted head of lettuce, a bottle of lite Italian dressing, and a box of Chinese take-out that she is afraid to even open. As she stands at the kitchen counter thinking about what to do now in the absence of any edible food, the smell of freshly brewed coffee beckons her. As she opens the kitchen cabinet, she considers for the first time the possible effects of caffeine on her unborn child. "I probably shouldn't be drinking this," she says, "I'll pick up some decaf when I go grocery shopping later today, but right now I need a cup of Joe." She removes her favorite cup from the shelf, but instead of heading back over to the coffee maker, she stands staring up into the open cabinet, frozen in her spot by a familiar craving. A craving that on most any other day she would have readily given in to. But with her promise to her child still fresh on her lips, she fights hard to resist the temptation. Standing staring up into the cabinet, tiny beads of sweat appear on the tip of her freckled nose. Suddenly, the bottle of whiskey is sitting on the countertop before her. She doesn't even recall taking it down, it's almost as if she willed it down; but regardless, there it sits. She unscrews the top and inhales deeply. "That smell...that lovely fuckin' smell," she murmurs as the musk of the whiskey tingles the hairs in her nostrils, causing her to salivate. She sets the open bottle down hard on the countertop and grabs the coffee pot and fills her cup to the rim. Suddenly having a cup of coffee doesn't seem like such a bad thing. As she leans against the kitchen countertop sipping her coffee, while absentmindedly stroking the neck of the whiskey bottle, she has the stark realization that she does not just want a drink of whiskey; she *needs* a drink. And the force that is driving this need is larger than her willpower, and more urgent than any promises made. In an attempt to assuage her urges, she plunges her thumb into the neck of the open bottle, swirling the bottle around until she feels the cool liquid lap against her skin. She sticks her liquor-drenched thumb into her mouth and hungrily sucks on it.

Her eyes well up and the tears start to fall as she feels the last of her willpower slowly ebbing away. She grabs the bottle and licks her lips. Her need for a drink is matched only by her feelings of self-loathing and shame. As the rim of the bottle brushes against her bottom lip, in the nanosecond that it takes before the first drop spills forth into her open mouth, she utters a quiet, desperate plea, *"Please, Father, help me."* Inexplicably, the bottle slips from her hand and falls into the sink below, shattering on impact. Vamp runs from the kitchen and gets into her car and drives until she spies a national brand coffee house, signifying that she has reached the Land of Gentrification. She goes inside and orders an expensive cup of coffee and a blueberry scone. As she sits alone staring out the window, she is shaken by the close call, but grateful that she had managed to keep her promise to her unborn child.

CHAPTER 35

As Vamp drives back into the inner city, her thoughts are on her parents and her promise to them to come by for dinner. She was not really looking forward to going over to her parents' house tonight, but she feared that if she postponed breaking the news of her pregnancy much longer, they might hear it from another source, namely Cat, who she still has not heard from since that fateful night when her worst fear had been confirmed. Since moving away from her childhood home, trips back had always been as an afterthought - a quick stop in on the way to someplace else. And even then, she did her best to limit the visits to no more than 20 minutes. Any longer than that and she swore she could feel her brain start to atrophy. After Vamp graduated from college, landed a job and moved in with Cat, Vamp began fabricating stories about her parents to her new friends. She told everyone that her recently retired dad had worked for the city in the newly formed sustainability department, while her mother worked in the education sector in student enrichment. In truth, her father was a retired garbage man, and her mother was the cafeteria lady at the local junior high school. Vamp lived in constant fear that the truth about her parents would be found out by her friends, especially her white friends, who would not understand that long before rappers were sporting gold and platinum grills, folks in her parents' generation sported gold capped teeth. And even though that trend had long since played out, Vamp's father insisted on keeping his gold-capped front tooth intact, arguing that what the young dudes thought was hip and new, was just them catching up to him. For years she had tried every possible tactic to persuade him to have it removed, stopping short of telling him that he looked like a damn fool. She finally gave up and decided that it would be far simpler just to keep her new friends away. Vamp viewed her mother as being still moderately attractive, but her soft, loose flesh could greatly benefit from regular trips to the gym, to distance her from the tragic statistic that one out of every three Black women was overweight or obese. Maybe once her mother rediscovered her womanly curves, she would finally get rid of those damn housecoats she insisted on wearing around the house, and start dressing in real clothes on days other than Sundays.

The long and short of it was that going back home made Vamp uncomfortable. She hated her feelings of annoyance toward her parents for being such simple people, and she blamed her mother, who seemed to rule the roost. She had once tried to add some sophistication to their lives by splurging and buying an expensive reproduction of a Monet painting. Even though she had been making good money at the time, the money was not so good that she could afford to buy an original, or even a limited lithograph, for that matter; still, the price she paid for the giclée reproduction had been nothing to sneeze at. But to her dismay, her mother had hung the painting in their bedroom instead of replacing the faded picture of Dr. King and the Kennedy brothers in the living room, as Vamp had recommended.

"Why does mother insist on keeping that outdated picture up on the wall?" Vamp says aloud, as she pulls up to the curb in front of the house on Ravenswood, "Doesn't she know that we've already overcome?" Trudging up the stairs, thinking that it would probably be a good idea to try and fit a nap in before heading to her parents' home, she sees something propped against her door. Once at the top of the stairs, she can clearly see that "the thing" is a book. She stoops to pick up the thick, dog-eared book on pregnancy and childcare, and quickly reads the sticky note with the tiny handwriting stuck to the front:

Not good at saying sorry.

 - Jamela

~~~

The nap did Vamp good. She woke up hungry and looking forward to a home cooked meal. Now there was just the matter of what to wear. Her once meticulously sorted wardrobe now lay scattered about the bedroom floor. As she sits among the heap of clothes thumbing through the book left at her door, she comes across an illustration of what a baby looks like at the start of the fifth month of pregnancy, and is astonished to discover that the fetus, as it is now called, already has well defined fingers and toes, as well as eyebrows and eyelashes. Another thing that becomes blaringly clear, as she continues to skim through the pages, is that prenatal care should begin at the onset of pregnancy. Further, under the most ideal of situations, which hers admittedly was not, a consultation with one's physician as a prelude to conception was highly recommended. But the loss of her job meant the loss of her medical insurance, and because she could not afford to pay the high premium on the COBRA insurance her former employer was legally obligated to offer her, she had not seen a doctor since that morning at the clinic. She had always suspected that there was more that she should be doing, but reality becomes harder to ignore when presented so graphically in black and white.

Finally settling on the one pair of pants she can still fit into - the black stretch pants with the elastic waistband, she pairs it with a roomy, men's white oxford shirt. Since weekly trips to her hair stylist had been one of the first luxuries to go, she carefully brushes her hair into a sleek French twist, rolls up the cuffs of the shirt, and slips her bare feet into a pair of Kenneth Cole oxfords, hoping that she has successfully managed to pull off a look of retro-beatnik cool, instead of simply looking like someone trying to camouflage a pregnancy.

CHAPTER 36

As she pulls up in front of her parents' house, a wave of nausea hits. "Oh God!" Her mind quickly scans the possible options to her pressing dilemma, and immediately rejects her body's initial impulse to throw open the car door, lean out and spew right there at her parents' curbside. Another, more dignified, option is to try and make a run for it and pray that daddy is not in the bathroom reading the Sunday paper, or that Marc's sorry ass is not in there with a smudged, outdated copy of *Maxim* magazine. She quickly concludes that the latter option has too many variables, making for too big of a gamble, so she guns her engine and takes off speeding down the street. She only manages to get as far away as three blocks away when she slams on the breaks, throws open the car door and heaves so forcibly that she almost topples out onto her head. She attempts to brace herself against the doorframe of the car, but her hand misses its mark, and lands in the gutter. Thoroughly disgusted, she shakes loose the sticky Popsicle wrapper from her palm before pushing herself back up into her plush leather seat. She spits one final time into the street, before quickly glances around to see how many people bore witness to her humiliation. A few brown faces stare back at her, their faces a mixture of curiosity and repulsion. She takes some tissue out of her glove box, wipes her hands and the sweat from her forehead, before tossing the tissue out the car window and speeding off.

Despite the fact that she looks pretty exactly the same as she did when she first left home, she feels tired and soiled. And her mouth feels, and no doubt smells, foul. After rummaging unsuccessfully through her purse for a stick of gum or a breath mint, she takes off in search of a convenience store. The dark-skinned bearded merchant does not acknowledge her as she enters the empty store. No words are exchanged as she points to what she wants and slides a crisp ten dollar bill through the slot of the plexi-glass barrier. The merchant slips her purchase inside a brown paper bag, sets it on the lazy Susan built into the glass wall, and then gives it a quick spin. She grabs the bag and hurries from the store, in her haste forgetting the four dollars and loose change that the merchant has placed in the slot. He does not call out to her as she departs, but takes the money from the slot and puts it in his pocket.

Safely back in her car, she unscrews the top off the pint-sized bottle of peppermint schnapps and quickly drinks half of it. As she is bringing the bottle down from her lips, her eyes meet the reddened gaze of a wino staring at her from a few yards away. But the unspoken rules of the streets dictate that the mere fact that she owns a car, or at least has access to one, automatically places her out of his league, rendering her unapproachable. The car is also an indicator to him that although they may both guzzle their booze from a bottle, she is still, for the moment at least, a part of main stream society, and has not yet sunk to that lowly social strata occupied by those who have lost everything, and now simply live for the next drink. The sight of the dirty, pitiful looking man huddled against the corner of the building shivering in 60 degree weather disgusts Vamp, and she dabs daintily at the corners of her mouth before screwing the top back on the bottle and slipping it into her purse. As she carefully reapplies the pale pink lip color to her mouth, a soft sigh of relief escapes her parted lips as she reassures herself that her purchase had been medicinal because of the soothing effect that peppermint is known to have on upset stomachs.

~~~

Even though she has a key to her parents' home, she rings the doorbell and waits impatiently for someone to answer. She had gotten a key to the house on her 18th birthday. It was her mother's official badge of approval, signifying that she had finally become a responsible adult, even though her baby brother had gotten his key at 16, something she still has not gotten over. Her father finally answers the door and flashes her one of his golden smiles, while holding the door open for her to enter.

"Hi daddy!" she sings, stretching her arms wide to give him a hug. As they embrace, their stomachs brush ever so slightly. She looks deeply into his eyes and is relieved to find no indication that he noticed that she now has a belly to rival his own beer gut. She loved her father something fierce, but since he's been retired, he always appears pensive and out of step with his life whenever she stops by to visit.

"Hi, Baby. Good to see you. You just don't come and visit your old man enough since you upped and got grown. What 'cha been up to lately?"

"Oh, the usual." she replies as she follows him back inside the living room where he resumes his position on the couch in front of the television set.

"Here, have a seat," he says, patting the sofa cushion next to him while reaching for a handful of salted peanuts. His eyes smile up at her, then dart back to the television set as the crowd roars. "Go on and catch the game, daddy. I'm going to go and say hi to mom."

"Mother's in the kitchen," he says, eyes still glued to the TV set.

"Who's winning?" Vamp asks, stepping over his outstretched legs and sitting her purse down at the far end of the cocktail table.

"The Pistons are putting a whippin' on those Bulls!" he

answers grinning, obviously loving every minute of it. Her dad lived for sports. *Thank God there's televised sporting events all year round. A man needs something he can look forward to, especially a retired one.*

When Marc was born, her father thought he had a sports buddy for life. But despite Marc's impressive 6 foot, 3 inch frame, it soon became apparent that Marc cared more about baking cakes and perfecting pastry dough, than he did about practicing his jump shot with his boys. While her father was understandably disappointed, Vamp merely saw it as an opportunity to further endear herself to her daddy, and she literally became a walking sports encyclopedia, able to spout basketball and football statistics at the drop of a hat. And although her high school had an outstanding track team and a promising girls basketball team, she had never tried out for any of them. She never wanted to actually *engage* in any strenuous sports, she couldn't bear the thought of breaking a nail or skinning a knee or, God forbid, being forced to play outdoors in the hot, brutal sun. But many an evening she had sat on that very sofa next to her daddy and helped him cheer on his favorite team. It was actually one of the few things she missed about being at home.

She makes her way to the kitchen under the watchful eyes of Martin, John and Bobby. That picture held so sacred a spot in her parents' house that she felt that each time she passed by she should make the sign of the cross or, at the very least, curtsy. She pushes her way through the swinging doors and sees her mother standing at the stove stirring a big pot of collard greens, her face flushed pink from the steam. As much as Vamp loved soul food, she hated the way her mother prepared collard greens, always insisting on adding the coarse stems and cooking them with hunks of fatty salt pork. On too many occasions she had warned her mother about the hidden dangers of saturated fat, as in heart disease and the possibility of a stroke; as well as the not so hidden dangers, as in a double chin and a big, lumpy ass. Vamp self-consciously tugs on the rear of her shirt, making sure that it is smoothed over her own big butt, and not stuck in some crevice above it.

"Hi mother!" she yells out over the gospel music blaring from the radio on the kitchen countertop. Her mother's philosophy was, if she was not in the Lord's house on Sunday, then He at least had to be in hers. Heading over for a quick hug and air kisses, Vamp stops short when she spies pork chops frying in a pan of hot spattering oil.

"Hi, Nessa," her mothers yells back, waving.

"Dinner will be ready in about 20 minutes."

Vamp nods, grabs a soda from the fridge and steps back through the swinging door into the empty dining room, grateful for a moment of solitude to compose herself and gather her thoughts before sitting down to dinner. She is unaware of how long she had been standing there watching the pulp floating in the sweating pitcher of lemonade, when she looks up and sees her mother watching her.

"Looks like you put on a few pounds," her mother comments casually, but what Vamp interprets as criticism.

"Come here and give me a big hug, or have you gotten too grown to hug your momma?"

Vamp winces at the thought of her mother actually touching the new softness of her body, and inhales deeply and sucks in her stomach before entering her mother's outstretched arms.

"How's my baby's doing?" her mother asks, squeezing Vamp tightly against her own plump body, moist with perspiration, while rocking Vamp's reluctant, rigid upper body from side to side. Vamp feels her mother's ample breasts crushing her own tender ones, smells the faint whiff of Estee Lauder, a perfume her mother has worn for as far back as Vamp can remember, and suddenly Vamp feels like a child, being cradled in her mother's arms.

Her mother had always been the one to soothe the hurt and wipe the tears away, calling her 'momma's little baby,' even when she was officially no longer the baby of the family. But once Marc started walking and talking, he became the star attraction, greedily stealing all of their mother's love and affection for himself, or so it had appeared to her little five year old mind. Even long after Marc had grown out of his adorable, cuddly toddler stage, turning first into a spoiled brat, then a royal-pain-in-the-ass teenager, Vamp still harbored memories of him being the apple of her mother's eye.

When Vanessa graduated from college and went on to graduate school, she watched from a distance, detached and unfazed, as the chasm between her and her mother continued to grow. But right now, she is mommy's little girl again, just like back in the time before Marc, when a tender stroke of her mother's hand across her brow could dissolve all of her worries and fears. And for the first time in many years, she gives herself permission to relax in her mother's embrace. Placing her head on her mother's shoulder, she surrenders to the moment and allows her body to be rocked in the gentle, easy sway of her mother's arms. She inhales deeply, and when she exhales this time, she lets go of her stomach and relaxes all of the muscles that had tensed up at her mother's initial touch. She feels the tears starting to well up in her eyes, but in her mother's arms she feels safe and secure enough to let them out…to let it all out. Her mother would hold her up and help her conquer her fears.

"Mother…" she begins hesitantly, speaking in a soft whisper, "Mommy, I'm…" The ringing of the phone slices into her sentence, and her mother's ears prick up like a dog's on point, "Hang on, baby, that might be Marc calling," her mother states as she places both hands squarely on Vamp's shoulders and in one deft motion, pushes her at arms length before hurrying off to answer the phone. The sudden motion sends the tears that had been welling up in Vamp's eyes flying from her face, and she watches in pained silence as one lands unnoticed on her mother's forearm. She brusquely wipes her face, and in less than the five minutes that it takes for her mother to complete her phone call and return to her side, Vamp's stoic facade is firmly back in place.

"Sorry, baby. That was Marc on the phone. He said to tell you hi!" she reports, literally beaming now.

"Oh, and I suppose that Marc dearest was calling to say that his meeting with his broker is running long, and for us to go ahead and start without him?" she asks sarcastically.

"What? Child, Marc ain't even in town, he's in Barbados!"

"*What* is Marc doing in Barbados!"

"Vacationing. I thought you knew. He told me he phoned you."

"Yeah. He called and left a message on my machine," she replies while thinking, *Which I immediately deleted as soon as I heard his voice.*

"Please tell me how is it that my dear, sweet, perpetually broke, chronically out-of-work brother gets to vacation in Barbados? Wherever did he get the money to pull that one off?"

"I gave him the money."

"How can you afford to send Marc on such a luxurious vacation? And why, when the farthest you've ever been is down south? Did you finally hit the lottery?"

"No, I didn't hit the lottery. I simply cashed in a CD."

"Mother! That money was intended to provide you with financial security *after* you retire. Does daddy know about this?"

"Of course your father knows about it; it was his idea. Listen, Nessa, you know how you're always traveling all over the place, and bringing us back those lovely souvenirs? Well, Marc's never been able to go to any of those nice places like that."

"That's because the boy won't keep a job!"

"I know, sugar, but daddy and I just wanted to do something special for him; show him how proud we are of him for landing his dream job."

"What job?"

"Your brother is going to be working at that fancy new four star restaurant downtown as a full time pastry chef! You know how he loves to bake. If he wasn't so good, I'd be ashamed to admit that most of his desserts are better than mine!"

"Well, I'll be damned!" Vamp whispers to herself.

"You know, Marc was never interested in attending college," her mother continues, "Told us not to waste our money. Lord knows at one point I thought that boy would be with us when he was old and gray, and daddy and I were too senile to care any longer. And all the while he's sitting upstairs getting educated by watching that food channel. Can you imagine that!

"So, I guess you could say that this trip is a graduation present, of sorts. Besides, it's a whole lot cheaper than four years of college." Even with thousands of miles and a sea separating them, Vamp feels that Marc has once again stolen the spotlight.

"So you're saying that you and daddy would have preferred sending me on a cruise instead of sending me to school?"

"Don't be silly, Nessa. A college education was what you wanted, and what apparently was right for you. You've done really good for yourself, and daddy and I are extremely proud of you."

"Right! A graduate degree in Art History really comes in handy in selling pharmaceuticals."

"Yes, well, Marc obviously was better suited for a less formal learning environment, something less structured and more hands-on. But the important thing is that you both got your feet firmly planted, so now daddy and I can rest easy and not worry. Not that we ever worried about you, dear. You've always been a go-getter, very ambitious. At a very young age, it was apparent that you valued nice, expensive things. I'm just happy that you're in a position to afford the type of life you've always dreamed of having, with the fancy car, expensive clothes and such."

"But you're right, daddy and I haven't done anything nice for ourselves lately. And as soon as I retire later this year, we're going to do us some traveling too. First stop - the Motherland!"

"Africa?!"

"Yes, Africa! Don't look so shocked, child. Where did you

think we'd be going, China?"

"First of all, I've never *ever* heard you express any interest in traveling, much less traveling to Africa. Why Africa? Why go to a continent full of emaciated people running around killing one another? Why not go someplace more dignified and refined like Paris...or Rome?"

"Nessa!" The tone and forcefulness with which her mother says her name startles and alarms her. She had only heard her mother say her name like that once before, and that was the time her mother left her and Marc alone in the car alone while she ran inside a grocery store for sodas, and Vamp had convinced Marc to stick his finger in the car's cigarette lighter to see if it was still hot after the orange glow that had lit their mother's cigarette had disappeared – it was.

"Do you hear how ignorant you sound? And to think, you're a college educated Black woman! Well, if you can go through six years of college and come out with backward thinking such as that, maybe we would have done better by you if we had saved some money and sent you away on a cruise too!"

"All I meant was..."

"I know exactly what you meant, and it pains me to hear you talk that way.

It makes me feel like I failed you somehow, by not teaching you how to be proud of your heritage."

"Aren't you the one always telling me that I've got so much confidence that I should bottle it and sell it?"

"Baby, it's one thing to be confident in the image that you present to the world, and quite another to be comfortable with the part of you that you can't dress up in designer clothes. That's one of the reasons I insisted on you and your brother going to church with me every Sunday. I wanted to surround you with positive, beautiful Black people. God knows I tried to do the right thing. I always made certain that you had a pretty little Black baby doll for Christmas each year, up until that one year when you begged your daddy to buy you one of those long-legged, blue-eyed Barbie dolls. God bless him, but that man never could say no to you. And after that first blue-eyed doll, you just didn't want nothing more to do with those little brown babies."

A sudden flashback of a little brown, plastic head being buried behind the house in the vegetable garden flits through Vamp's mind.

"I guess that could have been considered a red flag to a potential identity crisis, but if it was, God forgive me, because I missed it!"

"But seriously, Nessa, if you haven't by now experienced the unique joys and richness of being a Black woman, then my heart aches for you, baby."

"You feel sorry for me because I'm not piss poor, uneducated, and dealing with baby daddy drama?" *Damn, scratch that last one*, she thinks.

"Child, let me explain something to you - Being poor and uneducated is not synonymous with being Black. Besides, there ain't no sin in being poor, and there shouldn't be any shame in it either, but I'm talking about those things that make me proud to be a Black woman. I'm talking about the women who have managed to raise their children while taking care of somebody else's children; women who can take nothing and make something - how do you think we got soul food? When I was a girl, times were so hard my mother, your grandmother, made us ice cream out of freshly fallen snow. Do you hear me, gal! And it was good too! And that was without the aid of these newfangled machines!

Baby, I need you to take some time to observe Black women and really hear them and see them. The rhythm of Africa is in the way we walk, and the wisdom of Africa is in the way we talk. Observe the way our brown skin glistens like gold dust in the hot sun, the riches of Africa is in our pores. And the bold laughter that pours from our full lips past our big white teeth is the music of our souls. Because you see, Nessa, while most of us have never been to Africa...yet, Africa is inside of us. We are still her children."

"Mother, if I didn't know any better, I'd say you had the

heart of a poet."

"Oh, and you think you know better?" her mother asks, challenging her with a raised eyebrow.

"Baby, I'm just trying to tell you like it is. Something I'm obviously guilty of not doing enough of sooner.

"What I'm trying to say, Nessa, is that everybody's got a story to tell and something they can teach you, even your old ma. I always thought things would be better between us when you got older and became a woman yourself, but you never seemed to have the time or the interest in getting to know my story."

"So, what's you story, momma?"

Now it was her mother's turn to blush, suddenly unprepared for the moment she had over the years prayed would come.

"Well, beneath these here dusters, which I know you despise," she says, looking down and self consciously smoothing out the wrinkles of her flour covered housedress, "lies a spirit that's soft and tough, open yet reserved, wise but searching... always searching. "

"What are you searching for, ma?" Vamp asks softly.

"I don't know...God, I suppose," she says, and stands silently for a moment with a far away look in her eyes. "And the place where I most often find evidence of him is in the smiles of my sisters."

"Oh, Mom. That's beautiful!" Vamp says, her eyes moist with tears.

"Ma...that stuff I said about Africa...I didn't mean it like it sounded. It's just that wherever I go, I want to fit in so badly that I'm always altering some part of myself to give people what they want. And lately, I just feel like no one really knows me. I just want someone to know me, ma." Vamp confesses, gasping now for air between sobs.

Her mother steps forward and encircles Vamp in her arms. "Shush now, baby. I know that you couldn't have meant what you said. And even though you may not think so, I know you, Nessa. You revealed your true self to me early on - headstrong, intelligent, funny, and a big softy when you think no one is looking. And even though life's lessons can be kind or cruel, the core essence of a person rarely changes. So trust me when I say, I know you. You're still my Nessa. You're still my baby girl.

"Now hush, child," she says lifting Vamp's chin and gently wiping away her tears.

"You're gonna wear yourself out crying like that. Go on to the bathroom and splash some cold water on your face. And when you come out, we'll sit on down to dinner and enjoy this meal I cooked special just for you."

~~~

Vamp goes into the bathroom and places a damp washcloth across her forehead. She yearns to splash the cool water freely on her face as her mother had suggested, but that would mean ruining the mask she had spent 45 minutes perfecting. She stares at herself in the mirror - at her eyes, her mouth, her nose. She hated her nose. She had spent most of her 32 years trying to ignore the feature that sat squarely in the center of her face; had tried to train her eyes to light upon some other, more pleasing feature whenever she looked in a mirror.

She considered herself pretty lucky in the genetic crapshoot by inheriting her mother's light skin and softly curled hair, but she joked that Lady Luck had screwed her over by using the precise moment that her nose was being assigned, to go and take a piss. Her only consolation was in knowing that what the good Lord had not blessed her with, a good surgeon would. The plan was to cut away the part of her face that she despised, and replace it with a cute, perky, 'Becky' nose, effectively rendering her ethnicity an enigma. People would look at her and not know what she was. At worst, they would think that she was half-white and half-Black; at best, they might consider her Samoan or Polynesian. They certainly would not automatically assign her as a descendent of slaves, and would no longer associate her with 'them,' - the ones with deep, percolating anger who butchered the Queen's English, had ashy knees and nappy hair and rhythm for days.

Staring at her reflection in the mirror, it was painfully clear that the nose on her face was the nose of her father. It was the only thing about her physical appearance that people could look at and declare, "Yep, that's Leroy's child." After talking to her mother today and actually hearing her for a change, it occurred to Vamp that as a young woman, her mother, who possessed no outward characteristics of being of African descent, had been in the unique position to choose which ethnicity she wanted to claim. Black or White, neither would have been a lie.

Momma could have easily passed for white and led a very different life, yet is quick to tell everybody that she's a proud Black woman. She defied her own mother's plea to continue the deliberate whitening of their bloodline, and instead chose to marry the dark-skinned man with the prominent African nose – my nose. Wow, that's my momma! Vamp thinks as she lowers her tired, heavy body down onto the edge of the tub, feeling both shameful and proud.

She removes the white shirt that she has been carefully guarding all day, and goes and stands back in front of the mirror in a bra literally busting at the seams. Filling the basin with cold water, she looks at her reflection one final time, takes a deep breath, and plunges her face into the cold, icy water. The initial sensation is shockingly exhilarating, followed by a numbing calm. Grabbing a nearby bar of soap, she lathers her hands and washes away the layers of concealer, foundation, blush, eye make-up and smudged mascara. Dipping her face back into the frigid water, her mind flashes back to a day many years ago when she had been dipped in a pool of water and declared born again. When she lifts her head for the final time, her carefully applied beauty mask has been reduced to an oil slick that skims the surface of the murky water below. Patting her face dry, she slips back into her no longer crisp, white shirt, and as she smooth back the wet wisps of hair from her brow, the eyes that she meet in the mirror smile tenderly at her.

Entering the dining room, Vamp sees that her mother has loaded the table up with smothered pork chops, fried catfish, collard greens, candied yams and hot buttered cornbread! With the exception of the collard greens, these were some of her favorite dishes. Her parents are already seated and waiting for her to emerge from the bathroom. As she takes her seat in the same spot she sat as a young girl, and she places her napkin on her lap and rolls up the cuffs of her shirt in preparation to say grace. She glances briefly over at her mother and finds her staring at her with an odd expression on her face. She looks down at her white shirt, convinced that she had finally succeeded in soiling the damn thing, and is puzzled when she sees that it is still spotless. Glancing in her father's direction, she finds him also looking at her with a sad smile tugging at the corners of his mouth and a melancholy look in her eyes. Suddenly feeling exposed and self conscious, she brings her hands up to her head and smooth down her hair before risking another peek in her father's direction.

"Dad…what?" she implores.

"Oh, baby, I'm sorry. I didn't mean to stare. It's just that…"

"What?"

He looks across the table at his wife, who nods knowingly and gently places her hand on top of his.

"It's just…your face. I haven't seen your face like this, free from all that makeup you like to wear, in more years than I can count. And looking at you sitting there now, reminds me of when you were little; when you were my baby girl."

"Oh, daddy!" she gushes, as the lump reappears in her throat, "I'm still your baby girl. I'll always be your baby girl," she says, rising from her seat and planting an audible kiss on his balding head.

"Baby, could you do us the honor of blessing the food?" her mother asks, as Vamp again takes her seat.

"Okay…sure," Vamp agrees, visibly blushing. She is uneasy about publicly displaying her relationship with God, even in this brief, generally accepted way. But once she had agreed to do it, she suddenly has a desire to do more than just recite some prayer by rote. *There has already been too many wasted opportunities. I'm going to take this moment and say what's really in my heart; Charlotte ain't the only one who can get deep!*

"Dear Father, thank you for the wonderful food we are about to receive. Thank you, Father, for the loving hands that prepared the food. Thank you, Heavenly Father, for the love that is present in this room today. And thank you, dear Lord, for my family, and our family tree with its new little bud that will soon become a twig, and eventually grow into a strong, sturdy branch with little buds of its own. Amen." She slowly raises her bowed head and wipes her sweaty palms on her pants. She feels her heart thumping out a wild beat inside the walls of her chest as she eagerly waits for their response. Both her mother and father are again staring at her, but this time their deeply etched brows convey an obvious state of confusion.

"That was nice, baby," her mother begins, "but I didn't understand the part about the twigs and the branches - did you daddy?" she asks her husband. Vamp watches as her mother looks at her father, who is squinting up at the ceiling as if he's trying to solve an algebra problem that is written up there, while simultaneously trying to figure out what the hell the equation is doing on the ceiling in the first place!

One minute passes, then two... the silence is deafening and more than Vamp can stand. "What I was trying to say," she suddenly blurts out, disappointed that maybe her prayer was a little *too* deep, "What I meant to say," she says, a little more calmly, "is that I'm pregnant. Now let's eat!"

CHAPTER 37

With a piece of catfish in one hand and a fork in the other, Vamp watches in amusement as the message finally hit its mark. Her mother leaps from her chair and runs a lap around the dining room table, arms flailing and short legs pumping, crying, "Thank you, Jesus! Thank you Jesus!" before collapsing in her chair in a heap of sweat and tears. Her father simply beams a big golden smile at her from his spot at the head of the table saying, "Well, I'll be! I'm gonna be a grandpa!" Everybody is happy and elated until the inevitable questions start flying, delivered in rapid-fire succession by her mother:

"Do you know if it's a girl or a boy? Have you picked out any names yet? Do you have a good obstetrician? Where are you going to deliver?"

"No. I don't know the sex of the baby yet. I think I'd like to be surprised and not find out the sex of the baby in advance. Nope, no names picked out yet. Currently planning to deliver at The University Hospital, but I'm also considering other possibilities."

"When's the baby due?"

"Mid-September."

"Mid-September? Then that would make you...let's see...that would make you...5 months pregnant?!"

"Yeah, that's about right."

"Why'd you wait so long to tell us?" her mother asks, suddenly looking deflated.

"Oh, mommy, I'm sorry. It's just that I've had so much on my mind lately, the baby, the move...being depressed over losing my job."

"You lost your job!"

Vamp nods yes, with eyes downcast.

"Oh, baby, I'm sorry. Why didn't you tell us you lost your job?"

"Because I didn't want you to worry. Plus, I thought with my degrees and experience, I would be able to land another job right away. But if I don't get something soon, like in a week or two, I'm going to be in real trouble because nobody's going to hire me once I can no longer hide this belly.

"Well, don't go worrying about that too much and getting yourself and the baby all worked up. The Lord will provide. You know that, right?"

"Yes, mother. I do."

"Who's the lucky father? And when are you two planning on tying the knot?" These two direct questions come from her father and catch her so totally off-guard that she literally chokes on her corn bread. Her father never pried into her personal life. His usually M.O. was to wait for her to offer up information, and then to accept it without question. She had not prepared for something she could not have seen coming. She feigns coughing longer than necessary to buy some time as she tries to figure out how to respond to her daddy. She hated the thought of lying, especially to him, especially now.

"Of all the times for me to lose my job; this could not have come at a worse time," Vamp says, not really wanting to engage in a conversation about why she got fired, but preferring it over the line of questioning that her dad was pursuing.

"You'll work something out," her mother offers reassuringly.

"Yeah, I've just got to stay on the balls of my feet. Keep jabbing and moving, right daddy?" she says, beaming a megawatt smile in his direction, praying that the tactic of changing the conversation to sports will work.

"That's right, baby. Jab and move. Jab and move," he says, doing the famous Ali Shuffle beneath the table and throwing a couple of jabs at a phantom opponent before continuing,

"So, what's the young man's name, Vanessa, and when do I get to congratulate him?"

"Oh, daddy. It's nobody you know."

"So when will I get the opportunity to meet him? This ain't just another casual admirer we're talking about. This here young fella is soon to be the father of my first grandchild!"

Vamp cringes as she prepares to tell the truth, "I'm afraid that's not going to be possible, daddy."

"Not possible? Why wouldn't it be possible for me to meet him, he ain't in jail is it?" he asks, the furrows between his heavy brows deepening.

"No! Daddy! I don't date men who have been in jail or are jail-bound. It's just that...well daddy, you see...unfortunately... we're no longer seeing one another." *Not exactly the truth, but not a bold-faced lie either*, she tells herself.

"So, I am preparing to have this baby and raise it by myself. I will be the first to admit that this is not the most ideal situation, but a lot of successful women are parenting alone these days."

"So what you're telling me is that my grandchild ain't gonna have a daddy?" her father asks, stress and dismay clouding his strong features.

"Of course he'll have a father...and a mother, but only one parent.

"Come on, daddy, we're not talking an immaculate conception here," she continues jokingly, in an attempt to lighten the mood.

"Vanessa!" her mother calls her name sharply, "We don't take the Lord's name in vain in this house."

"Mother, I simply meant..."

"I don't care what you meant, young lady! Some things must be treated with the reverence they deserve. I think that's one of the problems with young folks these days, nothing is sacred anymore."

"I'm sorry, momma," she says, the mood at the table now heavy and solemn.

Her dad's golden grin is gone, and the sparkle in her mother's eyes is replaced by a dull, opaque stare.

"Mommy…daddy…" Vamp ventures pleadingly, "I'm sorry that this long-awaited day isn't more in line with what you had envisioned. It's not exactly how I pictured it would be either. But I hope that I have your blessings and support, because the reality of the situation is that a baby is coming in a few short months, and I'm going to need all the prayers and blessings I can get."

"Baby you know you are always in our prayers. Yes, I will admit that this is a bit of a shock, but daddy and I have never turned our backs on you and we don't plan on starting now. Right daddy?" she calls to her husband.

"Right, mother. We're always here for you, Nessa. I guess I'll just have to be the one who teaches the kid how to throw a curve ball."

"But what if it's a girl, daddy?" Vamp asks, her heart leaping as the smile returns to her father's face.

"So what if it's a girl!" he replies. "Hell, she can learn to throw a mean curve ball too!"

~~~

On the drive home, Vamp keeps replaying scenes from tonight's dinner in her head. She knew her parents were disappointed in her; hell, she was disappointed in herself. In her grand scheme for her life, never once did it include raising a child alone. Even worse, while her mother had assured Vamp that she would help out, she would not commit to being the primary caregiver when Vamp returned to work. She informed Vamp that she had already raised her two children, and now she wanted to do some of the things that had been simmering on the back burner for years – decades even. She told Vamp not to worry, stating, "Baby, you'll find a way. And if you can't find one, you'll make one. Nothing brings out the resourcefulness in a woman more than the need to care for her child. You'll be fine. We're confident of that - we raised you well."

Yeah, well, I'm glad somebody's confident, Vamp thinks, with one hand on the steering wheel, and the other fishing around in her purse for the remainder of the Peppermint Schnapps.

CHAPTER 38

Now back at home after having survived dinner, Vamp struggles to get out of her binding bra. She had developed the habit of sleeping in her bra after she learned that Marilyn Monroe, (another of her blond, American idols) slept in hers. But with her breasts growing larger each month, she's had to relax her efforts to try and outwit the laws of gravity by swapping out the bra for a more giving camisole. Clad only in the camisole and extra large cotton briefs, she climbs into bed and unconsciously curls her body into a fetal position. She yearns for nothing more than to escape into a deep, peaceful sleep. Sleep, where in her dreams she is still the sexy Vamp of old, and not the lonely, pregnant woman she has become. But the sleep she craves eludes her, and the knowledge that she consumed an entire bottle of Schnapps disgusts her. And yet, in the absence of sleep, and despite her disgust, the only other thing she desperately wants at this moment is a good stiff drink of whiskey. She is acutely aware that her own liquor supply has gone, quite literally, down the drain. "Lucky for me there's never been a shortage of liquor stores in Black neighborhoods," she says cynically. "A lack of a decent shoe store, yes, but a shortage of well-stocked liquor stores...never. In fact, if I were to hop in my car, I could drive less than 5 blocks in any direction and find one. Then I could just run in, make my purchase and be back in bed in less than 15 minutes." She looks down and is alarmed when she sees that while she was mentally entertaining the idea, she was also unconsciously acting upon it. A sweatshirt now covers her camisole, and the one pair of pants she can still squeeze into, covers her hips. "Oh, what the hell!" she says, and allowing self-pity to propel her forward, slips her bare feet into her loafers, grabs her keys and wallet she steps quickly and decisively into the hallway. After hearing the lock slide securely into place, she turns to creep down the stairs and bumps into Jamela.

Oh, no! Vamp groans, *Not her! Not now!*

"Whoa!" Jamela says, steadying herself and tightly clutching the plate she's carrying. She peeks beneath the edge of the checkered dishcloth covering the plate, then breathes an audible sigh of relief.

"Sorry," Vamp replies, with a sinking feeling in her gut that her simple little plan was about to get complicated due to this unwanted chance encounter. "I was just on my way to the store to get some ginger ale to settle my stomach. You know...heart burn."

"I know all about Mr. Heartburn," Jamela says, smiling.

"Oh, by the way, thank you," Vamp offers.

"For what?"

"The book you left for me. It contains a lot of helpful information. So...thank you."

"Yeah, sure. You're welcome. Hey listen, I was just on my way downstairs to take this plate of teacakes to Miz Mattie. She's been trying to teach me how to bake. I wanted to surprise her with my very first batch! So, if you're feeling daring, why don't you come on down and try a few. I can run to the corner to get the soda for you. Shaka's downstairs too, so while I'm gone, you can help Miz Mattie keep an eye on him. Believe it or not, he actually likes you. Even mentions you from time to time."

"Yeah? He knows my name?"

"Not exactly, calls you 'The Lady.'"

"Cute," Vamp says, amused. "But it's not so improbable, you know."

"What isn't?"

"Him liking me. This is new for me, I haven't had the opportunity to be around kids much."

"All the more reason you should come on down, 'cause that 'not being around kids much' thing is about to change, and in a very big way," she says, eyeing Vamp's protruding belly.

"Yeah, you're right about that, Vamp says, rubbing her stomach. "But you don't have to go to the store for me. I was just going to jump into my car..."

"It's no problem. The store's right on the corner, two blocks away; I walk there all the time. Besides, it's not even dark out yet, and there's still lots of folks hanging out on their stoops, so I'll be okay."

"That's really kind of you, but..."

"You got a problem with people trying to be nice to you?!" Jamela snaps, now becoming irritated. "Look! We both can agree that we got off to a bad start. I'm trying to make an effort. You turn me down now, and I ain't gonna try again. Got it?"

"Got it! Geez, since you put it that way, okay. Here's $2.00. On second thought, take $5.00, buy yourself something nice."

"Don't mind if I do," Jamela says, tucking the bill in her rear pocket and continuing on down the stairs.

~~~

"Come on in, babies!" Miz Mattie chimes happily as she sees the two figures entering the parlor together. "Vanessa, I was just thinking about you. Here, let me get one of these chairs down for you," she offers, and begins the rocking motion she uses to propel herself up out of her seat. Jamela rushes forward, "I'll get it, Grandma. Here, you just take this plate of cookies and sit yourself back down."

"I can do it," Vamp intervenes, "I'm not completely helpless; not yet, anyway."

"I don't doubt that you can do it and, trust me, under normal circumstances you'd best believe that you would," Jamela says, as she effortlessly hoists a chair down from the wall. "But at this stage of your pregnancy, you really shouldn't be raising your arms up over your head."

"What?"

"Lifting you arms up over your head can cause the baby's umbilical cord to get wrapped around its neck."

"You can't be serious!" Vamp snorts, as she slowly lowers her expansive body down into the chair. "Miz Mattie, please explain to Jamela that that is just an old wives tale."

"Well, I have heard it said to be true. Now, whether or not it's an old wives tale, I don't know. Jamela here is our in-house expert, so I'm inclined to trust her."

"What do you mean, Jamela is the expert? Shouldn't the wisest and most experienced person have the final word on the subject?"

"I totally agree with you, and like I said, in this case that would be Jamela. I never had any chil'ren of my own. Charlie and I had planned on having us a houseful of chil'ren, but the good Lord obviously had other plans."

"Oh, I'm so sorry," Vamp states, embarrassed by her presumptuousness. For some reason she had just assumed that all women of her mother's generation and older had children, and the older the woman, the more children she was likely to have.

"So, like I was saying," Jamela injects authoritatively, "Don't go lifting your arms up over your head!"

"Well, what am I supposed to do if I need to get something down from a shelf?"

"If I'm home, come over and get me; otherwise, it will just have to wait. Besides," she says, laughing now, "I don't imagine you've got chairs hanging up on your walls like Miz Mattie. She's the first Black person. No. I stand corrected...the *only* person I know who's got their furniture hanging up on the wall! And you know us Black folks can come up with some imaginative stuff!"

"I got the idea from a television show I saw about the Shakers. But you gotta admit it does free up more space for me to get about and more room for little Shaka to play."

"It does at that, grandma," Jamela responds, still giggling, as she takes a seat at the table.

"Here, grandma, take a look at these and tell me what you think."

As Miz Mattie lifts the edge of the dishcloth, a wide grin spreads across her face. "Oh, baby! These look just like mine! And I bet they taste just as good too!"

"Now, don't go jumping to conclusions," Jamela replies, her eyes wide with pride, "But please, help yourselves, there's plenty more where those came from. Man, *is* there ever! Whoever created that original recipe must have had one big family!"

"I just cook the way I was taught," Miz Mattie replies, "But now that you know all of the ingredients, feel free to cut it down to fit your family."

"Are you kiddin'? I ain't gonna go messing around with that recipe; I might mess it up. I'm gonna leave it just the way it is. By the way, I'm about to make a quick dash to the store - need anything?"

"No, baby. Thank you."

Jamela sits Shaka at the table, and places a teacake in front of him. "Back in a minute, sweetheart," she whispers, then kisses the top of his head and quickly departs.

"Those do look good," Vamp comments, as she unconsciously rubs her belly. "I think I might try one."

"Here chil'," Miz Mattie says as she pushes the plate containing the mound of golden colored, nutmeg scented teacakes to the center of the table, "Help yourself."

"I was actually on my way out to the store, but Jamela offered to go for me. No." Vamp says, holding up a finger to emphasize her point, "Jamela *insisted* on going for me."

"Hmm. And that surprises you?"

"Yeah, I suppose it does. But I've been getting a lot of surprises lately," she states, reflectively. "I had dinner with my folks today."

"That's wonderful, Vamp."

"I told them about the baby."

"I bet they were happy."

"Yeah. I suppose they were. You know, parents are a strange lot. I know for a fact that my parents have been waiting with baited breath for grandchildren. And now that it's about to happen, instead of settling into retirement and becoming a doting nanna, my mom's got her sights set on becoming a globetrotter. First stop - Africa!"

"Ahhh. A home going," Miz Mattie nods, appreciatively.

"Yeah, apparently. But don't you consider America your home? This is where you were born."

"Of course, America's my home, but Africa is where my people come from. I think of it like my first cousins twice removed on my daddy's side of the family. I ain't never met 'em, but I know they down there in Oklahoma somewhere, and to pretend that they don't even exist would be stupid. So I just look at Africa as a place full of my people I ain't met yet. And since I don't know which country my people come from, I just claim the whole continent as mine."

"But you've got no memories of Africa, nothing to bind you to that land," Vamp says, trying to reason with the old woman.

"Chil', the memories of Africa are imprinted on my soul. Erasing them is not as simple as taking me from my home. It's like raising a puppy with a bunch of kittens, and then go around not just wanting, but expecting that puppy to spend most of its day sleeping and grooming and not going around barking and playing and burying bones in the backyard, ruining your garden and digging up your tulip bulbs right before they're ready to bloom and show off their nice, pretty colors. And, even being foolish enough to believe that napping and grooming all day is what that little puppy *wants* to be doing instead of just being his true little puppy self."

"Huh?"

"Chil' all I'm saying is that some parts of your mother's trip to Africa will be different and strange, but I've got a hunch that in many ways your mother will feel right at home. It's a shame that you can't go along with her."

"Yes, well, traveling to Africa is the last thing on my mind right now.

"Just thinking about how I'm going to take care of this baby has me overwhelmed and scared."

"Don't worry, chil'. The Lord will make a way."

"That's the same thing my mother said."

"Your momma sounds like a wise woman."

"Yes, she is at that. You would like her. I would like one day for the two of you to meet."

"I'd like that, too."

As Vamp reaches for another teacake, she is startled by a loud "thump," as Jamela sets a plastic bag containing a 2 litter bottle of ginger ale on the table while proclaiming, "If that one little lonely teacake is any indication of how my first batch turned out, then I'd say I must have done all right!"

"Oh, my goodness! I'm so sorry!" Vamp says with an embarrassed smile as she realizes that all the while she has been talking with Miz Mattie, she has been eating teacakes non-stop.

"Oh, Lawd! We ate all them teacakes?" Miz Mattie asks, as her hand flies to her chest and then her cheek. She sits quietly for a moment staring at the near empty plate before continuing softly, her voice choked with emotion, "Chil', you done me proud!"

The two younger women exchange quizzical glances as they watch Miz Mattie busy patting first her left cheek then the right one, in an unsuccessful attempt to hide her falling tears.

"Are you crying?" Jamela asks, as she leaves Shaka's side and rushes around the table to where Miz Mattie is sitting.

"I've never cooked food that made anybody cry before. Were they really *that* good?" Jamela asks jokingly.

"Yes, baby. Yes, they were," Miz Mattie responds, looking at Jamela with a smile, even as the tears continue to trickle down her cheeks. "In fact, they were so good that up until a moment ago when you showed back up from the store, I was convinced that I was eating some of my own cookin' "

"Really?"

"Yes, ma'am!"

"Wow!" Jamela says, beaming, but her smile quickly turns to a scowl of skepticism.

"No. You don't really mean that."

"She meant it, girl. They're good. Really!" Vamp interjects.

"Well, thank you. And thank you, Miz Mattie, but explain to me again why it is you're crying."

"I'm crying because I get the chance to pass on my momma's teacake recipe that she got from her momma to someone who I love like she was my own daughter. That makes me mighty grateful because to me, these teacakes have always represented love. So now, even after I'm long gone, part of me will still live on."

Tears now fall from Jamela's eyes as she kneels and wraps her arms around Miz Mattie's middle and places her head upon the old woman's heart. Miz Mattie leans down and places a kiss on the top of Jamela's loced hair. Vamp looks on silently, sniffling and wiping her nose. She knows that Jamela and Miz Mattie are not really related, and that Jamela has known Miz Mattie for only a little bit longer than she has, but watching them together tonight, it is apparent that something special exists between them, and she is suddenly reminded of something her mother said earlier tonight at dinner, '...evidence of God in the smiles of my sisters.' Suddenly, Shaka runs over and wedges himself between the two women and is instantly folded into their circle of love.

For a fleeting moment Vamp sees herself rising from her chair and going over and being met with arms opening up and accepting her into the circle of love too, with her baby being gently rocked by their warm, loving energy. But she stays seated in her chair, embarrassed by the knowledge that at one time she had felt these women beneath her, had never before wanted to be included or associated with them. So as much as she yearns to go over now, she knows that she has not earned the right to do so. So she sits quietly watching while sniffling and shifting uncomfortably in her chair, feeling very much like the duly disciplined, bald-headed stepchild.

"Anyone care for some ginger ale?" she finally asks, in a feeble attempt to again feel included.

"No, thanks. We'd really better get going," Jamela says, rising to her feet and lifting Shaka up from the floor. Just as she's about to place him on her hip, she exchange glances with Miz Mattie and the two women chuckle at some private joke, as Jamela stands the toddler back on his own two feet and takes ahold of his hand. "This evening has been a blast, but we're gonna head upstairs. It's time for this little guy to go to bed, and for me to get ready for work tomorrow. Good night, all. Miz Mattie, we'll see you in the morning.

"Say good night, baby," she instructs her small son.

"'Night," comes his sleepy reply.

"Good night, baby," Miz Mattie says, as she blows the sleepy child a kiss.

"It has been a long day," Vamp says, as she pushes herself out of her chair and hoists her unopened bottle of soda up into her arms, "I think I probably better head up too. Good night, Miz Mattie."

"Good night, babies!" Miz Mattie calls out as they all head for the door with Jamela leading the way and Vamp bringing up the rear, cradling her soda in one arm and her belly in the other. As they near the upper landing, Vamp speaks up, "Thank you, Jamela, for going to the store for me tonight."

"You're welcome."

"No, really. *Thank you!*" Vamp says again, unable at that moment to find more expressive words to convey her gratitude.

"O.K. *You're welcome!*" Jamela replies with a tired smile, "It really wasn't any trouble," she says as opens the door to her unlocked apartment. When she looks back over her shoulder to say a final good night, she suddenly finds her face awkwardly buried in the warm curve of Vamp's neck, who had unexpectedly sidled up beside her and engulfed her in a brief, yet sturdy hug. Before Jamela has a chance to react, Vamp quickly navigates the six feet that separates the two apartments and disappears behind her closed door.

Wow! Jamela thinks as she closes her own door behind her. *Those really must have been some kick-ass teacakes!*

CHAPTER 39

Leaning against the closed door, Vamp feels her heart pounding loudly in her chest. If Jamela was annoyed or taken aback by her uncharacteristic display of gratitude, she didn't want to know about it now; she was certain she would hear about it soon enough. She feels proud of herself at being able to display what she felt in that moment, without first overanalyzing the hell out of it to the point where it was planned and staged, instead of just being natural and organic.

After she finishes scouring the kitchen sink and pouring a generous amount of lemon scented disinfectant down the drain, Vamp pours herself a tall glass of ginger ale and heads for her bedroom. Grabbing the remote control and clicking on the television, she mindlessly channel surfs for a brief time, and then turns off the television and grabs the latest issue of *Jet* magazine from her bedside table.

As she leafs through the pages, the magazine automatically falls open to the centerfold page, revealing a shapely young woman clad in a red bikini that was obviously not designed for swimming in. Her bio claims that she enjoys skating, horseback riding and dancing, and her measurements are listed as 36-24-36, which do not appear to jibe with her curves in the photo. "That suit's not working for you, girlfriend," Vamp states critically, "For starters, your thighs are a tad too fleshy to pull off the high cut of that suit." Glancing down at her own legs, she laughs mirthlessly at her hypocrisy before pulling the sheet over her dimpled thighs.

Flipping the pages of the magazine, Vamp does a double take when she see Cat, along with Danny, smiling out at her from the Society Page under the subheading: Wedding Announcements. "Oh, my God! Cat's getting married!" Vamp squeals excitedly, bouncing up and down on the bed, sending the magazine sliding to the floor. "What the hell am I sitting her for?" she says, pushing her bulk up from the bed and heading to her closet in the spare bedroom, "I've got a wedding to go to!"

She opens the doors of both closets and the armoire and stands staring blindly into them as the reality of the news sinks in.

"Wow. Cat's getting married," she says, as she pulls out a red strapless number, holds it beneath her chin, and lets out a loud sigh as she looks at her reflection in the mirror. "There's no way I can get my big ass into this," she says, tossing it to the floor. "She could have at least called and told me first, before going out and announcing it to the world," she says, as one by one the dresses are pulled out for review then quickly discarded on the growing heap at her feet. "Did she think I would be mad because she's walking down the aisle first? Okay, full disclosure, maybe I am a little jealous, but I ain't mad at her. I did always think that I would be the first to settle down and get married, but as I can personally attest, shit happens and life changes," she says, tossing two more dresses onto the heap. "I can't believe that Cat is actually going to marry down by marrying that fool. She could have done so much better," she snorts, although her disgust has more to do with her inability to fit into her clothes than it has to do with Cat's choice for a husband.

"She could have at least waited until after I had the baby – damn!" Vamp says, looking at the mound of clothes on the floor and starting to feel a little desperate at the challenge of finding something to fit her growing girth. And right when she feels she's about to lose it and start ripping those pretty little dresses in two, she pulls out a sleeveless, calf length chiffon dress in a soft floral pattern. Her eyes light up as she closely examines it, while thinking that the soft, fluid layers of chiffon was exactly what she needed – something to skim over, not hug, her voluminous curves.

"This might just do," she says, holding the dress beneath her chin, the soft green in the foliage on the dress picking up the green flecks in her eyes. "This might do nicely, indeed!" she says as a wide smile spreads across her face. "But, wait!" The smile disappears. "What if the event is formal? If it's semi-formal, this will work. If it's formal, Houston, we have a problem."

It seems weird that I haven't gotten my invitation in the mail yet. Cat probably couldn't remember my address, and is planning on dropping it off, Vamp thinks, as she waddles back to her bedroom to retrieve the magazine from the floor. "Maybe the announcement mentions where the wedding will be held, and the venue will give me a clue as to the required attire," she says as she picks up the magazine and quickly flips through it searching for her friend's smiling face.

"I might be pregnant, but I intend to look good!" she says, finding the happy couple and reading the caption out loud, "Mr. and Mrs. Avery are pleased to announce the marriage of their only daughter, Kathleen Marie, to Daniel Leslie Roberts. The couple exchanged their vows before close friends and family on Sunday, May 13, at Holy Cross Tabernacle Temple. The newlyweds honeymooned in Rio de Janeiro."

CHAPTER 40

Her eyes fly open, releasing the twin pools of tears that are trapped beneath her lids. She frantically scans her surroundings, quickly trying to assess the where, what and how of her present situation. The handmade patchwork quilt at the foot of her bed, a relic from her beloved grandmother, sends the message to her brain that she is home, safe in her own bed. She exhales deeply and relaxes against the pillows, breathing out the residual of a frightful dream that she can barely recall. Snatches of lingering images flit through her mind: her mother crying, as she kneels in prayer; Cat sitting at the kitchen counter lost in thought, cradling a cup of coffee with both hands; and finally, she sees herself floating, untethered, in a big void of blue.

Hunger pangs and a growling stomach bring her attention back to the present, and she slides her feet into fuzzy slippers and scuffs her way into the kitchen. "Damnit! I don't know why I even bother coming in here; it's not as if groceries are suddenly going to magically appear," she says, looking into the bare refrigerator. "This is so sad." As she pulls back on the clothes she had worn last night during her thwarted trip to the store, ever mindful of the dangers of shopping for food on an empty stomach, she attempts to piece together a shopping list in her head. But unlike most folks who shop on an empty stomach, she was more prone to end up with a cart full of bottles from a distillery versus junk food from a factory.

"Why didn't I bring home a plate of food last night like mother had insisted?" she admonishes herself as she swipes a lipstick across her lips, and grabs a pair of sunglasses to hide her unadorned eyes. When she opens the door of her apartment, a tantalizing aroma rises up to greet her. "Hello!" she says, hurrying down the stairs as quickly as she can propel her round body. But with each step she takes, the scent of teacakes grows fainter and fainter. Holding her belly, she turns and retraces her steps, only to discover that the unmistakable scent of baking teacakes is wafting out from beneath Jamela's door.

I wonder if she's planning on bringing them downstairs to the parlor? She brought a big batch down just yesterday, so that fact alone decreases the probability that she'll do it again today, she thinks, as she stands on the stairs nibbling her fingernail while growing hungrier and more frustrated by the minute.

She's probably just baking a small batch for her son. But she did say that she wasn't planning on messing with the original recipe, so she probably has more than any little boy needs. She did also say that if I needed anything to just knock. Maybe I can say I need help getting a book down from the bookshelf, she thinks, and before she has had a chance to think her newly hatched plan through, forgetting the crucial fact that there were no book laden shelves in her apartment, she raises her hand and applies 3 brisk raps to the wooden door. The sound of her knuckles on the wood is louder than she had anticipated, and her first impulse is to turn and run. "Okay, don't be stupid, Scarlett," she tells herself, while unconsciously inching away from Jamela's door. The door opens and Jamela stands wiping her hands on a dishtowel with an impatient air about her and a confused look on her face. Shaka runs up and joins his mom at the door, takes one look at Vamp, then runs away giggling.

"Hi," Vamp says.

"Hi, back."

Vamp looks at Jamela's smudged apron and the tufts of flour on her face and in her hair.

"Umm, remember last night when you said that if I needed help with anything, I could come over and ask?"

"Right! Are you okay?"

"Yes, I'm fine. Thank you." Vamp replies, looking over Jamela's shoulder and seeing a floral print sofa covered with books and toys.

Jamela raises both eyebrows questioningly and nods her head, silently urging Vamp to hurry up and tell her want she needs. Jamela glances back over her shoulder, then looks back at Vamp.

"Hey, I...do you mind?" she asks, gesturing with her oven mitt toward the kitchen, "I was just baking some teacakes, and if I don't... here, come in! Come inside!" she says, pulling Vamp in with her mitt-free hand, then abruptly turning and running back toward the kitchen leaving Vamp standing alone at the open front door. Vamp tentatively steps inside and looks around. The apartment is not at all what she had expected, although now that she thinks about it, she is not really sure what she had been expecting. She recalls once hearing a friend refer to a passing Rastafarian as "dirty." And now, to her dismay, she realizes that she had unconsciously internalized that belief as well. And although she didn't think Jamela was a Rasta, she realizes that she had expected to find Jamela's apartment dirty and disheveled. Looking around now, she feels ashamed that she would so readily accept someone else's distorted views against a group of people based solely on a hairstyle.

The sun pours in through three large bay windows on the southern wall, painting the room with a soft, golden glow. The energy in the room is warm and inviting, and Vamp has a sudden profound urge to kick off her shoes and curl up on the sofa and bask in the sunrays and the smell of baking teacakes. Inside the apartment a 12" television sits atop stacked milk crates. A bookshelf against the wall sags under the weight of numerous books. Still more books are neatly stacked on the floor next to the bookcase. Vamp recognizes a few of the names: Angelou, Walker, Baldwin, Morrison. Some of the others she has never heard of: hooks, Hurston and Danticat. Vamp has never read any of these books before her, even those with names she recognizes. She prefers to wait for books to premier on the big screen, and if they never make it, she was of the opinion that they must not have been any good to begin with.

A coffee table fashioned out of two cider blocks and a plank of wood sits at the center of the room. The wooden plank has been painted green, the color of baby peas, and picks up the flecks of green in the sofa, amidst tufts of sprouting stuffing. Yet more books adorn the table next to the sofa, and on the mantel above the decorative fireplace sits a mason jar filled with dandelions. *Now, who would ever think of picking dandelions for display in one's home?* Vamp thinks, *Nobody I know, that's for certain.* The dandelions are all cut to the approximate same height and tied at the tops of the stems, beneath the clump of yellow flowers, with a scrap of satiny blue ribbon. And although Vamp hated to admit it, the end result looked like something she would find described as 'urban chic' in any of the fashionable and trendy design magazines she subscribed to.

The two women's apartments were as different as the women themselves. Every scrap of Jamela's furniture probably cost less than Vamp's bed, and that's not even including the cost of the headboard and footboard. But the differences didn't stop there. One other difference, and arguably the main difference, was that you sensed, felt it even, that Jamela viewed her apartment as her home. Its contents reflected her personality and provided a place for her to house those things she loved and cherished most in the world; namely, her son, and from the looks of things, her books. Consequently, her apartment was furnished and decorated in a manner conducive to nurturing the bodies and souls that lived there. Conversely, Vamp viewed her apartment as a pit stop on the way to someplace better. And while her apartment was outfitted with beautifully crafted, expensive items, it had all the warmth and personal appeal of a furniture warehouse.

Jamela returns from the kitchen smiling, as she tosses her locs over her shoulders and pulls off a crispy oven mitt. "Sorry, but I was right in the middle of baking more teacakes, and I didn't want them to burn. Why are you still standing? Take a load off, and have a seat! You gotta excuse my manners. It's not that I don't have none, I'm just not used to having company. Usually it's just me and Shaka. So, what can I help you with?"

"Huh?"

"You said you needed help with something. You've got something you need me to get down for you?"

"Oh, right…" Vamp says, racking her brain trying to think of what thing and on what shelf. "Oh, what the hell!" she finally says. "Listen, girl, I'm not even going to lie. The reason I'm here, and I'm almost too ashamed to admit this, but I was on my way to the market and I smelled your teacakes baking. So, I just had to stop by and ask if I could have a couple. It's okay if you say no, I'd understand, considering that I ate a small boat load just last night."

"Ha! Girl, is that all! Yeah, of course! And you can have more than just a couple. I've got this huge ball of cookie dough that I'm convinced, even if I bake these suckers every day, this thing will last me well into next week. You came over here looking all serious and stuff, and all you wanted was some teacakes. Ha! You're funny! Who would've ever thought!"

"I was on my way to the market to pick up some food for breakfast, when the smell just drew me in."

"You haven't eaten breakfast yet? Girl you know you gotta feed that baby!"

"I know…I know. That's where I was headed," she says, pointing feebly toward the door.

"I'll tell you what," says Jamela, "You come on into the kitchen with me, and while I'm waiting for this last batch to finish baking, I'll fix us a bite to eat."

"Oh, no! Don't go to all that trouble. I'm not all that

hungry, even. I was just thinking of maybe some toast and possibly some orange juice."

"It's no trouble," says Jamela, "I could stand to eat a little something myself."

"Really, no." Vamp staunchly insists, as her loudly growling stomach says otherwise.

Jamela hears the growling, looks at Vamp and shakes her head.

"Okay, I'm busted!" Vamp says laughing, feeling silly at being betrayed by her stomach.

"Yeah, I'll say!" Jamela says, as she places two teacakes on a napkin in front of Vamp, "Why don't cha have a seat."

"Remember that first day when you came by to check out the apartment?" Jamela continues, as she takes a carton of eggs out of the refrigerator, "I actually saw you from my window. You were sitting on the stoop below looking so cool, with your little beret. I hoped that you would take the apartment, and that we would become friends. But up until recently, we've barely said a decent word to each other." Mouth full of teacakes, Vamp silently nods in agreement.

"But this is nice, having someone over to sit and talk to for a while."

"I know what you mean," Vamp responds.

"No, I'm being serious."

"I'm being serious too" Vamp insists.

"Maybe you are," Jamela says, "'cause now that I think about it, I don't see nobody coming by to visit you, either. I would have thought that you would have an army of folks beating a path to your door. What's up with that? Don't you have any friends?"

"What!? Sure I've got friends. Tons of 'em. But since you were so bold to bring it up, I don't exactly see anybody beating down your door either. Don't *you* have any friends?"

"No. Not really," Jamela says matter-of-factly, and curiously devoid of any self-pity. "No. Wait!" she says, after a moment's pause, "Miz Mattie. Miz Mattie is my friend."

"Well, consider yourself lucky. You know, it's true what

they say about finding out who your true friends are when you're down on your luck. Fair weather friends will want to ride your coattail and bask in the rays of your light. But let that light dim, even just a tiny bit, and they're off and running, leaving you sad and distracted with nothing but an expensive light bill and a tattered coat tail."

"Come again?"

"Nothing, girl," Vamp says, but then feels an obligation to try and explain further, "You know, I've got a lot of nice clothes - none of which I can currently fit into, mind you. And I drive a nice car, and generally have nice things. But right now I don't have a job, and if I don't get one soon, I'm going to be selling all of my pretty things just to be able to eat and have a place to live. Look, I'm going to be frank with you. I don't know why, but I just feel that you deserve to hear the truth. People like me, who are constantly buying things to impress others are, by definition, insecure." Seeing the confused look on Jamela's face, she continues. "Let me try and explain. You see, I'm like the fat chocolate bunny in the big fancy Easter basket, looking all rich and tempting that the child cries and pleads for. Then she finally gets it in her two chubby hands and sinks her teeth into it, only to discover that it's hollow inside. And worse, not only is it hollow, there's no marshmallow filling, no caramel nougat. Nothing. That's me, I'm that Easter bunny. But you... Well, look at you! Your clothes are old. Your hair is wild. You don't seem to care about these things, and you certainly don't obsess over them like I do. And yet, you're able to pull it all off with a certain savoir-faire," Vamp says, with a flourish of her hand.

"I don't understand," Jamela says, self-consciously straightening the collar of her shirt.

"The point I'm trying to make is that you possess something that money can't buy - the confidence to just be yourself."

Jamela doesn't know how to take what halfway sounds like a compliment, so she says, "Here, girl, have another teacake."

"So, how do you do it? What's your secret?"

"My secret to what?"

"For being you."

Jamela looks puzzled and then replies, "Who else could I be?"

"More profound words were never spoken."

"I think I understand what you're trying to get at, and that is, why don't I try to look like the girls on television? I don't concern myself with trying to be like the girls on television because purposely don't watch a lot of TV for that exact reason. I've learned that the media is some pretty powerful stuff; it influences not just how we see ourselves, but how others see us as well. Now, I can't do nothing about how other people choose to see me, but I don't to be told how I should look, what I should wear, and what I should think. That might also explain why I don't have a lot of friends. Anyway, I don't really care because I can have a good conversation with myself. Except I don't really consider it talking to myself, it's more like talking to a big sister...you know?"

"Hmmm...not really. I gotta admit, you kinda lost me there."

"Well, have you ever sat and stared at your face in the mirror for so long that everything, except your eyes, just disappeared?"

"No. I can't say that I have."

"Okay. Don't laugh, but it's what I used to do when I was scared and lonely and didn't have nobody to talk to. I would just sit and stare into my eyes for so long that after a while, it seemed as if I was looking into someone else's eyes. And those eyes saw deep into me. They saw things in me that a lot of people don't see because they get caught up on my hair, or the color of my skin, or my clothes.

"What, exactly, did those eyes see?" Vamp asks.

"Well..." Jamela ventures tentatively, glancing first into Vamp's eyes to see if they are sincere or mocking. "Well," she continues, "They saw me, or rather, what I feel is the essence of me - someone's who kind, passionate, funny and quirky. But they also saw my vulnerability and sadness at being misunderstood. But then they told me not to feel bad at being misunderstood by people who don't even understand themselves. And so, in answer to your question, that's the secret that allows me to be me."

"Whoa, girl. That's deep!"

"Yeah...I know."

~ ~ ~

In the relatively short time it takes for Jamela to prepare breakfast, Vamp discovers firsthand that she *is* funny, smart, kind-hearted, philosophical, generous and courageous. She was, in short, a pretty decent person. Plus, she could cook, which was always an asset in Vamp's eyes. But to hear Jamela tell it, before Miz Mattie moved in, she had barely mastered the art of boiling water. So, obviously she was a quick study too, because in no time at all, she is pulling biscuits made from scratch from the oven, while removing strips of bacon from one frying pan and scrambling up eggs in another. Vamp makes herself useful by placing pats of butter inside each hot biscuit. As Shaka scrambles up into a chair, Jamela places a bottle of Algra syrup alongside the pan of hot biscuits, and sits down with a look of contentment on her face. While Jamela and Shaka say grace, Vamp bows her head respectfully while furtively eyeing the bottle of syrup.

With the food blessed, Jamela passes a plate to Vamp, "Dig in, girl." Jamela then takes a biscuit out of the pan, breaks it open and places it face up another plate, revealing its fluffy, buttery insides. Finally, she picks up the bottle that had been bugging and puzzling Vamp from the moment it first appeared, and drizzles syrup over each half of the open biscuit. She adds a small scoop of eggs and one strip of bacon, and then places the plate in front of Shaka, delivered with a kiss. Intrigued, Vanessa decides to follow Jamela's lead. After just one bite of the sweet, buttery biscuit, she's nodding her head and dancing in her seat. After she finishes off her biscuit, and right before she starts in on her eggs, she slips her shoes off beneath the table, which doesn't go unnoticed by Jamela.

Fighting to suppress a giggle, Jamela asks, "I though you grew up in the city?"

"I did. Why?" Vamp inquires as she licks away the syrup that had escaped down her wrist.

"Because, from watching you eat that biscuit, I woulda sworn you was born and raised in Mississippi!"

Vamp grins and shrugs. "What can I say?" she asks, "I'm a sucker for down home cooking. Now, pass the biscuits, please."

~~~

After breakfast, despite Jamela's ardent protests, Vamp insists on washes the dishes. "It's the least I can do. Besides, I find it relaxing, not to mention the fact that it is one of the few domestic chores that I do well."

"Well, okay, if you insist," Jamela responds, finally giving in. "Listen, while you're doing that, I'm gonna run to the back and finish packing Shaka's bag. I'm almost done, so it won't take long."

"Take your time, I'll be just fine," Vamp replies, as she immerses her hands into the hot, soapy water, humming a little tune while she washes and rinses the breakfast dishes, then places them in the dish rack to dry. As she glances at her handiwork, she notices for the first time that no two plates, forks, or glasses, for that matter, seem to match. She also notices that this passing observation is not accompanied by a feeling of superiority, as it would have been only a few short days ago. But just a few short days ago, she thinks, I never would have imagined finding myself in Jamela's apartment washing dishes.

Just as she places the greasy frying pan into the soapy dishwater to soak, the doorbell rings; she jumps at the sound of the buzzer, so rarely has she heard it. Shaka instantly comes tearing out of the bedroom heading straight for the front door. Jamela is close on his heels, leaving in her wake the faintest whiff of freshly applied perfume. Had Vamp known that Jamela was expecting company, she would have departed beforehand. Now, trapped in the kitchen and not knowing what else to do, she takes her seat back at the kitchen table. From where she sits she can hear the low murmur of adult greetings, abruptly interrupted by a loud roar, followed by squeals of laughter. Jamela suddenly appears at the entrance to the kitchen and, with an impish look on her face, beacons Vamp into the living room. When Vamp enters the living room, she sees Shaka being held upside down by a bigger version of himself. A quick flip, and he's back on his feet, where he quickly gains his equilibrium before pouncing on his dad again.

"Vanessa, this is Clyde, Shaka's daddy," Jamela says with a small wave of her hand in his direction. "Clyde, this is Vanessa, my new neighbor who lives across the hall."

In the midst of flying feet and elbows, Clyde calls out a "hello" to Vamp, as he throws Shaka back over his shoulder.

Keeping a safe distance, Vamp waves hello back. She had never before seen Shaka so loud and energetic, or Jamela so meek and quiet. As she watches Clyde totally absorbed in playing with his son, a sudden ache in her heart reminds her that moments like these are exactly what her child will never have. *This is what daddy meant when he said that his grandchild wouldn't have a daddy*, she thinks. Most any man could impregnate a woman, but to be present in your child's life as provider, nurturer, protector, playmate and teacher is what separated real fathers from sperm donors.

Silently watching the three of them together, Vamp senses that aside from trying to successfully co-parent their beautiful son, there was something else between the two of them. Suddenly feeling like a fifth wheel, she attempts to stealthily maneuver her big belly to the front door. "Hey, you're leaving?" Jamela asks.

"Yeah, I didn't know you were expecting company. I'm just going to head on home, get out of the way."

"Clyde's not company," Jamela says grinning in his direction, "Besides, he just stopped by to pick Shaka up for the weekend. They're gonna be leaving soon."

"Let's go, daddy!"

"OK, little man."

"See?"

"Yeah, but I really should be leaving too. I still need to go to the grocery store. I can't very well expect you to feed me three times each day, every day. Unless, of course..."

"Ha! You're funny. But wait here just a second," Jamela says, and heads back to the kitchen and returns with a cellophane covered plate stacked high with teacakes for Vamp, and a hefty foil wrapped bundle of teacakes for Clyde, all tied up with a little blue ribbon. *Just like the one around the flowers on the mantelpiece*, Vamp thinks, and then noticing the drooping dandelions, realizes – *It is the ribbon from the flowers*. And now, without that little strip of blue, what moments before had looked like a chic flower arrangement, now simply looks like a bunch of weeds in a jar. *Yeah, there's definitely something still there*. She hoped that they could work out whatever was keeping them from being together because Shaka deserved and needed a full time dad. And despite her bravado at dinner with her parents about being a new millennium kind of woman, she secretly prayed that one day she would find true love, and have a full time, live-in dad for her own child.

~~~

Back at home after breakfast, feeling fortified and full, Vamp realizes that she had better make time to finally go to the market and stock her kitchen with healthy, but easy to prepare foods. But first, she wanted to do something that, up until this moment, she had not thought she would be able to do - call Cat and congratulate her on her marriage. She sits down on the edge of her bed and dials the number. A man answers, "Hello?"

She starts to hang up. For some reason, she had not counted on Danny answering the phone. Instead, she asks, "Is Cat home?"

"Yeah. Hold on."

She is relieved that he did not appear to recognize her

voice. As she waits, she wipes her sweaty palms nervously on her pants, when Danny yells out loudly, "Babe, phone!"

Good God, man! Didn't anyone ever tell you that you're supposed to move the receiver away from your mouth first! she thinks, irritably.

Cat finally picks up and breathes a winded, "Hello?"

"Hi, Cat. It's me."

"Oh, hey girl. How ya doing? I've been meaning to call you."

"Yeah? Well, I'm fine, thanks. Did I catch you at a bad time?"

"Naw. I was just finishing up a 5 mile run on the treadmill, trying to keep my glutes tight for my man, if you know what I mean."

"Yeah, yeah, I know what you mean," Vamp answers automatically.

"Listen," she continues, "I don't want to come between you and your glutes, so I'll keep it brief. I'm calling to congratulate you on your marriage to Danny. I read about it in *Jet*. I must confess it was quite a surprise. I opened the magazine and there you were...there you both were...Yeah, I was in bed flipping through the pages, and all of a sudden there you were. Imagine my surprise when..."

She suddenly stops talking when she realizes that she is starting to babble. *Just congratulate her and hang the damn phone up! She already knows you must have been surprised; remember, she didn't invite your ass!*

"Well, congratulations!" she says again, with forced enthusiasm.

"Thanks, girl! I suppose that must have been some surprise, opening a magazine and finding me, of all people, in it. Listen, I wanted to tell you, but I knew your plate was already full, girl. And I didn't want to be the one to put another morsel on it. But since you asked about the wedding, it was a lovely affair. One hundred guests, and my gown was exquisite! It was, of course, virgin white, and it had a low cut, tight fitting bodice with 1,000 tiny, hand-sewn pearls. It's true! I counted them! Well, most of them, anyway. And girl, that bodice was hugging the twins so tight, I was afraid that they would either spill out or those pearls would start popping off!

"But, oh, I was simply breathtaking, if I must say so myself! It cost crazy phat dough, but daddy said nothing but the best for his angel! Still, every time I would give him another receipt from his credit card, he would toss down a shot of scotch," she says giggling. "But it was worth every penny. Plus, we got a shit load of expensive gifts." She pauses for a moment before continuing, "Listen, Vamp, I heard that you lost your job, and with the baby coming, and all, I didn't want you spending any of your money buying me an expensive wedding gift. Because you know me, anything less than exquisite will get you laughed at and talked about. So you see, I really had your best interest at heart."

My best interest? She is still too hurt to try and challenge Cat's twisted logic, so she manufactures a quick exit. "Listen, girl, I've got to go. I left the water running in the tub. I just wanted to call to say that my wish for you and Danny is that you both get all the things that you deserve."

"You really mean that?"

"Yes. I really do."

"Well, thanks! But hey, are you doing okay?"

"Never been better."

"Are you sure?"

"Yes, I'm sure. But I've got to..."

"...go. Right. You left the water running."

"Right. Take care."

"You, too."

"Good-bye."

"Bye."

Vamp does not try to suppress the tears as they start to fall, nor quell the sadness that threatens to engulf her. With her head in her hands, she watches as the teardrops fall and land on her stomach, where they bleed together, forming a large wet splotch on her flesh colored camisole. Through the thin, translucent fabric, her protruding belly button glares up at her. Within the last few months, her belly button had somehow managed to transform itself from a cute inner to a not so cute outie. And lately, she's been having growing concerns over whether it will ever return to its original state. But right now, her belly button just looks like one big friggin' eyeball, and she cannot suppress the giggles that push through her tears. She laughs until her nose runs and her sides ache, and when she is finally done, she says a silent prayer of thanks for the old preaching woman downstairs, and the Rasta rebel across the hall.

CHAPTER 41

The following months pass in a flurry of doctor appointments, as the preparations for the beginning of new life intensify. Once a month doctor visits give way to weekly visits, as in the blazing August heat, Vamp enters her 35th week of pregnancy. Vamp's mother had recently retired and instead of immediately starting her long awaited travels, has opted to stay put a while longer. She stated that when her grandbaby finally makes its grand entrance into the world, she wanted to be there to give the kid a standing ovation! Vamp still was not sure whether she meant it literally or figuratively, she was just relieved to know that her mother would be by her side when the big moment finally arrived.

The August heat was unbearable, until that blessed day when Miz Mattie had an air conditioner unit installed in the parlor. With little else to do, and to escape the hot summer heat, Vamp began spending several hours each day downstairs in the parlor with Miz Mattie and Shaka. She noticed that Miz Mattie spent a lot of time in her kitchen cooking or eating, or talking about cooking or eating, or just rummaging and sorting through kitchen drawers while enjoying a cup of tea. Vamp also noticed that it was there, in her kitchen, that Miz Mattie became spirited and talkative and told stories that seemed to spring forth from some seemingly bottomless pit. Vamp grew to look forward to these stories almost as much as she looked forward to the pans of warm teacakes fresh from the oven.

At least once a month, everybody in the house helped in preparing dinner, even Shaka, who was a good go-getter. *"Shaka, go get me a paper towel, please. Baby, can you get grandma that wooden spoon out of the drawer."*

Dinner conversations ran the gamut from talk of Vamp's baby to whether there was life after death, and everything in between. After dominating the dinner conversation the first few times, Vamp quickly learned that sometimes it was better to just sit and listen. In the past, her friends had seemingly accepted everything she said as if it were the gospel, whereas these two women expected her to be able to substantiate her point of view. In the process, she discovered that a lot of what she stated as fact, was merely an opinion based on conjecture and hearsay.

This sobering lesson was made glaringly clear one evening as Jamela talked animatedly about a book of poetry by Alice Walker. The little Miz Mattie knew of Alice Walker she had learned from earlier conversations with Jamela, since she had never read any of her books. Apparently, neither had Vamp, but that little tidbit of information did not prevent her from having the audacity to state that she did not care for Ms. Walker's writings. When pressed for a reason, all she could say was that she found her work weird. For some reason, her use of that word to describe the entire body of work of a prolific and respected writer greatly irritated Jamela, who then pressed Vamp for clarification. On and on, Jamela was unrelenting, until finally Vamp finally admitted that while *she* had not personally read any of Ms. Walker's books, she had seen one of her movies on television and thought that *it* was weird.

Despite Vamp's admission, Jamela still felt more needed to counter Vamp's slanderous statement. So, she cleared her throat as she rose from her chair and in a clear voice ringing with conviction, proceeds to recite Ms. Walker's poem entitled, "Three Dollars Cash." As she spoke the words from memory,

Miz Mattie closed her eyes, and Vamp crossed her arms and closed her mind. Moments later, a smile lit across Miz Mattie's lips as a light of recognition shone in her eyes, while Vamp's face remained frozen in a blank stare. That humbling incident stayed with Vamp for a long time afterwards. It taught her that she could learn a thing or two from these two mismatched women, so long as she learned to keep her mouth shut, especially when she didn't know what she was talking about. Vamp was, for the first time, learning how to relate to other women in a mature and healthy way, instead of trying to control their thoughts or buy their allegiance. No sophomoric kid stuff here, these women were dealing with life unapologetically and on their own terms. And as a consequence of living in their midst while her body was undergoing a life changing transformation, Vamp began to think and feel like a real woman herself.

A few weeks later Vamp, the woman, found the courage to do what Vamp of old would never have done – she telephoned her ex-supervisor and apologized for slacking at work and letting her team down. She had expected to get a robotic, bureaucratic talking down to, but was pleased that the conversation was mutually respectful, pleasant, even. And right before she hung up the phone, she found the courage to ask for her old job back. She was informed that at the end of the year the company was doing some restructuring, and that they could welcome her back into a junior level position (not the senior level position she had recently vacated) that would become available mid-December. After hanging up the phone, Vamp gives a shout of "Hallelujah!" The timing for her return to work could not have been more perfect then if she had planned it herself.

"Wow! Momma and Miz Mattie were right! God *will* take care of you…you just gotta believe!

CHAPTER 42

The little house on Ravenswood was a constant hum of good food, honest conversation, music and laughter. These days, Vamp felt like she was now a part of the extended family. And as such, she was no longer afraid to reach out and embrace Miz Mattie when she felt moved by her caring words or kind gestures; or Jamela, who fussed over her like a protective mother hen guarding her chicks. And always, there were rubs and pats and songs and smiles for "little baby," as her unborn child had come to be called. Each time that they would greet her, both Jamela and Miz Mattie always made a point to greet little baby as well. The first time Miz Mattie asked if she could rub her belly, Vamp had said yes without a moment's hesitation. And she had been moved by the tenderness with which the old woman caressed her stomach. And in that one gentle touch, Vamp swore she could feel the long-buried longing of the old woman, mingled with a sense of awe at the life growing inside her womb. But what was most prominent was the love being emitted from those strong, crooked fingers. Love that was so strong, it rocked Vamp back on her heels. And like a sponge, Vamp soaked up all the loving energy she received, and soon discovered that positive energy to be as vital to her unborn child's well being as the food she ate and the very air she breathed.

Throughout the pregnancy, Jamela proved to be an invaluable source of information and inspiration. She had whole shelves of her bookcases devoted to pregnancy and child care, not to mention the magazine articles that she had clipped and filed away, all of which she was more than willing to share with Vamp. But more importantly, Vamp got the added benefit of seeing Jamela's parenting skills at work up close and personal. Jamela was a good mom. Actually, she was a very good mom, exercising great care, patience and dedication in caring for her young son, making her the model that Vamp secretly choose to emulate. Time was quickly winding down, and now it was simply a waiting game. Waiting for little baby to knock at the wall of her womb and announce, "Okay. It's time!" But at least she was prepared, having researched and secured an affordable delivery plan at an alternative facility, at a fraction of what it would cost at a traditional hospital. The facility was staffed mainly with midwives, doulas and interns, with a few doctors on call in case of emergencies. Because the mere thought of going into labor petrified Vamp, she tried to keep herself busy by focusing on finishing the little booties that she was knitting - just one more thing that she had learned from Miz Mattie.

But what scared her even worse than the pain of labor, was the thought of the enormous responsibility in caring for a small, totally helpless baby. She had never bathed, dressed or fed an infant before. Still, there were moments when her fears were quelled by the thought of finally being able to look into little baby's face, to hold its tiny hand in hers and say, "hello." She also had to acknowledge the strange sadness she felt at the pending loss of her current pregnant self. Despite the dimply shelf butt and the tender boobs, after 9 months of pregnancy, she had grown accustomed to the extra weight, the round curves, and her constant silent companion.

Yet, she knew that little baby could not stay inside of her womb forever. The doctor had already given him his eviction notice. If he didn't show up by the due date, he had exactly two additional weeks to pack up and move out; otherwise, they were planning on coming in after him. But now that she had finally gotten her drinking demons licked with the help of prayer and countless teacakes, she was anxiously looking forward to the next phase of her journey - the sacred role of mommydom.

She lay in bed on a hot Sunday going over her 'Things to Pack for the Hospital' checklist, she has an feeling that she is forgetting something really important. And just as an image is pushing its way to the forefront of her mind, the telephone rings.

"Damn it!" Vamp cries irritably, as she grabs the receiver and barks a gruff, "Hello!!"

The sound of sobbing on the other end startles her, causing her to bolt upright, sending a sharp pain across her middle as a not so subtle reminder that quick, sudden movements are a thing of the past. "Hello?" she says again, concerned and frightened at the same time. Her broke status does not allow her the acquisition of non-essentials, like Caller ID, and the unidentified woman crying on the other end of the receiver is starting to freak her out. Just as she is about to hang up the phone, she hears the whispered response, "Vamp. It's me."

"Cat?"

"Yeah, I didn't wake you, did I?"

"No. What's wrong, girl! Why are you crying?"

"Girl, that Danny ain't no damn good!" More muffled sobbing. Vamp sits, waiting patiently for her estranged friend to regain her composure. "Did you know that he was fooling around on me before we got married?"

Suspected it? Yes. Would I have bet my entire paycheck on it? Yes!

These are the thoughts that run through Vamp's head, but she does a quick edit and empathetically replies, "No, girl, I didn't know."

"Yeah, well, he promised me he'd straighten up and get his shit together. Asked me to make an honest man out of him, so I thought if anybody could save his sorry ass, it would be me. And now, come to find out, he's about to become a daddy!"

"Whoa! How did you find that out?"

"Because the heifer called me up and told me!"

"Oh!" Vamp replies, since there was not much else one could say after that.

"The bitch even went so far as to describe the thongs I bought for him to wear for me on our honeymoon! As if my shit ain't good enough. I know my shit is good!"

Vamp cringes and winces at the coarse language streaming into her ear. Ordinarily, such language would not faze her, because she herself had a wicked tongue that even a sailor would admire. But tonight, she keeps seeing the sound waves of the words echoing off the walls of her womb and swirling around little baby's head with the destructive energy of a small tornado. She knows that she must either redirect, tone down or end the conversation.

"Girl, this marriage simply ain't working out," Cat whines. I should have known when you just upped and baled on me that something was wacked!

"Right after I file for an annulment, I'm gonna take back all the shit I bought for him, including the tiger print thongs, and kick his no good ass outta here!" she says, sounding like the determined Cat of old. "So how about it, Vamp?" she asks, without missing a beat, "Wanna be roomies again?"

"What! Are you serious?"

"Of course I am. Before I messed up and let Danny ruin everything, we had a good thing going on. We worked hard, and played even harder. Besides, I heard through the grapevine that you got your old gig back, so now you'll be able to afford the rent. And even though there's soon to be a new addition to your act, compared to what I've been going through, even your little crying crumb snatcher would be a welcomed change. And, no offense, girl, but I've seen where you live. I can have Danny's crap outta here in a couple of weeks, and you can move your things back in right after you get out of the hospital. Wait a minute! Light bulb moment! Just give me the word, and I'll arrange to have your stuff - furniture, clothes, everything, moved back here while you're *in* the hospital. I'll even foot the bill. It seems only fair, seeing as how I'm primarily responsible for you moving out in the first place. That way, once you and the baby are released from the hospital, you can come back to your rightful home, and that precious little baby of yours won't have to spend one day of its life living in the ghetto. Girl, I still don't know how *you've* managed to stay there this long."

She is serious, Vamp thinks incredulously, as she listens to her roommate telling her that the place she lived, the place she now called home, was not fit to raise her child in. But Vamp clearly understood what she meant, because less than a year ago, she had held similar views herself. As she listens to Cat rant excitedly on about parties, hot men, shopping and picking up where they left off, Vamp mutters softly to herself one of Miz Mattie's often repeated phases, "I ain't yet what I'm gonna be, but thank God I ain't what I used to be."

"What? What did you say?" Cat asks, having finally stopped talking.

"Cat," Vamp begins, with a heavy sigh. "I'm sorry, but I'm trying to live a different sort of life now that I'm about to be somebody's mother. I don't party anymore. I don't drink. Seriously, I don't drink! Nothing! Ever!"

"Well, hot damn! How'd you ever manage that? Well, whatever, I'm just glad to hear you finally got that shit under control, 'cause ain't nothing worse for a kid than having a drunk for a mother. Kids can be cruel, and they won't let you live that kinda shit down, you know?"

"Yeah. I know. But you don't have to worry, because like I said, I finally got it beat."

"Good for you! How'd you do it, A.A.?"

"No, teacakes."

"Teacakes? What's that, some kind of new program for alcoholic mothers?

"No. It's...forget it, you wouldn't understand. Quite honestly, *I* don't even know how to begin to explain it myself. But listen, Miz Mattie, my landlady is throwing me a baby shower next week. Small group, nothing fancy. If you're not too busy, I'd love it if you could come by."

"Consider me there."

"Great!"

"And Cat," Vamp begins hesitantly, not wishing to ignite a war of words, yet feeling the need to honor her feelings, "My new home is not what you make it out to be. My neighbors are awesome and kind, and believe it or not, I actually like living here."

"Hey, whatever floats your boat."

"Alright," Vamp replies, relieved. "But listen, girl. I hate to cut this short, but I'm really exhausted...pregnancy does that to you."

"Yeah, okay."

"But, Cat..."

"Yeah?"

"I'm sorry to hear about you and Danny."

"Yeah?"

"Yeah, I am."

"Thanks, Vamp. And I'm sorry I didn't invite you to my wedding. I wanted to, but Danny didn't want you there."

"I figured as much."

"Yeah, but I could have insisted, but I didn't because I didn't want to cause waves so early in our marriage. Can you forgive me?"

"Yeah girl, you're forgiven. What is it that we always vowed?"

"To never let a man come between us!" they say in unison, laughing.

"You got that right! Good night, girl."

"'Night!"

CHAPTER 43

The baby shower had been Miz Mattie's idea, but she sought the advice of Jamela to help ensure that the day would be perfect. The biggest challenge turned out to be the guest list. Since they had never met any of Vamp's friends or family, they had to assign the task of inviting the guests to the guest of honor.

The day before the big event, Jamela was finally able to coax Miz Mattie into sitting still long enough to let her braid her hair. She had been dying for some time now to do away with that little braid of hers with the colored rubber band on the tip. Aside from that, Jamela felt that she didn't have anything of any real value that she could give to Miz Mattie for all of the kindness she has shown her and her son. So, she decided that she would attempt to show her gratitude by letting her fingers gently tap out the message of love on the scalp of the woman with a heart of gold. She instructs Miz Mattie to settle down into her favorite chair, and then Jamela goes and prepares her a cup of her favorite tea, puts on some of those old scratchy gospel records she likes so much, and goes to work. She wasn't sure how she was going to style her hair, just that she needed a design suitable for an older, mature woman. And since she knew that Miz Mattie didn't like her hair hanging down onto her neck, which is why she kept her hair in that scraggly old braid in the first place, she factors that into some of the potential styles she is mulling over. She takes the braid down and gently combs through the hair. She is surprised at how long Miz Mattie's hair actually is, and also at how fine and limp it is. *It's just like white folk's hair*, she thinks, amazed that someone as dark as Miz Mattie would have hair so naturally straight. She had never braided a white person's hair before, and in her opinion, some styles were just naturally better suited for the denser, stronger hair of Black folks, cornrows being one, and dread locs being another. For one thing, the braids, once completed, would simply unravel. *Well, I guess that explains the rubber band. But it's cornrows I promised her, so it's cornrows she's gonna get! But with hair this straight, I'll have to put something like those ugly rubber bands back on the tips to get it to stay braided, and that's exactly what I'm trying to get her away from. Unless...*

Her hands begin to fly with a sudden surge of inspiration. She works standing, deftly maneuvering her body around the large recliner. She parts the hair from ear to ear, then starting at the front hairline, and working from front to back, she expertly braids row upon row of neat cornrows across the front half of Miz Mattie's head. Then she repeats the process on the back half of Miz Mattie's head, starting and the nape and ending at the center part; the rows on the front half of her head are a mirror reflection of the rows on the back half of Miz Mattie's head. Ordinarily, when she braids someone's hair, which could take anywhere from 2 - 6 hours depending on the intricacy of the design, she prefers to sit in a straight backed chair and have the person sit on the floor between her knees – old school style, like momma's all over the world do when they're braiding their little girl's hair. But to ask Miz Mattie to take a seat on the floor would be sacrilegious. Not this woman, whom she loved and adored and maybe even idolized a tiny bit. It would have been easier even, had she asked Miz Mattie to sit in the straight backed chair, but Jamela wanted Miz Mattie to be as comfortable as possible, so she willingly enduring the discomfort and awkwardness of having to stretch, bend and twist her body around the big, boxy chair. Two hours later, when Jamela is finally done, she hands Miz Mattie a mirror to inspect her work. Miz Mattie takes the mirror, sees the smooth braids in the front and smiles, pleased. Then she moves the mirror higher up and sees the clump of loose braids at the top of her head; some sticking up like antennas, others just hanging down like sad, noodles.

"Lawd, chil', what have you done to my head! I look like I've been 'lectrocuted!"

The smile is quickly replaced with a frown. When Jamela sees the confounded look on Miz Mattie's face, she can't hold her laughter in any longer. She grabs hold of her sides to ease the pain that she feels slicing beneath her ribcage, and each time she glances at Miz Mattie, she can't help but laugh even harder, and the cramp in her side causes her to double over in pain. "Okay! Okay!" she sputters, "Stop it! You're killing me!" she says, literally rolling on the floor now.

"Well, it's a good thing somebody's getting some joy out of this," Miz Mattie says, placing the mirror face down on her lap, "And I know it took an awful long time for you to do this here," she says, gesturing with a wave of her hand toward her head, "But baby, I'm sorry! You're just gonna have to take these here braids outta my head!"

Jamela had finally managed to stop laughing enough to sit up, and she realizes that the joke has gone on maybe a little too long. "No! No! Calm down now, Miz Mattie. I ain't done yet. You think I'd have you walking around looking like Buckwheat? No way! We're the descendants of African royalty remember? Now wait here, I've got to run upstairs and get something." She leaves and comes back minutes later, still chuckling and wiping tears from her eyes. "Okay! Now, for the finishing touch!" she states, placing her hands reassuringly on Miz Mattie's shoulders. Then starting at the right ear, Jamela gathers the soft, loose braids in both hands and braids them, cornrow fashion, all the way across to the left ear. The resulting singular braid that extends beyond the ear is woven back into the cornrowed braid and secured in place with rhinestone-studded bobby pins. Jamela strategically adds several more rhinestone pins across the braided ridge. "There! Finished!" Jamela says, as she takes a step back to admire her work. Miz Mattie picks up the mirror from her lap, but before looking into it, she looks up into Jamela's eyes. Jamela gives her a small reassuring nod, and Miz Mattie hesitantly glances down into the mirror and takes a peek. "Oh!" the word involuntary escapes her lips. Her hand comes up to gently touch her hair, and then down to cover her mouth as she stares at her reflection in the mirror. "You made me a crown," she exclaims, "You made me a braided crown! Oh, how wonderful!!" she says, her eyes dancing with delight.

"You like it?" Jamela asks, anxiously.

Miz Mattie nods her head yes, as her eyes remain transfixed on her image.

"Well, good!" Jamela says with a tired sigh of relief. "Looking at you reminds me of a quote by James Baldwin that goes, 'Our crown has already been bought and paid for. All we have to do is wear it.' So, there you go, grandma. Now you have your crown."

CHAPTER 44

The next day while Shaka naps, Jamela dresses for the party then heads downstairs to check to see if Miz Mattie needs help with any last minute preparations. Before heading over to Miz Mattie's apartment, she peeks her head into the parlor; this has become a newly acquired habit of hers. And there in the living room stands a woman in a beautiful royal blue dress with her head bent, as if in prayer. Jamela had not expected any of the guests to arrive so early. *Is that Vamp's mother?* she wonders. But because she was not very good at initiating or engaging in small talk with strangers, Jamela quickly pulls her head out of the doorway and quietly backs up toward Miz Mattie's open apartment. But in the very last instant before she turns away, the stranger in blue raises her bent head. Jamela's brows furrow as she's struck by a vague sense of familiarity.

"Miz Mattie" she calls out timidly. The old woman turns at the sound of her name, and for a brief instant she appears to Jamela like some mystical creature, as the royal blue of her dress blends with the dark richness of her skin, reminiscent of the deep blue waters of the ocean caressing the starry midnight sky.

"Grandma, you look beautiful!" Jamela whispers.

"Thank you baby! I feel beautiful, and I have you to thank."

"Heck, all I did was braid your hair. But, wow, look at you! I love your dress! You've been shopping without me?"

"Shopping? Me! No, baby, I just took me a swatch of cloth I had lying around and put a tuck here and a hem there."

"No way!"

"Yes, way!" Miz Mattie says grinning at her silly attempt at sounding hip. She can't suppress how she feels - happy and giddy, like a young girl again. "This is the first time I've had my hair fixed up in a way that could actually be called a style. I haven't felt this beautiful in a long time. Thank you, Jamela, for helping an old lady feel pretty again," she says, her voice cracking and tears welling up in her eyes.

"Now don't you go turning mushy on me," Jamela says firmly, wiping away the tears from her own eyes before they can fall, "We've got a party to throw!"

"You're right," Miz Mattie says, smiling and patting the tears from her face, then she reaches up with both hands and touches her hair in such a manner that it appears as if she is adjusting a crown. Her eyes meet Jamela's, and it is as if Jamela has read her mind and replies, "Don't worry, that sucker's not going anywhere!"

Jamela goes over and puts her arm around Miz Mattie's shoulder, a gesture that she has done countless times over the year, always accompanied by the words, "I love you." But today, no words are necessary because the act now speaks for itself. Miz Mattie pats Jamela's hand, and with a look of determination in her eyes instructs her, "Come with me." Walking at her fastest clip, Miz Mattie leads the way out of the parlor and into her kitchen, then goes over to the cabinets above the sink, and very carefully lifts down a covered serving tray and gingerly sets it on the table.

"You know," she says, as she removes the cotton cloth from the tray. "I got this here tea set as a wedding present from my parents 50 years ago. And in all these years, I've only used it once."

"It's beautiful. I remember seeing it that day Shaka and I came by to help you unpack, but you had so much stuff everywhere, there wasn't really much we could do to help."

"Yeah. That's me. Hanging onto stuff and waiting for what? I don't even know what I've been waiting for. But today is a special day because we're celebrating life. And if that ain't special, I don't know what is! So, come on baby. Help Miz Mattie get these things back on across the hall before our guests start arriving."

CHAPTER 45

Cat arrives first, followed by Vamp's mother who heads up the stairs to retrieve the guest of honor. Vamp makes her grand entrance moments later looking happy and radiant, and displaying the universal sway-back gait of a very pregnant woman: one hand on her waist, the fingers pointing to the small of her back for added support, while the other arm slices through the air propelling the enormous belly forward. As she slowly makes her way into the living room to have a seat at the dining room table, the women gathered applaud her entrance. "Cat!" she cries, at seeing her friend's face in the crowd. "You made it!" Cat comes from around the table and gives her old friend an embrace.

"I wouldn't miss this for the world," she whispers in Vamp's ear.

"I've really missed you," Vamp replies, her voice heavy with emotion.

"I've missed you too," Cat replies, her voice sounding equally strained. There was so much more that she wanted to say, but realizes that now was not the time or the place, so she whispers an earnest plea into Vamp's ear.

"Friends forever, okay?"

"Friends forever." Vamp whispers back.

Cat takes a step back and examines Vamp from head to toe, then proclaims loudly for all to hear, "You're looking good, girl. I hate to admit it, but you're working this pregnancy thing!"

"Stop!" Vamp laughs, grateful for the compliment. At 40 extra pounds, unable to see her toes, and the back of her neck having turned four shades darker, she was grateful for any and all compliments, sincere or not.

Next, Vamp steps into the outstretched arms of Miz Mattie and Jamela.

She places her head on Miz Mattie's shoulder as the three of them share in a group hug. "You guys have no idea what you mean to me. Jamela, you're like the little sister I never had. And Miz Mattie, you've been a Godsend since the very first day I met you. And may I say..." she says, sniffling and looking up at Miz Mattie's hair, "...that you are looking mighty fine today. And your hair is something fierce!"

"You like it?" Miz Mattie asks, beaming as she gently pats her hair. "Jamela did it for me."

"You did that? Whoa, girl, you've got skills."

"Of course I've got skills," Jamela says, smirking and playfully rolling her eyes. "But I'll take that as a compliment, coming from you, Ms. Thang!"

"Mommy!" Vamp calls out, looking over Jamela's shoulder and waving her mother over to the circle, then adding, "Cat, you come here too, girl."

"I don't know if everyone has met, but everybody, this is my mommy, Charlotte. And this is Cat, my college chum and old room mate; and Jamela, my neighbor and friend; and Miz Mattie, my landlady and part-time spiritual advisor," she says, smiling. Out of the blue, Shaka runs up and wraps his arms around Vamp's expanded hips. "Oh, everybody, this precious little boy is Shaka, Jamela's son.

"Sweetheart," she says, looking down into his bright face, "As soon as I am able, I'm going to pick you up and give you the biggest hug ever!" she says, playfully tousling his hair. That proclamation appears to be satisfaction enough for Shaka, who grins up at her, pats her belly, and then darts off again.

As Vamp slowly lowers her body into a chair, she confesses to her guests, "As some of you may already know, my drinking had gotten a little out of hand. But, as a result of the numerous teacakes I have eaten over the past few months, in what can only be described as a miracle, I have completely lost my desire to drink. So, Miz Mattie, I would like to thank you for all of the teacakes you have personally baked for the entire household and, for teaching Jamela how to bake them in extra large quantities. I would also like to thank you both for the biscuits, the butter rolls, gingerbread cookies, and the sweet potato pies…Okay, *now* I understand why everyone's been telling me that I'm having twins!" she says laughing, while instinctually placing her hand on the side of her belly and caressing her unborn child.

"But seriously, Jamela, thank you for being my friend, I know I didn't make it easy. And Cat, girl, you know we've been through some of the best times and some of the worst times together, thank you for not throwing it all away. Miz Mattie, you were a beacon of light during some of my darkest days. Thank you for being there for me. And mommy…" she is unable to finish, as she choke back the tears. Her mother comes up behind Vamp and wraps her arms around her ample middle. As Charlotte stands silently holding her child, while simultaneously embracing her child's child, she feels in that moment the convergence of the past, present and future.

The sacredness of the moment is not lost on the women present, and they each look on in wistful awe.

"Mommy," Vamp says, taking her mother's hand in her own, "I need to tell you that I love you, and that I am proud to be your daughter."

"Baby, I love you too, and I am extremely proud to be your mother. You do know that, don't you?"

"Yes, mommy. I believe I finally do."

After everyone has dried their tears, they take a seat and feast on ribs, potato salad and fried corn. After the table has been cleared and the dessert plates are being passed out, Miz

Mattie turns to Jamela, "Sweetheart, would you mind serving the tea?"

"Mind? Of course not!" Jamela replies, bounding from her chair, almost tipping it over in her haste. With a huge grin and a noble air, she carefully makes her way around the table, serving Miz Mattie first, then the guest of honor next.

"What a beautiful tea set." Charlotte exclaims, holding the delicate cup up to the light for closer examination.

"Why, thank you. It was a wedding present from my folks. It's the only thing I have left from them, aside from a headful of memories. I used during the very first meal I ever cooked for my husband, Charlie. I remember all through breakfast I was so nervous, thinking that the fragile little cup would get crushed in those big hands of his, that afterwards I stored it away and haven't used it since...until today."

"Oh, Miz Mattie! Are you certain you want us using it now?" Vamp asks, sounding alarmed, her tea cup frozen in mid-air.

"Chil', I've come to realize that there ain't no sense in keeping something so beautiful all covered up and locked away, especially when it is intended to bring some joy into your life."

"Well, thank you, Miz Mattie. I feel happy and honored that you chose this occasion to use your beautiful tea set again," Vamp says, as she takes a sip of tea and lets out a happy sigh of contentment.

After tea has been served all around, Vamp places a generous slice of the German Chocolate cake onto her dessert plate, and then shores it up on either side with stacks of teacakes, then looks up and sees that all eyes are upon her.

"What!? I'm eating for two, remember?!"

"Looks more like four or five to me," Cat jokes.

"Don't you worry, baby, whatever extra you gain, that little baby will keep you so busy it'll burn right off!" her mother consoles her.

"Plus, if you breast feed, not only is it good for the baby, but the fat will just melt off of you like butter!" Jamela offered.

"Alrighty then, breast feeding it is!" Vamp says, through a mouthful of cake. After she has worked her way through most of the hunk of cake on her plate, and one stack of teacakes, Jamela suggests that she start opening her gifts.

"Okay," she agrees, grinning sheepishly.

"I can't believe that you guys did all of this for me. You make me feel like this is a big deal, like this is something special."

"But you know," she continues, after having paused long enough to really hear what she just said, "Despite the whole daddy debacle, this *is* a big deal! And I feel blessed that you all apparently think so too. I love you, guys!"

"Baby, one thing I've learned over the years is that life ain't perfect. But the Creator's got a master plan, so you just gotta trust in him!" Charlotte asserts.

"Amen!" Miz Mattie shouts out, waving her hand in the air, then closes her eyes and starts humming a familiar spiritual.

"Yeah, well, it's hard, but it's not impossible to raise a child alone," offers Jamela.

"I hear what you're saying, but you've got a man!" Vamp states playfully, blowing her nose, which has the habit of running and turning bright red when she gets emotional."

"I ain't got no man! You see me with a man!?"

"Girl, you know that Clyde is sweet on you. Hey, I ain't mad at you! In fact, I'm happy for you. I'm just wondering when you're gonna give the brother a break, and give him another chance. Take it from me, Jamela, a good man is hard to find."

"Amen to that! Can I testify?" Cat adds, thinking about her own failed marriage.

"Testify, sister! Testify!" Vamp shouts, waving her hand in the air.

"Y'all truly don't want to get me started! We can dish the dirt about my failed marriage some other time, but right now, Missy, you should start opening your presents."

"Oh man, and it was just getting good!" Vamp says grinning and licking the chocolate frosting from her fork.

"Okay, which one should I open first?"

"Just pick one, girl, hurry up!" says Cat.

"Okay! Dang! You would think you've never been to a party before, girl."

"Well, you of all people should know that I've been to my share of parties. But it ain't everyday that I get to attend a baby shower for somebody who's like a sister to me. Hell, you *are* my sister! As of today, I'm going to stop referring to you as, 'someone who's *like a sister.*' Besides, saying sister is a whole lot quicker! So, go on sister-girl, pick a gift, any gift!"

"Girl, you are still crazy!" Vamp says with delight, as she picks up the gift closest to her, the one wrapped in antique looking ivory paper, with strips of blue and pink ribbons tied around a sprig of baby's breath. "Oh, what beautiful wrapping," Vamp says as she holds the gift in both hands. "It's so pretty I almost hate to open it. Who is this one from?"

"That one's from me," her mother replies shyly.

Vamp eagerly unties the ribbons, and sticks the baby's breath behind her ear. She then carefully unwraps the thin, fragile paper and lifts out a leather journal. As Vamp leafs quizzically through the pages, which are already filled with neat, precise handwriting, her mother explains, "It's a collection of some of my poetry."

"Oh, mommy, thank you! It's precious! I'll treasure it always. But I must read at least one page before I continue," she says, randomly flipping to a page in the book, then looking into her mother's eyes. "May I?"

"Oh, gosh!" Charlotte replies, visibly blushing, "I've never had any of my poems read out loud before, other than to myself. I didn't imagine that you would want to read them aloud."

"If it's going to make you uncomfortable then, of course, I won't."

"No. Go ahead. I can't think of a kinder group of people to share my work with. So, please, go ahead." she urges. "Which one did you select?"

"The one called, "The Essence of Me." Is that okay?"

Her mother nods her head yes. Vamp clears her throat and begins reading in a strong, clear voice:

"The Essence of Me" by Charlotte Lawson.

My heart beats within the inner chamber of my temple.
But, the true essence of me
is housed
inside my temple
in a yet
unidentified
room.
And though you cannot see it
or touch it,
it is as old and as wise as the moon.
And when my heart no longer beats,
And my temple is buried deep,
the true essence of me,
now untethered and free,
will dance amongst the clouds
until my Father creates a new temple for me.

"Oh, mommy!"
"Whoa, Mrs. Lawson," says Cat, "That's beautiful!"
"That was lovely, Charlotte," Miz Mattie agrees.
Jamela also nods her head in agreement, "Nice. Very nice."

"Thank you. Thanks, everyone," Charlotte says humbly, eyes shining with pride. She slides an envelope underneath the edge of Vamp's dessert plate. "Here's a gift certificate from daddy and me, for you to buy something pretty for the baby." To her astonishment, she sees that Vamp is crying uncontrollably. She hurriedly gets up from her chair and rushes over to Vamp, "Shush, baby. It's gonna be okay," she whispers softly as she gently strokes Vamp's hair.

"No, Ma, you don't understand! That poem…it was so beautiful! I never knew…I never knew you were so wonderfully creative…to be able to write so beautifully…I never knew."

"It's okay, baby. We're making the time to learn about each other now, and that's what's important. So dry those tears, because this is a joyous occasion."

"Mrs. Lawson, maybe we should have saved your gift for last. I don't know what the rest of y'all got, but that's gonna be one heck of an act to follow," Cat says, only half jokingly.

"Yeah, you got that right," agrees Jamela, "But what the heck! Here's one from Shaka and me," she says, handing Vamp a clumsily wrapped gift. Vamp tears at the paper, which she now can't see clearly due to the tears flooding her eyes. Her hands feel the soft, warm fur, and as she wipes her eyes on her sleeve, she sees two little eyes looking out at her from a chocolate coat of fur. "Oh, he's adorable!" she says gleefully as she rubs the soft furry face against her own. "Thank you, Jamela! Thank you, Shaka! He's too cute! And check out this darling little kente cloth vest that he's wearing."

"I made that myself," Jamela says proudly, "With Shaka's help, of course."

"Of course! Thank you both, I love it! Girl, I 've got to say that I am truly impressed with all of your hidden talents: hair stylist, baker, and seamstress. What's next?" Vamp asks.

Jamela shrugs her shoulders and replies, "There's something else in the bear's vest for you."

"What's this?" Vamp asks, as she pulls out a cassette tape hidden inside the bear's vest.

"Those are some of Shaka's favorite lullabies that I used to sing to him when he was a baby. I still do, but not so much anymore."

"Oh, how sweet! You copied a tape of lullabies for me; you shouldn't have!"

"No. I didn't copy a tape. I made a tape. The song's aren't originals, but that's me singing on the tape."

"Oh! Then in that case, you *really* shouldn't have!" Vamp says with a feigned look of fright on her face, which causes everyone to laugh, including Jamela. "Come over here girl, and let me give you some love!" she says, holding out her arms to embrace Jamela. "You know I'm just kidding. That was very thoughtful and very sweet. Thank you."

"Okay, here's my gift," says Miz Mattie, pushing forward a package wrapped in the identical blue fabric as the dress she is wearing, and tied with a pink satin bow. "Thank you, Miz Mattie," Vamp says softly. She slowly unties the bow and folds back the blue cloth, then lifts out a miniature quilt. The swatches of fabric form no particular design, but Vamp knows firsthand that each stitch was woven with love, and the colors selected and their arrangement in the little rectangle resulted in a finished piece that was sunny and vibrant. Vamp looks at Miz Mattie and with a small wave of her hand, tries to convey her gratitude because the words she wants to say have lodged themselves in her throat, and her eyes are once again brimming with tears. She buries her face in the quilt, giving in to her emotions. Finally, she lifts her face from the quilt, reveling red eyes and a shaky smile. And although she's feeling a bit more composed, she is still unable to speak. Instead, she places both hands on her heart and then brings them to her lips where she kisses them, and then releases the kiss in Miz Mattie's direction.

"Well, I'd better hurry up and give you my present," Cat says, " 'Cause from the looks of you, girl, I don't know how much more of this you can take!" she states in the rapid, quick fire way she has of talking when she's excited.

"Has anyone noticed a theme here?" Cat asks, without pausing to give anyone a chance to ponder, let alone, answer the question. "Everyone has given Vamp something that they made themselves! Now I know you don't think I've got a creative bone in my body, but I made you something too! But, to be on the safe side, I bought you something as well!" she says dragging over a tall, 13 gallon capacity plastic garbage pail with a big red bow stuck on top.

"Don't tell me. Let me guess!" says Vamp, "You made me... compost!"

"Ha. Ha. Funny, funny girl. No, I did not. This is what I bought for you.

"A garbage pail?"

"Yes! Girl, you're gonna need it with all those dirty diapers you'll be changing! But we'll get to that in a minute. First, I want to present you with the gift that I made with my own two hands!"

"Oh, excuse me." Vamp laughs, shaking her head at Cat's silliness, remembering that this fun playful side is one of the things she truly misses about her old friend.

"Go on, girl!" she says, "I promise I won't interrupt again."

"Thank you! Okay!" Cat says as she leafs through her purse, pulls out some papers, and then shakes them free of heaven only knows what, before proudly announcing, "I'm so glad I thought of this idea. I would have felt left out had I not made something for you, since everybody here is so creative and cleaver. Okay! Here you go, darlin'," she says as she proudly hands over the crudely stapled slips of paper to Vamp, who accepts them with a confused grin.

"Coupons! Get it? I made coupons!" Cat states proudly.

Vamp laughs as she flips through the pages, "Oh! Okay! I get it!" she says, and reads aloud: "One evening of free baby sitting service. Well, all right! I'm sure I'll need that! One free manicure - I could use one of those now! And, one home cooked meal - you know I do love your cooking!

"Thank you, Cat! That's so sweet and creative of you. I must say that I am impressed!"

"Thank you, and you're welcome. I had about a dozen or so more, but I tore those suckers up. While I'm happy for you and all, I didn't want to go and place myself into voluntary servitude over your little pending bundle of joy. So, to make up for all the coupons that you're not getting, I bought you this," she says, and with the studied flair of a game show hostess, gestures elaborately with both hands in the direction of the garbage pail.

"Do I open it now?"

"Now!"

Vamp timidly lifts the lid and lets out a high pitched squeal followed by giggles, as she lifts out several packages of disposable diapers in various sizes, two large tubes of diaper rash cream, baby wipes, a box of cotton swabs, a jumbo bag of cotton balls, one bottle each of baby lotion, baby powder, baby shampoo, and baby detergent, along with a dozen or so tiny wash cloths. And, at the very bottom of the pail sits a small wicker basket containing bath salts, body cream, a loofah mitt, and a journal to record all of baby's first milestones.

"Wow, this is unbelievable! Thank you, girl! You really outdid yourself."

"Glad you like it! Because now that you've opened all of your gifts, you get to wear the ceremonial bonnet of the mother-to-be!"

"Oh no! Not that silly thing!"

"Oh, yes!"

"Well, who am I to argue with tradition," Vamp says, as she takes the sprig of baby's breath out of her hair and gently places it on the table next to the journal.

Charlotte stands and places the completed bonnet, fashioned from a paper plate and all of the ribbons from the gifts, atop Vamp's head and ties it beneath her chin.

"Oh, I must get a picture of this!" her mother giggles, as she reaches for her camera and runs around the table for a better vantage point.

"Strike a pose, Miss Thang!" shouts Jamela, to which Vamp frames her face with her hands and gives serious face.

"Oh, this has been such a glorious day!" Vamp says, "You all have no idea what this means to me."

"Speech! Speech!" Cat yells.

"Okay," Vamp says, picking up a piece of nearby paper and as if reading from it begins, "First, I'd like to thank the Academy..." Everyone laughs, and then Vamp begins again, this time sounding solemn and sincere.

"Seriously, I want to thank you all from the bottom of my heart. I am so touched, and feel incredibly blessed to have in my life mothers and sister-friends who are such phenomenal women. I used to think that I had this thing called life all figured out, but I've learned that life doesn't travel a linear path, and that it's not a game to be won. It's about the journey and the person that you become along the way. All of you know that this has been a really challenging year for me, but with everybody here offering me a shoulder to lean on, a smile and a hug, and a warm teacakes or two, I'm managing to make it through. It puts me in mind of something that Reverend Doyles from *waaay* back in the day used to preach. Remember, momma, how she used to say, 'God didn't bring me this far to fail me now!'"

"Oh! Hallelujah! Praise Him!" shouts Charlotte.

Vamp smiles broadly at her mother's exuberant outburst, and then asks, "Now, can I get an Amen?" The room reverberates with a loud chorus of, "Amen!"

CHAPTER 46

Two days following the baby shower, Vamp goes into labor and is taken to the birthing facility sweating and cussing. Fourteen arduous hours later, at 6:03 a.m., she gives birth to a cuddly 8 lb., 10 oz. baby girl, who arrives bearing a stock of jet black curls to complement the big brown eyes shining out from her little chocolate face. They made quite the compelling pair, Vamp with her hazel eyes and pale skin, and her little chocolate cherub. Vamp falls hopelessly in love with her daughter and names the baby girl Charlotte Imani. Charlotte, after her mother, and Imani, after learning from Jamela that it was Swahili for the word faith.

Vamp is grateful when her mother accompanies her home from the birthing center and stays with her for three glorious weeks, taking care of all of the shopping and cooking and cleaning, leaving Vamp free to rest up, bond with her daughter, and make the physical, mental and emotional transition from pregnant woman to full-time mom. Little Charlotte developed beautifully. She was always either happily cooing, sleeping, or eating. The baby girl was lavished with much love and attention, going from one lap, to a pair of strong arms, on to someone's soft bosom, and back again. Life was good!

The days quickly melted into weeks, and the weeks turned

into months, bringing falling leaves and gusting winds. Shortly after little Charlotte turned two months old, Vamp's parents departed for their trip to Africa; her mother was finally going home. It was around that time that Vamp realized that it would soon be time for her to return to work. Her heart ached at the thought of having to leave little daughter for any length of time. How she was going to be able to do a full eight-hour day was beyond her comprehension. She longed to stay home and nurture her child, but as much as she wanted it, as much as she prayed for it, being a stay-at-home mom was simply not an option for her. After many tear filled nights, and at Jamela's urging, with a shaky voice and sweaty palms, Vanessa found the courage to ask Miz Mattie if she would be willing to look after Charlotte when she returned to work. She knew that Miz Mattie was fond of Charlotte, loved her even, but to ask for her to dedicate her days, five days a week, was asking for a lot. Looking after Shaka for five hours a day could not compare; he was potty trained, and could walk and talk. Miz Mattie looked up at Vamp from her recliner, grinned and replied, "I was wondering what was taking you so long. I was starting to think that you didn't think I was fit to look after your baby girl, and that you had found somebody else."

"I thank God for you, Miz Mattie," Vamp cries, as she gives the old woman a bear hug. It was the perfect arrangement. Vamp places a bassinet in the parlor so that she can just carry little Charlotte downstairs while still asleep in her jammies, instead of getting up extra early to dress her in a snowsuit, trudge across town in the snow, only to leave her in unfamiliar surroundings looking up into the apathetic eyes of strangers. Here, in the safety of her own home, she would spend her days in the presence of people who loved and cared about her well-being and happiness. Also, Vamp knew that she could count on Shaka being Miz Mattie's helper. He could do helpful little things like bringing Miz Mattie clean diapers for the baby. And considering the number of diapers that child went through in a day, that alone would be a huge help. Plus, he got a big kick out of clowning around for Charlotte, or

Charlie, as he called her.

And so, on the coldest day of the year, with a sad yet grateful heart, Vamp carries a sleeping Charlotte downstairs, gives her a teary kiss goodbye, and then places her into Miz Mattie's outstretched arms. Miz Mattie looks into Vamp's sad eyes and reassures her, "Don't you worry bout a thing, chil', everything's gon' be alright." Sniffling and nodding, Vamp heads out the door into the dark of the pre-dawn morning as Miz Mattie makes her way to her armchair and carefully sinks down into it. With Charlotte snuggled safely in her arms, she looks out the window and marvels at the large fluffy snowflakes drifting silently to the ground looking like liquid diamonds in the glow of the streetlights.

As she places Charlotte's bottle down on the table, on which sits a steaming cup of tea next to a silver picture frame, her eyes are drawn to a disturbance in the snow directly beneath her window. Her brows knit tightly together as she squints into the darkness, feeling remnants of fear echoing winters past. All of a sudden, a singular tear rolls down Miz Mattie's face and lands on the sleeping child's cheek as the rising sun reveals the imprint beneath her window to be that of an angel - a little snow angel. "Ooh, Charlie," she says, nuzzling the sleeping baby cradled in her arms, as her gaze comes to rest on the eyes smiling out at her from the picture frame, "God sho is good!"

As the sun continues its steady ascent into the wintery sky, sweeping away the last vestiges of the night, Miz Mattie picks up her delicate, hand painted teacup, and before taking a sip of the tepid amber liquid, softly whispers, "Thank you, sweet Jesus, for another day!"

ABOUT THE AUTHOR

Dorothy Griggs is a native Detroiter who early in life developed a love of books. It was through books that she gained a broader perspective of life and the diverse experiences of Black women, and books that helped her to expand her knowledge of spirituality.

She has a Bachelor of Arts degree in Business, with a focus on Entrepreneurship, and is currently finishing up her studies toward a Master of Arts degree in Educating Adults. She resides in the Chicagoland area with her husband and two sons.

www.ingramcontent.com/pod-product-compliance
Lightning Source LLC
Chambersburg PA
CBHW070920260626
47162CB00007B/2737